I0761974

BOOKS BY AVA STRONG

REMI LAURENT FBI SUSPENSE THRILLER
THE DEATH CODE (Book #1)
THE MURDER CODE (Book #2)
THE MALICE CODE (Book #3)
THE VENGEANCE CODE (Book #4)
THE DECEPTION CODE (Book #5)
THE SEDUCTION CODE (Book #6)

ILSE BECK FBI SUSPENSE THRILLER
NOT LIKE US (Book #1)
NOT LIKE HE SEEMED (Book #2)
NOT LIKE YESTERDAY (Book #3)
NOT LIKE THIS (Book #4)
NOT LIKE SHE THOUGHT (Book #5)
NOT LIKE BEFORE (Book #6)
NOT LIKE NORMAL (Book #7)

STELLA FALL PSYCHOLOGICAL SUSPENSE THRILLER
HIS OTHER WIFE (Book #1)
HIS OTHER LIE (Book #2)
HIS OTHER SECRET (Book #3)
HIS OTHER MISTRESS (Book #4)
HIS OTHER LIFE (Book #5)
HIS OTHER TRUTH (Book #6)

DAKOTA STEELE FBI SUSPENSE THRILLER
WITHOUT MERCY (Book #1)
WITHOUT REMORSE (Book #2)
WITHOUT A PAST (Book #3)

CHAPTER ONE

When Kevin Anderson stepped out of the yacht club, he knew he was in trouble.

He staggered slightly as he jolted down the low step. The December wind hit him like a smack in the face, the icy air clearing his head as he glanced reluctantly back inside toward the buzz of conversation and laughter, the atmosphere mellow with cognac and cigars.

The company here was always fascinating. Joining this club was the best thing he'd done since moving to Connecticut earlier this year. There sure were some interesting guys in this echelon of society.

He'd have liked to have spent another hour there. One more cognac, maybe two. But after checking his phone, he'd seen the three missed calls from Jasmine. And two texts – the first annoyed, the second angry.

He called her as soon as he was out the door.

"Hey, babes." The wind whipped his words away, but her reply crackled down the phone, and he could hear every sharp word.

"Kev, where are you? You said you would be home two hours ago! We leave for the airport at six tomorrow morning. You still have to pack!" When she lost her temper, the tone of her voice could cut through glass, as could the glare from her frosty blue eyes.

"I'm sorry, babes. I was waiting for Patrick Coleridge to arrive. You remember, the finance guy I told you about? He was going to bring me some details on the investment portfolios."

Kevin tried his best to sound sober and contrite, as if it had been nothing more than a responsible desire to invest that had kept him in his armchair and drinking cognacs way past dinnertime. "I'm leaving now. On my way to the car."

"You're what?" Jasmine's outraged tone stopped him in his tracks. "To the car? I can hear you are way too drunk to drive. *Way* too drunk."

"I'll be fine," he protested.

"I am not having our overseas vacation ruined by having to bail you out after a DUI."

Her words were a harsh reality check. In the sequestered atmosphere of the yacht club, Kevin felt as if normal rules didn't apply and that he was somehow protected from them. But once he'd left the club, real life would prevail. He couldn't argue with that.

"Okay, okay, babes. Can you ask Clayton to come pick me up?"

"No, I can't. Clayton went home at five today. I'm not calling him back in now. He can fetch your car tomorrow morning. Take a cab. And when you get home, we are going to have a serious talk about the amount of time you've been spending at this club. I wish you'd never been granted membership. It's damaging our family life!" She sounded furious.

"I don't –" Kevin began, weakly protesting, but he was talking to himself because Jasmine had hung up.

He sighed. He guessed she was right about the DUI. At eight-thirty p.m. on a Friday night, driving the ten-mile route from the yacht club to his home would be downright stupid. Of course there'd be roadblocks. Even so, he felt oppressed. Her criticism was unfair.

"Babes, you need to get off my back," Kevin muttered to himself. It was so much easier to sound defiant when the fiery-tempered Jasmine wasn't actually on the line.

Now he had to call a cab, despite employing a family driver. It was literally years since he'd last had to do that. And furthermore, there were issues with it at the moment. One of the guys had been talking about it recently.

They were renovating the club's parking lot, and the temporary parking was accessed via a series of side roads. The route was almost impossible to find unless you knew about it. At this hour, in the dark, the chances of the average cab driver showing up at the right place were close to zero.

The guy who'd taken the cab last week had said it was better to go up through the construction zone to the main road. Remembering this advice, Kevin veered away from the sporadically lit pathway that led to the temporary parking, its makeshift railing clanging in the breeze, and headed in the direction of the main road.

The parking lot was a full-on construction site. None of the lights were working. The paving had been ripped up and there were piles of sand everywhere. It was a mess. He guessed they'd gotten a lot further with the renovations since the other guy had gone this way. Now, it was practically impassable.

Kevin stumbled over a plank invisible in the gloom, cursing briefly as he staggered forward. Seriously, he could break an ankle out here.

And it would all be Jasmine's fault. In any case, it wouldn't be his fault, he thought, self-pityingly.

He could use his phone's flashlight! That would allow him to navigate this obstacle course.

But even as he had that good idea, a warning prickle of instinct sharpened the blurriness of his inebriated thoughts.

Was someone following him?

Following a rich guy wearing thousand-dollar shoes and a Brioni suit, clutching the latest model Apple phone, with a thick, white gold wedding ring on his finger. A rich guy who'd thought he was invulnerable in the sheltered club environment, but who was now on his own in an unlit construction zone, drunk and unaware.

Kevin stood still, breathing hard, puzzled by the sudden, powerful feeling he had that something was wrong.

What was that to his right? It looked like movement. Or even the faint shape of a person.

His heart accelerated, and he felt suddenly much more sober as he strained all his senses in the direction of the perceived threat.

It was difficult to see or hear anything at all on this breezy night. He picked up the flapping sound of a tarpaulin, the shifting grind of something else that sounded like wooden planks, but he couldn't see where it was coming from.

The shape of the other person, if there had been one, was no longer visible. But he still felt that sick certainty there was somebody close by.

"Who's there?" he called, feeling self-conscious about yelling such a thing, but he was convinced now that someone was lurking nearby. His eyes strained through the darkness.

There was no reply.

Had he seen someone? Or had it just been a trick of his surroundings, an optical illusion created by the piles of sand and bricks, the tilted planks. He could have made a mistake. But better to be sure.

He snapped his phone's light on and shone it around, an exercise in futility since the beam didn't reach more than a couple of yards before it was swallowed by the darkness.

Then his heart lurched as he saw a menacing shape loom ahead of him and he let out a cry of fear.

The beam wavered and leaped, before settling on the dark tarpaulin draped over a pole.

He let out a sigh of relief.

That was all it was. Just a tarp. It had looked exactly like a threatening man lurking in the shadows – but no. An innocent piece of plastic was all.

Kevin surprised himself by uttering a short laugh. How the guys would have teased him if they'd seen how flustered he was. He could imagine the hilarity if they'd watched what had just played out. Just as well nobody had seen. It would have been embarrassing. Anyway, he wasn't going to carry on making a fool of himself out here. Directing the cab to the temporary parking was a more sensible option.

There was an explanation for the lurking man he thought he'd seen. It had been a tarp. The same tarp that was flapping behind him now, making a sound just like footsteps.

One-two, one-two.

It didn't matter, because now he had reached the walkway that led to the temporary parking. Feeling disproportionate relief, he stepped onto the smooth, paved surface. He put his phone away. No need to draw attention to himself any longer.

It was very dark, but twenty yards ahead, the first of the lights glowed faintly. On level footing again, he sped up to an almost run.

One-two, one-two.

Just the flapping, he reassured himself, feeling fear surge again as he glanced back into the darkness.

And then, Kevin's feet were knocked out from under him, and he crashed to the ground.

The impact slammed the breath out of him. The rough paving stones scraped his hands and ripped the knees of his expensive suit. He gasped in shock and pain.

What – what had happened?

At first, he thought he'd been attacked. But he hadn't. Wincing as he clambered to his feet, Kevin pieced together that he'd tripped over something in his way. Something big and immovable that surely shouldn't had been there.

He looked back at the shape that was almost invisible in the darkness. Reaching into his pocket, he snapped his phone's light on, peering down at what the bright beam illuminated.

A horrified cry burst from Kevin's numb lips.

He was staring at a sprawled, lifeless body, with a lake of dark blood pooled around it. Sightless eyes stared into the darkness. The mouth was half-open as if asking the unanswerable question, "Why me?"

Nausea wrenched his stomach, causing him to stagger away, leaning on the rickety railing as hot vomit spilled from his mouth.

He knew this face. He knew this man.

How had the larger-than-life Patrick Coleridge, everybody's best friend and go-to investor, ended up brutally murdered on his way into the club?

CHAPTER TWO

FBI agent Stella Fall glanced up from the files she was perusing, pushing a lock of long, dark hair away from her face as she stared at her apartment window.

Something had alerted her instincts enough to distract her from the work she was busy with. She sensed something wrong, with a cold, sure feeling that was a combination of intuition, and picking up subtle signals in her surroundings.

What was it?

She was seated in her apartment's small lounge, on the fifth floor of a new condo in downtown New Haven. The lounge window overlooked the apartment's corridor, which was glassed in.

Stella kept the room's white blinds closed, but she could always see people passing by, gray shadows against the blinds, made visible by the brightness of day or by the night-time lights. It was night now.

She looked harder, realizing what she'd missed while preoccupied with her work.

There was a shadow beyond the blind. But it hadn't moved. It was there now. She could see it faintly.

It looked like someone was standing in the corridor outside her apartment.

Stella swallowed down her fear. Right now, she knew there were people who might be watching her. Powerful people who wished her harm.

Stella regretted the day she'd ever become involved with the Marshalls. If only she'd never become engaged to Vaughn. If only she'd never gone back with him to Greenwich, and met his toxic, evil family. Just as she'd started to realize the depth of the trouble she'd landed in, a murder had been committed.

In her efforts to clear her own name, Stella had uncovered the criminal activities of the corrupt Marshall clan. They blamed her for everything that had happened since then. After the recent suicide of his wife, she knew Vaughn's father, the ruthless ex-senator Gordon Marshall, would be pursuing her with no holds barred.

Standing up, she walked quietly to the front door, noticing the security chain was in place. She kept it fastened because every layer of protection helped. But now, it would be slow and noisy to remove, and would warn whoever was outside.

She did it anyway. Yanked off the chain, grabbed the Yale lock and wrenched it open before flinging the door wide.

Staring out, she saw nothing. The corridor was empty as far as she could see – which was only as far as the corner beyond the next-door apartment.

But as she'd moved the chain, she was sure she'd heard the rapid patter of running footsteps.

"What do you want?" she called. "Why are you watching me?" Then, picking up the scared tone in her own voice, she added more forcefully, "You'd better not come back. I'll be waiting and you'll regret it!"

Her right hand dropped to her service Glock. She'd arrived home from work a few hours ago but it was still belted around her hips.

Automatically, she flexed her hand, feeling the tug of the scar. Three weeks ago, her palm had been cut to the bone while fighting a murderer who'd almost killed her. The wound had healed fast and well, and yesterday she'd been cleared for active duty again, but she still woke up in the night, gasping and screaming, reliving the trauma she'd endured.

What would be best to do now?

Leave the chain off, she decided, locking the door again and returning to the table where she was working. The small wooden desk opposite her leather couch doubled as a workstation and a dining table. It was big enough for one, or even two, but Stella hadn't yet had two for dinner in her apartment. And she didn't want to think about that painful subject right now.

Sitting back down, she took a sip of coffee, now lukewarm, before returning her focus to the screen. At quarter to nine on a Friday night, she was immersed in a private project, and a desperately important one.

She was following up on her father's disappearance.

When Stella was ten, Detective George Fall had gone to work at the local Kansas police precinct and had never come home. For years, Stella had agonized over his whereabouts, fearing that he was dead but not ready to believe it. A few weeks ago, she had found evidence that he'd been alive after the date of his disappearance. She'd confronted her abusive mother and demanded to know the truth. To her surprise, her mother had eventually relented and had sent her his last known address.

Stella now knew that her father had gone to Ouray, Colorado, where he had lived for a few years after his disappearance. He'd taken on a new name – Frank Newman – and he'd rented a post office box in town that was still emptied occasionally. He'd become a different person. Quiet and withdrawn, not making friends or integrating with his community.

These fragile clues were all she had, but they were a start.

At first, Stella had thought that her father's inexplicable actions were linked to some kind of mental breakdown. But now, she was researching another theory, which was that George Fall's disappearance was linked to a case he was working on.

She'd finally gotten hold of the right decision maker in the Leavenworth police department. Although very busy, he had listened to her explanation, as well as her introduction of who she was. Stella hoped that her being an FBI agent might mean he'd be more willing to share information which she understood could not be distributed to the general public.

Even so, he hadn't sounded keen about sending off case details to a random stranger. Stella was worried that he would decide against it; and in that case, she'd have to go there and plead with him in person to at least view the old files. That would take time and money she didn't have right now.

He had promised to call her back when he had time and had thought about it. For now, Stella was doing her best to research what was available in the public domain.

So far, her research had uncovered that George Fall had been an extremely hard-working detective. He'd run a tight ship, he had a high solve rate, and the police department where he worked had been well managed, trusted, and highly regarded by the community. The press reports she'd seen had shown that he had a good relationship with the local press.

How Stella wished she could sit down with her father and speak to him again. Now that she was in law enforcement herself, she had renewed admiration for the way he'd done his job.

At that moment, her phone rang. She grabbed it anxiously.

"Stella Fall?" she said.

"Agent Fall? It's Detective Harding here from Leavenworth."

"Thanks so much for calling back," Stella said.

She felt nervous and expectant as she waited for his verdict.

"I have considered your request about the case files." He paused. "I wasn't working at the precinct at that time. I transferred there a few years ago. But even so, your father's disappearance has never been forgotten and people here still talk about it. It must have been very difficult for you," he said.

Stella felt grateful for his brisk sympathy.

"It was," she acknowledged.

"I don't allow case information to be circulated outside of the precinct," he said firmly.

"I understand," Stella said softly, trying to fight back the disappointment she felt, even as she considered her next move.

But then, he continued.

"However, I've decided to make an exception for you, since you're also in law enforcement, and because of the family connection. So I'll require you to send through your ID and proof of employment at the New Haven branch, and also sign a disclaimer to say you'll keep the information confidential, that you won't forward or share it, and will delete all the records as soon as you are done with them."

"Oh, thank you so much!" Stella felt her spirits lift.

"I trust as an FBI agent you're on board with that?"

"Yes. I will keep it totally confidential," Stella promised.

"Okay then. I'm going to ask my assistant to scan all the files, from the date of Detective Fall's disappearance, going back sixty days. That will probably be about ten criminal cases."

"Thank you. I'm really grateful," Stella replied.

Even though a small Kansas precinct was not a typical hotspot for serious or organized crime, there must have been something that caused him to take this drastic action.

Quickly, she emailed through her ID as well as her recent letter of employment. She felt surprised, as she sent it through, that the date of employment was October, and it was already mid-December. She'd been working at the FBI New Haven branch for two months. Time had flown.

As Stella sent the mail, a flicker of movement from outside caught her eye.

She leaped to her feet.

There was a shadow visible again from behind the window blinds. Someone was outside her apartment again. Watching, listening, waiting.

For a moment, Stella felt choked by fear. Then, steeling herself, she moved quietly.

She was not going to let the intruder get away, and she was going to find out who was lurking outside.

She ran to the front door and wrenched it open.

CHAPTER THREE

Bursting into the corridor, grasping her gun, Stella faced up to the shadowy observer who'd been lurking outside her window.

To her astonishment, she found herself aiming her weapon at the equally shocked Special Agent Rick Maxwell – until recently, her investigation partner and potential love interest.

"Stella! Why are you holding your gun?" he asked, sounding as startled as he looked.

Stella's ice-blue eyes narrowed in fury as the fit, dark-haired Maxwell stepped toward her, his hands open in appeal.

He hadn't come straight from work, because he was wearing jeans and a black sweater. Emotions boiled inside her as she looked into his dark eyes, taking in his repentant expression, the broad strength of his shoulders, the firm lines of his jaw.

"What are you doing here?" she snapped as she holstered her Glock.

She never wanted to see Maxwell again. She thought she'd made that very clear after recently discovering that he was still married. Separated, but still married to the blond, attractive Brigitte.

She wouldn't have minded if he'd told her. Why hadn't he been open about it when romance had first blossomed between them? If he'd explained he was still married, that Brigitte was desperate to try again but he didn't want to, Stella would have understood the complications. But he hadn't said a thing and that made Stella feel as if the rug had been ripped out from under her.

Maxwell had been her investigation partner. They'd depended on each other in life-and-death situations. How could he have kept such an important fact from her, knowing that she had trust issues because of her past, and that honesty was such a critical aspect of a relationship? She was terrified of becoming trapped in the same nightmare that she'd had with Vaughn.

Now, she hated that all the anger and betrayal was surging inside her again. She wanted to forget about those feelings, forever. All Stella could think of was to run, as far and fast as she could. There was no other possible option. There was too much pain. Too much old scarring.

"I came by because you weren't answering my calls," Maxwell said. "I want to discuss this issue with you, Stella. I really want to resolve this. I was an idiot. I knew what you'd been through, and how important truthfulness was to you, and I still kept things from you. I want to explain why I made such a bad decision. To help you understand."

Now Stella felt frustrated. Why was Maxwell being so reasonable? How could he plead for resolution when he'd caused her so much anguish?

She shook her head. "I told you before, I don't want to have anything to do with you. And you were standing in the corridor and watching my apartment. Now, and earlier, too. Why?"

"I wasn't here earlier. I only got here a minute ago. I did stop before I reached your door. I was trying to figure out what to say. I should have realized you'd notice me outside. You never miss a detail."

Now Maxwell sounded embarrassed.

If he was telling the truth, it meant there had been someone else earlier. And that brought in a whole new set of complications.

Fear gripped Stella as she thought about what this might mean. Right now, she couldn't afford to be close to anyone.

"Maxwell, I'm not ready for this," she tried to explain.

"Stella, let me at least apologize." He spread his arms again.

Even as she hesitated, she heard the trill of her phone from the lounge.

It could be the Kansas detective on the line, needing more information. That was at the forefront of Stella's mind as she rushed back inside and grabbed it.

It wasn't the detective. Instead, Stella found herself speaking to Special Agent Roth, who was in charge of the FBI New Haven branch.

"Fall. Do you have a minute to speak?"

"Of course, Roth," she replied quickly.

Hovering in the doorway, Maxwell looked intrigued at the mention of their boss's name.

"We have an urgent case that's just been called in. A murder down at the South Sands Yacht Club. You'll be handling it, and I'd like to brief you on it as soon as possible. Can you come in now?"

A case! Three weeks of office work while her hand healed had felt like an eternity. Now, she'd be back in the field. Doing what she felt called to do.

She had no idea what the circumstances were, or who Roth would decide to partner her with, but those were minor issues compared to the sheer exhilaration that she was on active duty again, and Roth needed her.

"Yes. I'll be there in fifteen minutes. See you then."

She disconnected and turned to Maxwell.

"I have to go," she said.

"What's up?" She could see Maxwell had clocked how excited she was.

"There's a new case that's just come in," Stella said. "Roth is going to brief me on it now."

Instinctively, Maxwell's hand flew to his phone.

"A new case? He hasn't called me yet. Do you want to ride there together?" he asked.

It was time to drop the bombshell that Maxwell clearly didn't yet know about.

Stella couldn't help feeling guilty as she drew a breath to speak. Even though his own actions had caused the rift between them, she still knew he would feel betrayed.

"I asked Roth if I could be partnered with someone different for a while," she explained, seeing the consternation appear in his face. "Roth said he'd consider it. So, if he hasn't called you, it means I'll be handling this with another agent."

"But, Stella –"

"I have to go," she repeated. "There's a case waiting. I can't discuss this now."

"Okay." Maxwell sounded angry and defiant. She knew he wanted to argue his side further, but his professionalism wouldn't let him interfere at such a critical time. He turned away and she heard the annoyed stomp of his retreating footsteps.

Trying to put her conflicted feelings about Maxwell firmly out of her mind, Stella grabbed her purse and her jacket, closed her laptop, and put it into her bag. She slung the bag over her shoulder and was ready to go.

*

She reached the New Haven FBI office in just ten minutes. By the time she climbed out of the car, a light dusting of snow was falling. The cold flakes brushed over her hair as she hurried toward the well-lit FBI building.

Stella rushed through the security checkpoint at the main entrance and headed down the corridor to Roth's office. On the way, she passed two agents leaving. Another three hurried in behind her, speaking in stressed voices as they took the stairs to the second floor. Crime never slept, and an urgent case could land at any hour.

She felt glad she'd been available immediately when Roth called. At the start of a case, every moment counted, and the sooner she could get onto this, the better.

"Fall." Roth was waiting at the door. His harassed expression and untidy chestnut hair belied the fact that he was an extremely competent and skilled workaholic. In the two months Stella had known him, she'd grown to admire his dedicated work ethic, and also his strong focus on integrity.

"Evening, boss," she greeted him with a smile.

"Glad you could get here so quick. This is going to be an urgent case. I'll explain why in a moment. Come through," Roth said.

He gestured to his office.

Looking through the glassed window, Stella felt her heart thud into her shoes.

Carrie Potts was glowering back at her.

Ever since Stella had rashly requested to be partnered with Carrie, she'd regretted her decision, and had hoped that Roth would choose somebody else to pair up with her. Someone more experienced. Someone who didn't have a long-standing grudge against her and who hadn't actively tried to sabotage her career.

Unfortunately, Roth had taken her words at face value, and in that moment, Stella realized how difficult this case was going to be. The tall, lean brunette clearly hadn't expected to see her arrive, and was looking furious. She glowered at Stella through narrowed eyes.

Ignoring the tense atmosphere that had descended, Roth bustled into the office ahead of her.

"It's a madhouse here this weekend. We have two senior agents off duty – one broken leg, one gunshot wound," Roth summarized. "As a result, we're very short staffed. I'm going to help where I can, but I can't be involved full time. So, let me brief you two."

Quickly, Stella sat down, noting that Carrie edged deliberately away from her.

"The victim's name is Patrick Coleridge. The murder took place at the South Sands Yacht Club, in Greenwich," Roth said.

Greenwich. Stella felt sick inside. Greenwich was where the Marshalls lived. She did not want to venture onto their home turf at such a time. The South Sands club wasn't the same one that her ex's family had frequented. She hadn't heard of it, but being in the same area, it was way too close for comfort.

"One of the other club members found the body about half an hour ago. The victim's car was in the parking lot, and he was lying on a walkway between the temporary parking area and the club. The main parking is currently under renovation," Roth explained.

"Any cameras, any footage?" Carrie asked.

"No. Due to the renovations, there were no cameras operational in that area," Roth said. "There are cameras in the club's lobby, I believe."

"And why are we involved? Is there a political angle?" Stella asked. She needed to get this question on the table but dreaded beyond words that Patrick Coleridge would be politically connected. If so, then without a doubt, she'd be rubbing up against the Marshall family again.

"No. We're involved because he's a British national. The case is urgent, as he's a prominent member of the local community and it was a very violent crime. The city council has already been in communication with the local police. They're worried about bad press affecting tourism and business in the area. I don't know more details at this stage. I'm sure there will be much more information available at the scene, but it's a long drive to south Greenwich, so you should probably get going now."

Stella nodded. She guessed it would take an hour and a half to reach their destination, and it was already after nine p.m.

Carrie stood up and marched out. Quickly grabbing her things, Stella followed.

Without speaking, Carrie led the way out of the FBI New Haven building, and to the parking lot.

"Do you want to drive, or shall I?" Stella asked.

In silence, Carrie opened the door of her unmarked and climbed in the driver's side.

Well, Stella guessed that was an answer of sorts.

“I wonder what the circumstances were,” she thought out loud, as she got in the passenger side.

Carrie didn’t answer. She started up the car and drove out of the parking lot in silence.

“Have you been to that yacht club before?” Stella asked. “I haven’t heard of it.”

Carrie was a local who had grown up in Bridgeport, and Stella hoped that her knowledge of the area might provide them with an advantage. But again, Carrie didn’t answer. Her response was nothing more than a small headshake.

Giving up on conversation, Stella lapsed into silence. This was going to be a long and awkward drive, and she was aware it represented only the first step in what she now knew was going to be a personally difficult investigation.

The sooner this case could be solved, the better, Stella thought. The combination of Carrie as a partner, and the crime having been committed in the Marshalls’ home turf, was making her feel scared, vulnerable, and way out of her depth.

She was heading into trouble, in more ways than one.

CHAPTER FOUR

It was ten-thirty p.m. by the time Stella and Carrie reached Greenwich.

Driving into the town itself, Stella felt more and more ill at ease. She was reminded how compact the town center was. It wasn't a big place. As Carrie wove her way past restaurants, theaters, and bars still doing a busy Friday night trade, Stella noticed landmarks she'd forgotten about.

There were the signs to the main street, where Vaughn had promised they'd visit the annual Arts to the Avenue display. That plan had fallen by the wayside as his family's influence prevailed. There had been no chance for them to be a functional couple once the Marshalls' stranglehold over their son's heart and mind had resumed. *What chance had she ever had*, she thought sadly.

There was the avenue that led to the historic district. They passed it by and headed out along the coastal road. A mile later, she noticed a signboard ahead. Her heart sped up as she saw it was for the South Sands yacht club. Beyond it, red and blue lights flickered in the dark and she could see the white glow of a powerful spotlight nearby. Police were on the scene.

"How do we get in?" Carrie frowned, slowing the car as she stared at the boarded-up main entrance, dark and desolate.

It was literally the first question she'd asked Stella, and Stella had no clear answer. They seemed to be doing major renovations.

"Perhaps it's back that way," she hazarded. She'd noticed a small side road a short while earlier. It seemed to be the only option, because from this point the road curved sharply to the left, away from the club.

Sighing as if Stella had personally caused this inconvenience, Carrie did a swift U-turn, and sped back the way she'd come. She headed down the side road, passing a couple of exclusive residential homes. Then the road branched. Carrie hesitated, chose left, and after one further wrong turn, they ended up at what Stella guessed was the club's service entrance.

These renovations had certainly been lucky for the killer, Stella thought, as Carrie parked the unmarked between a Porsche and a Range

Rover. The parking lot was still about half full. Stella guessed that the police were still taking statements from the patrons. Then she rethought. That guess was wrong. A better theory was that none of the drunk patrons had wanted to climb into their cars while detectives were on the scene, and they had all used drivers or cabs to get themselves home.

"None of these guys wanted to get behind the wheel with the police there," Carrie commented, staring around at the expensive vehicles. Stella felt surprised they'd been thinking along such similar lines.

She grabbed her purse from the car as Carrie slammed the door and powered down the walkway, clearly keen to arrive first and establish herself as the go-to person.

Marching irritably along to catch up, Stella realized she'd forgotten exactly how annoying Carrie's ultra-competitive nature was. Worse still, it was distracting Stella. Instead of being focused on the crime, she was worried about outpacing her rival.

She forced herself to slow down. Let Carrie charge ahead and introduce herself. Stella decided that it was more important to get an impression of this crime scene.

The walkway was dimly lit. Temporary lights had been set up at intervals. Even so, between the lights, it was dark enough that Patrick might only have seen his assailant when he – or she – was a couple of steps away.

Had it been a chance encounter, or had he arranged to meet his killer there, Stella wondered. Perhaps he'd innocently walked to or from the club with the murderer. It could also have been an entirely random crime. An opportunistic robber could have taken advantage of the temporary change in the club's setup.

All options needed to be considered, Stella reminded herself.

Ahead, she heard Carrie say a brisk, "Good evening, detectives. Agent Potts from FBI New Haven." She glanced around. "And this is Agent Fall," she added dismissively.

Stella caught up, arriving at the point near the end of the walkway that was the scene of the crime.

Yellow tape already barricaded the walkway and a portable high-intensity light had been set up, bathing the area in its unrelenting white glow. To her relief, the body had been removed, but she saw dark bloodstains on the paving. The evidence of this violent death chilled her. Two detectives wearing PPE were combing the surroundings.

Stella knew this essential search for evidence could sometimes uncover important details.

Unfortunately, she guessed that in this case their efforts would be futile. The persistent icy drizzle, the gusting wind, and the spray blowing in from the sea would have combined to whip away any trace evidence that might have survived in a more sheltered environment.

On her right, a makeshift railing separated the walkway from the cold, restive waters of the harbor. On her left, there was a temporary fence barricading a construction zone beyond, where she saw a high wall was being built. It would be very easy for someone to have hidden there, leaped out, and disappeared again into the darkness.

All this raced through her mind as she walked up to the police detective in charge. When she reached him, she stared at him in surprise. She recognized this stocky, tough-looking man, with shrewd dark eyes and close-cropped dark hair.

He stared back at her, equally flabbergasted.

This was Detective Bradshaw, who'd led the investigation into her fiancé's murder. He'd first suspected Stella, and eventually arrived in the nick of time to help save her from the real killer. After the crime was solved, he'd suggested she go into law enforcement. Now, here she was, assigned to a murder case he was managing.

"It's you. Stella Fall," he said, sounding astounded. "Agent Fall, I mean," he hastily corrected himself.

"Yes, it's me," Stella said, feeling proud.

As well as pride, she was deeply relieved that this capable detective was in charge, and that she had a connection with him.

"Well, this is a surprise. A welcome one," a smile briefly warmed his face. Stella guessed, from the stress she saw, that there hadn't been many opportunities for such an expression in the last couple of hours.

She glanced at Carrie. As expected, the tall, slim brunette was looking furious at the fact Stella knew the detective in charge.

"Unfortunate circumstances," his words brought them firmly back to the matter at hand.

"Can you tell us what you know so far?" Stella asked.

"Patrick Coleridge appears to have been on his way in to the club. A couple of the witnesses said he'd promised to stop in for drinks but hadn't yet arrived inside. He drives the Porsche back there. His body was discovered at about half past eight by one of the club members leaving. He literally fell over the body. From all accounts, another man left half an hour before that, and saw nothing. Since the body was lying in the middle of the walkway, that narrowed down our time of death, which the coroner confirmed as being between eight and eight-thirty p.m. Probably closer to eight-thirty based on the body's temperature."

"So the club member might have just missed the crime," Stella said. "Or is he a suspect?"

"His name's Kevin Anderson, and he's still here. Based on his version, we've cleared him as a suspect, but I'm sure you'll want to interview him."

Stella nodded.

"How did the victim die?" Carrie asked.

"He was stabbed. Multiple times, in the chest and stomach. They'll confirm on autopsy, but there were at least four separate stab wounds. The two to the heart would have been fatal."

With dizzying suddenness, Stella's mind swooped back to that terrible moment on the Marshalls' property, when she'd awoken to find Vaughn dead beside her, with a knife in his chest. In that moment, she recalled the raw, metallic stink of the blood that had been on him, and the sheets, and had oozed onto her.

She took a deep breath. Stared down at the ground.

She sensed that Carrie was looking at her curiously, as if assessing whether this behavior represented a weakness she could use. Detective Bradshaw, who knew the full circumstances, was regarding her with somber sympathy.

"What about his possessions?" she asked in a wobbly voice.

"His wallet was in his pants pocket, with credit cards and a few hundred dollars inside. His phone was in his jacket," Bradshaw said. "So it's extremely unlikely that this was an attempted robbery. We are looking for another motive."

"I have a lot of questions," Carrie said briskly, obviously wanting to take charge and show leadership.

"Please," Bradshaw invited.

"Firstly, the guest who left the club before Mr. Coleridge died. Does he have any connection with the deceased? What was his reason for leaving and does he have an alibi?"

"He knew him," Detective Bradshaw explained. "But the guest who left at eight p.m. rushed out because he received an urgent business call which he needed to deal with immediately at home. He was on the call from that time, until he arrived at his house, a few blocks from here, where he gave the caller the information he needed. He's still home and has already sent us proof of the call. So he wasn't the killer."

Carrie nodded. Stella could see her mind was turning over as she processed this information.

"Who could have had a motive? Any leads thus far?" she asked.

Bradshaw glanced at the detective next to him.

"That's the challenge," he said.

The sturdy detective next to him, a red-haired man swaddled in a jacket and scarf, nodded.

"We all knew Mr. Coleridge. He was very active in the community. Supported anti-crime initiatives and charity events. No known conflicts, no obvious enemies. No criminal record whatsoever. A couple of speeding fines, paid on time. That's it," he said.

"His family?" Stella asked. Family wasn't always as loving as society perceived them to be.

"He has a wife and two sons, aged eighteen and nineteen. The sons are both at Oxford University in England."

At that moment, one of the detectives combing the scene called out.

"You can come through. We're done on this side."

He unhooked the crime scene tape, and they walked past. Stella realized she was shuddering, although whether it was more from cold or tension, she couldn't say. Out here, by the ocean, the elements were fierce, and she hadn't dressed warmly enough for standing outdoors on a winter night. Up ahead was the clubhouse. In this cozy and well-lit environment, Stella hoped that answers, as well as warmth, would be found.

Detective Bradshaw pushed open the door and they walked in.

Stella breathed in warm air scented with the aroma of coffee and cognac as she looked around the elegantly decked out clubhouse. Sophisticated and plush, with gold detailing around the wooden counter and muted, red-shaded lamps, it reminded her of an old-fashioned gentlemen's club.

A reception area, with an anxious-looking waitress in attendance at the front desk, led to a large and comfortably furnished restaurant and bar area. With a mix of lounge furniture, armchairs, and table seating, this clubhouse clearly catered to everyone's needs, and could sit about fifty if it was full.

Glancing up, Stella noticed a camera discreetly positioned on the wall above the reception desk. At least this would confirm who'd been here, if needed.

There were only a few men still inside, sitting on wingback chairs surrounding a coffee table. About five staff members were still present, standing against the walls looking uncomfortable and stressed. The atmosphere was somber. The place was very silent. Someone must have turned the music off at an earlier stage.

"This is Kevin Anderson, who found the victim. We asked him to stay, as we thought you might have some questions," Detective Bradshaw explained.

The expression of dire stress didn't sit well on Kevin's good-looking visage as he turned to them. She thought easy confidence was a far more usual default.

"Agents Potts and Fall, from the FBI," the detective introduced them.

Kevin stood up, looking alarmed. It was only as he stumbled slightly that Stella realized he was still quite drunk.

"Evening, ladies," he said.

Stella felt a surprising flicker of amusement as she saw Carrie draw herself angrily up. Her partner was irate at being addressed as 'ladies' instead of 'agents.'

"Tell me how you found the body, Mr. Anderson?" Stella asked, perching on one of the available chairs.

Officiously, Carrie began arranging the setup.

"Before we start, if you other gentlemen could please move elsewhere. We need to interview you one at a time. We'd like your version, not what you've heard other people say."

Effectively, she cleared the seating area in time for Kevin to sit back down and start with his stammering account.

"I – I was leaving. I'd had an argument with my wife about staying here too late," he said, looking shamefaced. "She'd called and messaged, telling me to come home. I called her as soon as I'd walked out the club. She said – she told me I must take a cab because I was too drunk to drive. I started walking through the construction zone to the main road to get the cab, because it's easier from there, but it was impossible to find a way through, and I – I felt spooked for some reason."

Stella nodded. She was sure there was a reason, even if it was a subliminal one. Kevin could well have heard, or sensed, something that had alerted him to the crime.

"Anyway, I changed my mind and decided to go to the temporary parking and try to direct the driver. And I literally didn't see the body until I tripped over – it – him." He stared at Stella, looking distraught. "I turned my phone's light on and recognized who it was immediately.

I threw up. I ran back inside. I told a few people. The manager, and a couple of guys in reception. After that, it's a blur. I sat down. Someone brought me a cup of tea. Everything was going mad, people were shouting, panicking, asking me what had happened. The manager stopped them from going out and said they had to stay where they were."

Kevin glanced at the tall, dark-haired man in a waiter's uniform who was standing near the reception area, looking concerned and alert.

"I can't believe I missed it by – by only a few minutes, most likely, the police said. I don't know if I would have been able to prevent it if I'd been there. Or if I would have been stabbed, also. He was – there was so much blood. There was a big cut on his hand, too. It was horrific. I see his body every time I close my eyes. It all feels so surreal."

Stella sympathized with his words. She knew what it felt like. It wouldn't offer Kevin much comfort if she told him that the shock, the fear, and those gory images, would stay with him for a long time to come.

Looking more closely at Kevin, she could see the signs of his fall. His palms were grazed, and one of the knees of his suit was ripped. With shaking hands, he took his phone and showed her the list of recent calls.

Stella was reassured that the police had been correct in clearing Kevin as a suspect, based on the phone call and what had followed. He had been comfortably ensconced at the club and hadn't wanted to leave until his wife had forced him to.

She felt grateful for the manager's quick thinking. Even though there was a lack of trace evidence thanks to the wintry weather, at least the scene had remained relatively uncontaminated.

Carrie bustled back.

"Mr. Anderson, you say Mr. Coleridge hadn't yet entered the building?"

"No. I didn't see him, and I was looking out for him. He'd promised to go through a few investment options when we saw each other again. He owns Zenith Wealth, which is a local finance firm. It's very well regarded, and I was looking forward to hearing more. He was a friendly guy. I mean, he never walked into a room unnoticed. It was more like a celebrity arriving. Lots of attention, lots of greetings, lots of fuss. In a good way."

“Did you notice anyone unusual here tonight? Anyone you didn’t recognize?” Stella then asked.

“No. I only saw the regulars.”

Stella exchanged a glance with Carrie, who stared coldly back.

Kevin’s version seemed pretty watertight, Stella thought. That meant they would now have to interview the other people at the club – the remaining patrons as well as the staff.

So far, this had all the indications of turning into a difficult case. Murderous intent was behind every vicious stab from the knife. Someone had hated this seemingly well-liked man enough to do this.

They needed to interview the staff, and Patrick’s contacts, and find out who had known he would be arriving at the yacht club at this late hour.

Hopefully, among the people present, someone would know something that would take them a step further in this disturbing case.

CHAPTER FIVE

Carrie Potts sat down opposite the stressed-looking yacht club manager who was the last of her three interviews. The pressure was on, because this was her first murder case. Up until now, the cases she'd handled had been related to drug trafficking and money laundering.

She took a moment to prepare, making sure her training protocols were firmly entrenched in her mind. She was going to succeed in this. She had to succeed.

Her father's words rang in her mind. "*Carrie, I can't believe you're going into the FBI. As a woman, too? It's unacceptable! Endangering yourself – and for what reason? Becoming some sort of glorified policeman, when you have a business brain? You got the highest grades in university. You're our only child and I always saw you taking over our law firm one day!*"

With her mother's support, Carrie had chosen to defy him and prove the critical, difficult-to-please man wrong. She was hell-bent on showing him that she was the best. The most successful female agent the FBI had ever had. And eventually, he'd begin to respect the fact that she had chosen this field and would soon rise to the top.

She would have been there already. She'd have been the only female agent to have graduated in her intake, and the only woman to have been hired at New Haven that year, on the path to succeed in a man's world. But Stella Fall had put a spoke in her wheel. She'd graduated with Carrie, won the Directors Award, and then, in a further blow, she'd also been hired at New Haven.

Carrie didn't trust her. She was too quiet, too restrained. She had connections, somehow, who'd wrangled her into the Academy and Carrie felt deeply suspicious. Had she bribed her way in? Slept her way in? Carrie felt certain she was the type of person who would do that, and who would stab you in the back as soon as she got a chance.

The only solution was for her to do it first. Destroy the threat, whatever it takes. That was what her father had told her, over and over again. That was how you succeeded. You didn't get to the top by being nice, but by being tough and ruthless.

Carrie glanced at Fall, who was interviewing the last remaining patron on the opposite side of the comfortable room.

Carrie had concluded the brief interviews with the guests first, so that they could leave. Now, she was seated opposite what she considered to be the most promising source of information, and she was sure she'd get better results from her interview than Fall would.

Suppressing the fierce competition that always burned in her mind, Carrie turned to the manager.

"Your name, please, sir?" she asked him.

"Victor Perry," he replied.

"Mr. Perry, do guests sign in when they arrive? Do you have a record of who was here tonight, and their contact details?"

"Guests are signed in by us. We know all the members personally, and this club is for members only. Of course, they may bring friends, or guests, as we call them, and if so, we take the time to find out their names also."

"Will you be able to provide tonight's list of members, with all the contact details?"

"Yes, I will."

"Anyone here tonight who you hadn't seen before?"

"Two people arrived with guests, but they left much earlier."

"What happened when you heard about the murder?"

Perry shook his head sadly. "I was serving drinks when the member, Mr. Anderson, left. He rushed in again, a few minutes after leaving. He was in a total panic. Grazed hands, his suit was torn. He looked terrible. At first, I thought he'd been mugged. But then I realized what he was shouting. That there had been a disaster. That Mr. Coleridge was outside, covered in blood, that he was dead. Luckily, I was serving a table near the door, so I heard immediately."

"What happened then?" Carrie asked, needing to piece together the entire sequence of events.

"The members closest to the door all jumped up in a panic. It was pandemonium inside for a minute," Perry remembered. "I acted fast. I ran into the reception area, closed the entrance door and requested that all members please be seated, be calm, and remain inside. I rushed out straight after that. I wanted to check if he was really dead or just badly injured so that I knew who to call."

Perry paled at the memory. Carrie could see that the gruesome sight would remain with him forever.

"Since he had clearly been murdered, I called 911 immediately and waited outside until the police arrived," he said.

"And you say Mr. Coleridge didn't enter the club?"

"No. It's definitely his car in the parking lot, but he didn't make it inside," Perry said sadly.

"How long have your renovations been going on?" Carrie asked.

"Four weeks, so far. At any rate, that's how long the parking has been rerouted. They were delayed due to weather, and then we had a problem with the supply of bricks for the perimeter wall. They've promised us it'll be done in two more weeks."

"When was the last time Mr. Coleridge was here?" Carrie then questioned.

"He was here last Friday for drinks. He sat on one of the couches and there was a lot of talk and laughter with the other guys. They were discussing an upcoming charity fundraiser," Perry explained.

"Is he often here on Fridays?"

"Quite often. I believe he often hosts client meetings at his work on a Friday. He's mentioned that once or twice. He then comes by the club after the meetings."

"What was your personal impression of him?"

"He never spoke an angry word. He was very sociable and always in the center of the conversation. He paid well; he tipped generously. I never saw him have a fight or a conflict with anyone. I don't think you'll find anyone here who says otherwise."

Perry glanced around, toward the other staff.

One of the waiters, who'd edged close enough to hear their conversation, nodded approvingly. Carrie glared at him. She'd cleared the area for a reason. People needed to do what she told them.

Hastily, the other waiter retreated a few steps back.

"Was he involved in any controversial issues that you know of?" Carrie asked, keeping her voice down.

Perry shook his head sadly. "He supported charities, but I never heard that he was involved in any controversy. Perhaps people who know him better might know more."

Carrie felt disappointed. So far, it seemed nobody could possibly have had a motive to kill Patrick. Even so, she wasn't going to take anyone's word for it but was going to closely investigate his life. Leaving out one small detail could mean losing instead of winning. The fear of losing smoldered inside her.

Equally powerful was the fear that Stella Fall would stumble upon a solid lead and end up solving the case and taking the credit. That would be humiliation at its worst. She imagined herself, her usual confidence in tatters, trying to stammer out to her father why her partner in this case – worse still, another woman – had been the one to solve the crime.

Her father would know. Or else, he would find out. He had connections high up in the police force, and also many business contacts in the media. Carrie cringed at the thought of what would happen if Stella Fall was on the scene when the crime was solved, and the local news interviewed her first.

Briefly, Carrie's thoughts veered to what she thought of as the ace up her sleeve. It was her friend, or rather acquaintance, who was close to the Marshalls. This friend had told Carrie before now that the Marshalls wanted to get Stella Fall removed from the Bureau.

But Stella's own strength of character, and the aggressive way she'd stood up to Carrie recently, had caused Carrie to hesitate. She didn't want Fall turning the tables on her, or getting her in trouble with Roth, who ran the New Haven FBI branch and, Carrie suspected, thought of Fall as his favorite.

However, the option was always there and perhaps now the time had come to take advantage. Carrie decided to get in touch with her acquaintance as soon as she had time.

At that moment, the entrance door banged open, and Detective Bradshaw rushed into the club.

"Agents, would you like to speak to the coroner who examined the body at the scene? The postmortem is scheduled for tomorrow afternoon, but he's at the Greenwich police precinct now, signing off some paperwork. If you have any questions, I can call him and ask him to wait. His name's Shane Oliver."

Carrie glanced over to Stella, who nodded, looking hopeful. Any additional information could be very valuable, and they might learn more about the crime than they already knew.

"Good idea," Carrie said. "Let's go."

CHAPTER SIX

Stella stood up from the wingback chair where she'd just wrapped up her last interview and hurried to the door.

She felt glad that they would have a chance to learn more about the actual crime scene rather than listening to opinions. So far, the opinions had not been helpful. Every person she'd spoken to had said the same thing. That Patrick Coleridge was a good guy, a pillar of the community, a contributor to charity and good causes, and an ethical and successful business owner.

Nobody, in fact, had found anything bad to say about the victim, or come up with any ideas about why someone would want to kill him.

Stella found herself feeling more and more suspicious of these worshipful accolades. Who was the real person behind the likable charity benefactor? People didn't get murdered for no reason. Someone had been angry enough with this pillar of the community to stab him not just once, but multiple times.

She and Carrie rushed down the windy walkway, got into the unmarked and set off on the short drive to the local police precinct.

"The guys I spoke to all said that he was often at the club on Fridays," Stella said, determined that she was not going to let this trip pass by in stony silence.

"Yes, mine said the same," Carrie agreed.

"They said he had definitely not been at the club earlier, and that there were no unusual or suspicious people at the club that night," Stella said.

Carrie shrugged irritably. "Likewise. Nothing out of place in the stories at all."

"Did yours also say he was a good-natured guy, no enemies, always the life and soul of the party?"

"Pretty much word for word," Carrie agreed.

Stella shook her head. "This isn't going to be as simple a case as I hoped," she said.

Was it her imagination, or did Carrie look briefly gleeful, as if she was pleased Stella was stumped? As she drove, Stella wondered whether the ultra-competitive Carrie had been fearful that Stella would uncover crucial evidence and end up solving the case.

This attitude presented a problem, especially since Carrie had already tried to sabotage Stella's career in the past. Stella needed to make sure the investigation truly was a team effort, even though she didn't feel the remotest speck of team spirit.

This situation was all Stella's fault. She was the one who, at the worst possible time, had asked to change partners. Who knew what the Marshalls might do at this point, and how Carrie would end up helping them?

"Here we are," Carrie said, pulling up outside a large, red-brick building, positioned in what seemed to be the banking area of downtown. They hurried inside with Carrie, as usual, shouldering ahead of Stella.

In exasperation, Stella almost said something. She almost snapped out words that would have been sarcastic and inappropriate, like "Shall I wait in the car?" or "Planning to speak to him all on your own?"

She bit back the angry comments that simmered in her mind. Instead, for the first time, she started wondering why Carrie was this way. It wasn't just a dislike of Stella. Now that she'd spent time with the other woman, Stella was picking up that Carrie was deeply insecure.

"FBI to see Mr. Shane Oliver," Carrie announced to the sergeant at the desk.

The young woman had clearly been briefed. She immediately got up and let them in the side door.

"Mr. Oliver is in the back office," she said, opening another door.

The back office was a cozy place, well-insulated with tidy ranks of filing shelves, and furnished with polished wooden desks. Only two desks were occupied at this late hour, and Stella's gaze was drawn immediately to the man at the closest desk, who was dressed in scrubs, with his sleeves pushed back, staring intently at the printed report he was reading.

He looked up when he saw them approach.

"FBI?" he asked.

Stella's first impression of Oliver was of brisk competence as he shuffled the papers into order and closed the file, gesturing to the seats opposite.

"Thank you for making the time," she said.

Stella felt relieved that she was face to face with this man in the warm, ordered environment of the police station back office, rather than having this discussion in the chilly confines of the pathology lab.

"I photographed the crime scene," Oliver said. "Let me show you the shots."

He opened a laptop that had been closed on the desk and turned it to face them.

Stella drew in a deep breath. Photographs were a step removed, but she'd still need to prepare herself to look at them.

"Here is where the body lay. It was lying across the walkway, but almost invisible in the dark."

In the bright glare of the crime scene spotlights, she saw Patrick was lying on his side, sprawled across the walkway, with his head turned in the direction of the parking lot. She could imagine that, with his black hair and onyx suit and without the benefit of lighting, he'd have been nothing more than a deeper shadow in the darkness from the clubhouse side.

"Here's a shot of his face."

Stella looked. The man had strong, handsome features. She guessed in another ten years they might be described as craggy. Superimposed over the pallor of death, his skin still held a faint summer tan, making Stella think he'd either vacationed somewhere sunny, or else maybe used a sunbed.

In the sharp close-up of the photo, she saw some evidence of the good life. His jowls were fleshy, his eyes slightly hooded. She saw small broken veins in his nose. She'd expected that he might look surprised, but weirdly, in death, his features looked somehow resigned.

"His right hand was close to his chest. There were defensive wounds on his right palm, but basically only one deep slice. So he tried to defend himself, as you can see from this next close-up photo, but the attack was violent and it's likely that all the blows were made in quick succession while he was standing. Fast and lethal. Two of the stab wounds were in the area of his heart. At least one must have been fatal, and he would have collapsed very soon after that."

"The other wounds?" Carrie asked.

"To the chest and stomach. I'm guessing the attacker was right-handed, although the pathologist will need to confirm that. And the blows were forceful. Someone was very angry. The victim was a tall, big man and if he'd had more warning, or the chance to defend himself, it might have ended differently. So my personal feeling is that he wasn't surprised by a stranger, or he'd have been more on his guard out there in the darkness. My guess is this was someone he knew, who took him unawares."

"Do you know what type of knife it was?" Stella asked.

"No. Again, the pathologist might be able to narrow it down, but my guess is from the size of the blade, it could be a hunting knife, or a chef's knife, or a good utility knife. Any sharp, quality blade could have made these wounds."

"Anything else you noticed?"

The pathologist shook his head. "Only that it was noisy out there, as I'm sure you observed. There was a wind. That railing rattled. The waves were crashing. It would have drowned out any sound, any shout for help. And it was dark. Whoever wanted to kill the victim certainly had a 'perfect storm' of ideal conditions to surprise him, do the deed, and vanish."

He stared at them with a rueful twist to his mouth.

"Thank you. I appreciate seeing the pictures, and your insight," Stella said.

They got up and left the warm, ordered back office. As they climbed back into the car. Stella sensed that Carrie was feeling discouraged by the lack of progress.

"That didn't provide as much evidence as I'd hoped," she said.

Stella shrugged. She felt differently. She thought Oliver had given them a lot of valuable insight. Particularly that the evidence showed he'd known and trusted his attacker. That meant it was time to confront the person who was always a prime suspect in a murder.

"Even though it's late, I think we should question Patrick's wife now," Stella said.

CHAPTER SEVEN

It was close to midnight when Stella and Carrie arrived at the Coleridge family home. Patrick's wife, Liane, had agreed to see them when they'd called her a few minutes earlier. Stella felt huge relief that this interview could be done tonight.

There was a good reason why the spouse was always the main suspect. They needed to probe for any possible motive and confirm Liane's alibi.

If she wasn't the killer, she would still know much more about his life than the superficial acquaintances at the club, and this might result in some new leads.

As they headed up the driveway, she took in the home. Its similarity to the Marshalls' mansion sent a chill down her spine. It was set in spacious grounds, and the house itself was a two-story architectural masterpiece. Stella guessed, from the exquisite façade, that millions had been spent renovating one of the area's historic houses into a stylish, modern home, while retaining the feel and flavor of the original building.

The impression of ultra-wealth scared her. She couldn't help this fear. Not after her association with the Marshalls and seeing how they had abused their money and power.

They parked next to another small vehicle in the paved circle at the top of the drive. Stella guessed that the local police were still here and wondered why they were taking so long to question Liane.

"Nice place," Carrie said casually, as if she was averagely impressed by its magnificent façade, with ranks of symmetrical bay windows on either side of the double doorway.

She strode up to the door and rapped the knocker.

A moment later, a housemaid opened it. She looked tired and stressed, and Stella was immediately triggered by her memories of the abuse that the Marshalls' staff had endured.

"FBI agents. We're here to speak to Mrs. Coleridge," Carrie said.

Fortunately, Stella's concerns about abusive staff practices were put to rest by the housemaid's warm, if sad, smile.

"Please come this way," she said softly, leading the way through the enormous hall, dominated by a twinkling chandelier, and then veering right into the formal lounge that Stella had expected to see.

Perched on one of the elegant, antique-style couches were two detectives. Seated on the other was the grieving widow. She looked up as they walked in.

Stella was immediately struck by Liane's beauty. She had a perfect oval face, porcelain skin framed by cascades of dark, wavy hair. Even though her eyes were reddened, Stella picked up that they were a deep, intense blue.

She was wearing a gray jacket, and black pants that hugged her slim figure. As she and Carrie approached, the officers stood up. She recognized one as Bradshaw's red-haired partner who'd spoken to them at the crime scene.

"We're done here, agents," one of them said. "Mrs. Coleridge asked us to stay until you arrived."

"I don't want to be alone at this time," Liane explained, in a soft, husky voice that was as beautiful as her appearance, even though it trembled with grief. "My sister is arriving soon. She's driving here from the Hamptons. She's going to stay with me for a few nights. My sons are thankfully in Oxford, England. We're making plans for them to fly back."

As the detectives left, Liane gestured to the nearby chairs, and Stella found herself taking a seat as if bidden to do so. Carrie sat down likewise.

Liane certainly was a powerful personality, Stella thought. She seemed to create an ambiance around herself. Right now, the overpowering feeling was of tragedy and loss.

Stella wasn't sure how authentic it was. *It was certainly compelling; but was it genuine*, she wondered. Real grief was often more ragged, more undignified and uglier. But, on the other hand, she warned herself not to be too mistrustful, since everyone's response was different.

The housemaid hovered with a tray, offering steaming cups of coffee. Stella accepted one gratefully and Carrie did the same.

A box of Kleenex also stood on the immaculate glass table. As Stella watched, Liane reached over and took one with her pearly-manicured fingers. She wiped her eyes carefully. The shaky catch in her breath was soft but audible. For a moment, the only other sound was retreating footsteps as the housemaid discreetly left the room.

“Mrs. Coleridge, please accept our condolences. And thank you for being available tonight,” Stella opened the conversation. She felt, rather than saw, Carrie’s quick, annoyed glance in her direction. Carrie had wanted to start this interview and now she’d gotten in first

“We may have to ask you some personal questions,” Carrie quickly added, putting down her cup on the glass-topped table. “I hope you understand we need to get as much background as we can and rule out certain obvious suspects.”

Liane nodded.

“Absolutely, agent. I understand what you have to do.”

“Did you know that your husband was going to be at the South Sands yacht club tonight?” Carrie asked.

“Yes.” Liane confirmed. “He likes to go there on a Friday. Probably three out of four Fridays he will socialize there. Would socialize, I mean,” she paused, looking briefly bewildered as if the reality of her situation was hitting home yet again. “Tonight, I believe he worked late. They often have client cocktail evenings, with drinks and snacks at his business on Friday. He’d go to the club after that, and usually be home by midnight.”

“And your movements tonight?”

“I went out for dinner with a girlfriend. That’s also quite normal. I see my friends most Fridays because of his work commitments. It never ends up being a late night. I got home tonight at around ten, I think. I was watching television in the family nook when the police arrived.”

So Liane had an alibi, but Stella needed to test it in more detail.

“Where did you go to eat?” Stella asked.

“A restaurant on the seafront called Gio’s Prawns. I love seafood. Patrick, not so much,” Liane explained.

“And who were you with?”

“A friend called Amelia Engels. She also lives locally, a few blocks from here. The police have her details.”

Stella decided it was time to push forward and ask the more difficult questions. She wanted to find out more background on the Coleridges’ relationship, and on Patrick’s close friends that Liane might know.

“What was your marriage like, Mrs. Coleridge?”

Liane looked at her, sadly, but with an astute sharpness in her eyes that told Stella she knew exactly why this question was being asked.

“Our marriage was good. Strong. And I say so knowing that a lot of marriages do go through ups and downs. I would describe ours as very steady and that was partly due to the type of person Patrick was. He was a rock," she said.

"Would you say he shared a lot about his life with you?"

Liane nodded. "Yes. We were close."

"Any recent conflict you know about? Work problems? Any falling out with family members or friends?" Carrie asked, leaning forward with an intense look in her eyes.

Liane shook her head. "This is exactly why all this is such a shock. There was nothing like that going on at all. Absolutely no friction with clients. His business was very successful. He's a very likeable, sociable man. One of those people who'll end up being friends with everyone he meets. I just do not know who could have wanted to kill him."

She gazed from Carrie to Stella in appeal. "Is it possible that he came face to face with a robber, some criminal element, a drug dealer? Patrick is very anti-drugs. That's literally the only thing that I can think of that could have triggered him. If he'd told a drug pusher to get the hell out."

"We're looking at all angles," Stella agreed, even though a robber or drug pusher would surely have taken his money before they ran.

She glanced at Carrie. She was all out of questions and couldn't think of anything more to ask that might help to direct their investigation.

At that moment, the sharp rap of the knocker echoed through the house. It was followed immediately by the hurried footsteps of the housemaid heading to the door.

Liane stood up, relief softening the stressed, miserable expression in her eyes.

"That will be my sister," she said.

Stella glanced at Carrie. There was no reason for them to stay here any longer. They'd managed to get a lot done since arriving in Greenwich. It was just unfortunate that none of it, so far, had yielded any valuable information or leads.

"Thank you for your time, Mrs. Coleridge," Stella said, as she and Carrie got up.

Carrie handed her a business card.

"If you think of anything else, please call me. And you can expect us back here again in the next day or so. As the case progresses, we will most likely need to interview you again."

They headed out, passing a dark-haired, slim woman who was clearly Liane's sister. Barely glancing at Carrie and Stella, she rushed into the lounge, and a moment later, Stella heard muffled sobs and soft words of condolences as she hugged her sister tightly.

So far, Stella thought in frustration, it was looking like Patrick was a disturbingly perfect man. There were no obvious problems in his life, his marriage was strong, he had no enemies and many friends. In fact, he seemed a paragon of virtue and a pillar of the community.

But this in itself was making Stella suspicious. Nobody had such a perfect life. Nobody had zero enemies. Everyone made mistakes.

"So. Where to now?" Carrie asked Stella as they got into the car, and Stella picked up the note of challenge in her voice.

It was half past midnight. A reasonable decision would be to call it a night and start up again in the morning. But Stella wasn't ready to do anything so sensible.

"We have the list of people who were at the club tonight," she said. "It's too late to interview anyone now, but why don't we go to the FBI's satellite office in Fairfield, and do some research on the list for a few hours?"

Carrie looked disappointed, as if she'd been hoping Stella would suggest turning in, and she could then prove she was the more dedicated agent, by arguing they should work late.

"Yes, I also think we should push on and do that," she said in surly tones.

They climbed into the car and drove out of the Coleridges' luxurious residence.

"We're not making as much progress as I'd hoped," Carrie said, sounding worried. "Perhaps we've missed that it was a random criminal. Who could have wanted to kill him otherwise? Nobody, so far."

Stella shook her head. "I don't trust that this is such a perfect situation. And that Patrick had such a blameless life."

"You really do have a problem with the upper classes, don't you?" Carrie said disparagingly.

It took all of Stella's self-control not to react angrily to this baiting. She, too, was feeling frustrated, and scared that they would end up failing and that Roth would have to step in.

"I don't have a problem with the upper classes, or with the ultra-wealthy," she explained calmly. "However, I do have a problem with so many versions all stating that Patrick Coleridge was only one step removed from being a saint. I don't trust that. I want to know who he was connected with at the club, so that we can look for any proof of something less than perfect going on."

"I still think you're prejudiced," Carrie insisted, with a smug, mirthless smile. "You're really being narrow-minded about this. Don't you feel that your mindset is going to start affecting the course of this investigation? You can't suspect a person of being an unsavory character just because he's wealthy and well liked. You're going to end up causing this whole thing to veer off in the direction you want it to go. And that's going to delay everything."

Stella shook her head.

"Someone had enough of a problem with Patrick to stab him multiple times. It wasn't a robbery, because why would all his cash not have been taken? It was someone who got close enough to him without him being defensive, late at night, on a dark walkway. Therefore, it was someone he trusted," Stella reiterated to Carrie.

"Okay," Carrie said reluctantly.

"There must have been a trigger. We have to comb through his seemingly blameless life, and all these good friends who thought he was a fabulous guy. And we have to find where things went wrong. That one person he screwed over. That one enemy that nobody talks about. I guarantee you that there is such a person. We have to find them," she said.

"I believe he was a genuinely good guy, and that someone had it in for him regardless," Carrie theorized. "The motive could be jealousy. Look at him. He had the perfect life, a beautiful wife, an amazing career, tons of money. Perhaps one of his friends or family did less well and couldn't handle it. Or they asked him for a loan or a handout, and he refused, so they got mad."

"That's certainly an idea," Stella said. "And when it's light tomorrow, we can question his friends and family about that, too."

"I can hear in your voice that you don't believe me, Fall," Carrie shot back, sounding as frustrated as Stella felt. "It's lucky there are two of us on this case, because at least I'm taking a wider view and not insisting that a local community hero was really a bad guy."

Stella shook her head, deciding to abandon the argument. She wasn't backing down from her stance, though. She was sure that there was more to Patrick's life.

She didn't trust perfect. It always meant there was something to hide, and she felt determined to find out what it was.

CHAPTER EIGHT

Stella stifled a yawn that threatened to split her face in half as she raised her head up from her folded arms. She'd lowered it down onto the desk to rest her eyes for a moment and she must have fallen asleep, because she'd had a weird dream that Maxwell had been rapping on the window, begging to talk to her.

Quickly, she looked across at the opposite desk, hoping Carrie hadn't seen this irrefutable evidence of exhaustion.

The desk was empty. Carrie must either have gone to the bathroom, or to the kitchenette to grab another coffee. Either way, she would have seen the shameful sight of Stella snoozing in the FBI Fairfield satellite office.

Feeling angry with herself, Stella checked the time, blinking her eyes, which felt grainy and dry.

It was already seven a.m.

Stella couldn't believe an entire night had passed. Fueled only by coffee, they'd sat in this well-equipped room, using all the Bureau's plentiful resources to further investigate the connections between Patrick Coleridge and the names on the list the yacht club manager had provided.

It wasn't that they'd found nothing. They'd found too much. The gregarious Patrick seemed to have connections with most of the men who'd been at the club.

Golfing, balls, charity walks, mountain bike clubs, investment ventures – Patrick was certainly active in his community and had networked with many of his yacht club friends. The evidence was out there in the public domain.

However, despite investigating all the links, Stella hadn't found anything unusual or irregular. There wasn't a whiff of scandal to be seen in the local newspaper reports and business snippets. Not so much as a sniff of any problems between him and his connections.

So their night of nonstop work had only reinforced Carrie's version. It hadn't progressed Stella's line of thinking at all.

Her phone beeped and she glanced down at it.

It was another message from Maxwell. He'd texted her late last night also and she hadn't had time to read it till the early hours.

This one was along similar lines.

"Stella, I hope everything's going okay. I know you're busy on the case. When you have time, we need to talk. Please call me."

She shook her head, closing the app on her phone, deciding to add 'short tempered' to her current mood as Carrie walked back in. She, too, looked tired and annoyed.

"What a wonderful night of progress we've had," she said bitingly. "Absolutely nothing uncovered, apart from that he's a pillar of society who has lots of friends."

"It hasn't been as productive as I hoped," Stella said grumpily.

Carrie stared at her through narrowed eyes that Stella could see felt as dry and tired as they looked.

"Maybe that's because we've been going in totally the wrong direction, thanks to your ridiculous suspicions that this victim has some skeletons hidden away in a nonexistent closet. How many more hours is it going to take for you to realize that this is absolutely futile?" Carrie snapped.

Stella was ready with an equally lashing comeback but caught herself. Sniping at each other would get them nowhere and they couldn't afford for the already stressed relationship between them to suffer further damage. Not when they had to partner together to solve this crime.

"I have a suggestion," Stella said.

"What's that?"

"Patrick's offices are in downtown Greenwich, and if we leave here now, I'm sure they'll be open by the time we arrive. Let's speak to his co-workers. That might open up new directions in both our lines of thinking. We might find out if a client was unhappy, or if a business connection was jealous, or if an employee left on bad terms."

"Okay," Carrie agreed. "I was going to suggest we should investigate his work as the next step."

Stella stood up on legs that felt stiff and cramped. She felt sick from too much coffee. What she needed now was sleep, but there was no time, and she'd have to draw on her inner reserves and push on. Even though she was exhausted, she had to be fully sharp when they arrived at the finance firm's offices.

There had to be a motive, and the more angles that were ruled out, the more important it became to investigate the remaining directions as thoroughly as possible.

*

Zenith Wealth was based in its own building in downtown Greenwich. With morning traffic creating backups, the main street was busy. As they crawled along, Stella looked again at the places she remembered from many months ago. Then, the graceful trees and planters had been wreathed in vivid spring greenery. Now, the trees were bare, but the storefronts twinkled with bright, welcoming Christmas lights. In the gray dawn, the street looked cheerful and attractive.

Thinking that this had almost been her hometown made her feel strangely disoriented. If things had gone right with Vaughn, she'd know every one of these restaurants and boutiques by now. She'd have spent many weekends exploring the stores, strolling along the clean, well-maintained streets.

Perhaps she would have found some personal favorites at that little bakery on the corner with a red-and-gold wreath above the door. Its tables were set for the few people who were braving the early morning cold, and colorful rows of cookies and cakes offered a mouthwatering enticement to enter. She looked longingly at the pies, realizing she was starving.

Maybe Vaughn would have gone shoe shopping with her at the store on the corner, selling a selection of sport and leisure footwear, with bright, twinkling lights threaded among the displays.

And if they'd moved into their own place, they would have spent many happy hours browsing the antique stores on the main street, hoping to find some hidden gems among the polished furniture and objects d'art.

Stella didn't like thinking this way, but immersed in Greenwich's town center, she had no choice but to dwell on what might have been.

Instead, she'd been caught in a horrific vortex of circumstances that had sucked her in and spat her out, changing her forever as a person and leaving her in a position where she'd made lasting, powerful enemies.

"We turn here," Carrie's sharp voice interrupted her thoughts. "And here, ahead of us, is the Zenith Wealth headquarters."

Stella stared in surprise at the glass-clad, three-story building set in a courtyard with a fountain as the centerpiece. Though imposing, the headquarters looked out of place among the more historic tone of the rest of downtown. Wealth, and the subtle promise of more to come, gleamed from every shiny facet of this ultra-modern structure.

"Quite a nice building," Carrie said approvingly, clearly on a mission to prove her point that Patrick Coleridge could do no wrong. "I feel in this town, the whole historic theme is overdone. It's refreshing to see a place that moves away from that look and dares to be different."

Stella didn't respond. She loved the historic feel of the Greenwich architecture and personally thought that new buildings should pay homage to their heritage and contribute to the character of the town. But Patrick had clearly thought the same as Carrie.

They parked in the basement and took the elevator up to the reception hall. Like the outside of the building, this too was ultra-modern, with large windows, bright lighting, blinding white tiles and trendy furniture.

The young, blonde receptionist looked distracted and harassed, and Stella was sure she'd just heard the sad news about her boss and was still processing her shock. She greeted them with a brave attempt at a smile.

"Good morning. How can I help you?"

Then her gaze traveled to Stella's gun and her eyes widened as she realized these were not, in fact, potential clients she was talking to.

"FBI," Carrie said.

"Oh. Oh, my goodness." The receptionist stared at them in consternation. "This is making it all so real. It's so terrible."

"Have you worked here long?" Carrie asked, clearly intent on forging ahead with questioning as many people as possible.

"I've been here a year."

"What are your impressions of the business?" Carrie asked.

"It's a wonderful place to work," she continued sadly. "Mr. Coleridge is – sorry, was – an amazing employer. He welcomed me personally on my first day and gave me a guided tour of the building. He calls – called – all the staff on their birthdays. I just cannot believe this has happened. That such a good man has lost his life."

"We'd like to speak to the senior staff who worked closely with him," Stella said. "Did he own the company in full, or were there other shareholders?"

"I think he was the sole owner. I never heard about other shareholders. But I'll call the management team and they can take it from here."

She picked up the phone and dialed.

"Harriet? The FBI is here." She put the phone down. "Harriet is coming now. She's the financial manager, and knows the business best out of everyone," she said.

A few seconds later, the elevator doors opened, and a black-clad woman walked out. She looked in her early forties – slim, attractive, competent, and exuding an understated aura of wealth.

"Good morning, agents. I heard about this tragedy last night. Liane called me as soon as she'd had a chance to take in the news."

Stella nodded, thinking this explained her somber black outfit and stark, scraped-back hairstyle.

"I'm extremely busy this morning," Harriet continued. "There's a long list of protocols in place to be followed in the event of Mr. Coleridge's passing. I'm working on it now. I can be available if you have any questions, but it would be easier if you could interview the other staff first."

"Sure," Stella said. She didn't think Harriet was being evasive. She looked like an efficient, get-things-done person who was genuinely stressed by the circumstances.

"Mr. Coleridge's PA is his right hand," Harriet said. "Her name's Yolanda Gregory. The accounts manager is Terri Booth. They supervise the rest of the team, comprising eight staff who work in areas from market trading to admin to client liaison, but they were all under me, not under Mr. Coleridge."

"So you're saying that the PA and accounts manager are the most important staff to interview first?"

"Yes. Perhaps you'd like to start with Yolanda? Come this way, and you can sit in the client lounge.

She turned and led the way back to the elevator.

Stella followed, with Carrie just about treading on her heels. She was glad they were going to see inside this building. Not only would they get a taste of what the clients had experienced, but they might also find out what happened behind the scenes.

As she passed the exquisite designer chairs set out along the wall, Stella noticed a tiny blip in the radar of perfection. One of the white tiles had a spreading, bluish stain on it, as if someone had dropped a leaking pen and the ink had set in before it could be cleaned. Once you'd seen the tile, you couldn't unsee it, even though it was all the way over in the far corner.

That made Stella think that, like the building itself, the staff were putting on a bright and shiny façade.

Hopefully, their time on the upper floor would reveal where their stains and blemishes were hidden.

CHAPTER NINE

On the top floor of Zenith Capital, Stella felt impressed when the elevator doors opened to reveal a magnificent lounge, with a massive plate-glass window on the far side. The panoramic view of Greenwich, and the ocean beyond, was a powerful sight.

"This is the client lounge," Harriet explained.

Stella had been so captivated by its layout that she'd barely noticed the gleaming wooden desk on the far left. Another pretty blond woman, who looked as if she could be the receptionist's older sister, jumped up from her seat behind the desk, and hurried over.

For a finance firm, Stella noted that there seemed to be a large contingent of female senior staff in what was usually a male-dominated industry. She was used to seeing finance firms comprised of mostly male traders and portfolio managers and financial officers.

"Good morning. I'm Yolanda," the blonde said breathlessly. "Please, how can I help? This is so shocking. Since Harriet called me, I've literally been in tears all night. Mr. Coleridge was such a good man."

She stared at them through wide, blue, and distinctly clear and unreddened eyes. Stella, by contrast, felt as if she'd had sand flung in hers after her sleepless hours of research.

"Shall we sit?" Stella asked.

Feeling for a moment like a prospective client, she moved to the lounge area and sat down on one of the supremely comfortable, brilliant white leather couches.

"We need background on Mr. Coleridge," Carrie explained to Yolanda. "Did you work closely with him?"

"Absolutely," Yolanda nodded decisively. "We met every morning and he'd be in touch throughout the day. I would run the ship here and adjust his schedule, and also liaise with the priority clients."

"Who were the priority clients?" Stella asked.

"Anyone whose investment or withdrawal needed urgent attention was a priority client," Yolanda explained.

"Any issues with priority clients in the past week or two?" Carrie asked, clearly latching onto Stella's line of thinking.

"No. There are no issues. That's why they're priority clients. So that all the admin can get done without problems or delays," Yolanda explained patiently.

"Did Mr. Coleridge appear worried about anything in the last few days? Any family issues, any personal problems, any clients causing trouble?" Carrie asked.

Yolanda shook her head.

"Everything was completely normal. This is why this has been such a huge shock. The past few days have been perfectly ordinary, although busy, and Mr. Coleridge behaved exactly as always. I didn't pick up that he was worried at all."

"What appointments did he have in the past week?" Stella asked.

"He spends a lot of time on routine client visits. I can show you his schedule. He likes to touch base regularly with clients and review their investments, find out about their changing needs. He tries to see at least six clients a week and the meetings are usually quite long and sociable. A lot of times, they are held here, especially on a Friday afternoon, and I provide drinks and gourmet canapés. It's all about the experience," she said earnestly. "Sometimes, he hosts them at restaurants or other premises. But I didn't hear about any problems in the last few meetings. They were all with long term clients. They all gave good feedback, and a few of them added to their investments."

Stella and Carrie exchanged glances. For once, Stella thought, they were in agreement.

"Please give me the names and contact details of the clients," Stella said as Carrie nodded approval.

"I'll email the list to you in the next hour," Yolanda promised.

"And can you show us to the accounts manager's office?" Stella asked.

"This way," Yolanda invited, rising to her feet and turning elegantly on her spiky heels.

She led them past the elevator and tapped on the door of a side office. She opened it, and a curvaceous redhead scrambled up from her desk, giving them a sad, welcoming smile.

"Good morning. I'm Terri, the accounts manager. I hope you're able to find out what happened. This is the most dreadful shock," she shared.

Beyond, in an adjoining room, with his head bent studiously over a laptop, was the first male employee Stella had seen at Zenith Capital. The dark-haired man looked up from his work, staring in surprise as they came inside. She guessed he was one of the 'support staff' that Harriet had mentioned and wondered what his role was.

"I think all of us are battling to focus on doing anything constructive this morning. What can I help you with?" Terri asked.

"How long have you been working here?" she asked.

"Two and a half years," Terri replied. "Mr. Coleridge started his own company about five years ago. I was employed at the finance firm where he worked before that. Then, when the accounts became too big a job for him to handle, he headhunted me. He's such a great boss! It was the best move I could have made."

Stella had a strong feeling that any further questions were going to bring up more of the same in reference to the awesomeness of the late company owner.

She remembered that Maxwell and Roth always said: when you reach a dead end with people, evidence and facts will take you further. Even though thinking about Maxwell gave Stella a pang of remorse, his advice right now was relevant.

"I'd like to have a look through the company's books, please. Can you supply a list of recent transactions?" Stella asked.

"Sure, of course!" Terri sounded eager to help out. "Of course, I can do that. How recent? The last few months, perhaps?"

Stella exchanged a glance with Carrie.

"Yes. That sounds good," she said.

Terri's office was well equipped, and the company was clearly digitally based, as it didn't have any of the piles of files or the smell of musty cardboard that Stella was used to breathing in whenever she accessed any of the FBI's record rooms.

"We are striving to be fully digital. Mr. Coleridge had such a passion for saving the environment and the planet," she explained, sadly. "I can print out the records, or else flash them up for you on our big screen.

"I think a paper printout will be best for the time being. We may need to add it to the case archives," Stella explained. "You can also email them to me."

"Of course!"

"A printed copy for each of us, please," Carrie insisted. Clearly, saving the planet was less important to her at this moment than not having to share documents with Stella.

The printer whirred, and in a few moments, crisp black-and-white sheets furled out of it. Stella took a look. She wasn't an accounting expert. There were forensic accounting specialists in New Haven, and if she spotted any irregularities, she knew she'd have to send the emailed records through for analysis.

But, at a glance, there didn't seem to be any. Taking a look at the workings of Zenith Capital, Stella saw that the company's income and also their outgoing payments were made up of lump sums – more commonly, and monthly annuity payments – less commonly.

Terri explained helpfully as they perused the pages.

"When clients invest with us, they normally contribute a lump sum of funds, although some do make monthly payments. We then filter this into one of our investment structures. These are dependent on the needs of the client, their risk index, the timeframe they want to invest for, and also whether they want an annuity from it or not. The investment portfolio is partly allocated to property projects, partly allocated to the stock market, and we also do a small amount of forex trading."

"I see," Stella said.

"Our clients usually enjoy growth of about thirteen to fifteen percent per annum. Slightly higher if they are keen to take on a bigger risk or invest for a longer term. This is well above the interest rate that banks and many other investments offer, but it's also not in the realm of high-risk, high reward. Zenith Capital does not operate according to that business model as our clients generally prefer a solid and reliable return that offers them better value than they can get elsewhere, but without the added risk factor."

Stella nodded.

It appeared that the company was run on sound principles, and the lack of serious risk also made it unlikely that someone had stabbed Patrick because he'd invested unwisely and lost all their money.

"We have payout reports per client. These are confidential, of course, but you are welcome to view them. I'll run reports on all our current clients."

Even though Terri's breathless enthusiasm for her company and boss made Stella feel strangely cynical, she did note that the accounts looked in perfect order, and that Terri herself was sharp and competent.

She wasn't finding anything noteworthy, though. Carrie's defeated sigh echoed her frustration. Staring at the records, Stella realized she felt lost.

It was that feeling which caused a long-forgotten piece of wisdom to surface in her mind, an old memory, completely unexpected.

She remembered herself and her father, driving along one of the rugged dirt roads in a rural area a few miles from their farmhouse. Her dad had old clothes in the back. They were going to drop them off for someone holding a charity sale.

They'd been lost. Nine-year-old Stella, in charge of navigation, had said, "Let's turn back. We must have missed it."

"I think we need to look further," her dad had countered. "Most times, when you think you're lost, you actually are giving up too soon and you need to push on to find what you're looking for."

Stella had felt doubtful about this advice, but a mile later, it had been proven true when the house they wanted came into sight.

Perhaps that advice could be useful here, too, she thought. It might have come to mind for a reason, and perhaps the reason was that she hadn't pushed on as far as she needed to.

"Can you print out all the records?" she asked.

"You mean, right back to the company's inception?" Terri asked.

"Yes, please," Stella said.

Sometimes, revenge was best served cold. If someone had been cheated, or felt as if they had been shortchanged, they might have bided their time.

The printer started rolling again, and Stella paged back through the records, keeping a close lookout for anything untoward that might have been buried in the past.

Month by month, the records paged by, shiny and clear and without any signs of irregularities in the incoming and outgoing payments.

And then, near the back of the records, she came across something unusual, which triggered her radar.

A few months after the inception of Zenith Capital, there had been a large lump-sum payout to a person, or entity, called Bruno.

No last name, no other details. Just the name Bruno, and an amount.

There was no incoming payment to match up with this. Had the mysterious Bruno been a client, or what was the reason for the payout?

It was the only false note she'd seen so far. The only imbalance in a perfectly balanced ledger. Instinctively, Stella felt it meant something, and that this needed to be questioned.

CHAPTER TEN

"Who's Bruno?" Stella asked Terri, pointing to the entry in the printout.

Terri smiled helpfully. "Mr. Bruno partnered with Mr. Coleridge originally. They started Zenith Capital together, but a few months later, Mr. Coleridge bought him out and went forward as the sole director."

"Is it a person or a company?"

"An individual person," Terri said.

Stella glanced at Carrie, who was scrutinizing the page, looking interested. She felt intrigued also. Although the payout was large, it was nowhere close to the company's first annual valuation. Investments from clients had flooded in during the first few months and Zenith Capital had already shown substantial growth. Why was this payout not reflecting this?

It was the only sign of anything untoward. But if she'd been Bruno, looking around at the massive building and the overt display of wealth, and the commissions that were taken on each investment made, Stella thought she would have felt cheated.

However, she had to admit, she didn't have all the information on this transaction and there might be a reason why the payout was relatively small. Perhaps Bruno hadn't been a full fifty-fifty shareholder and had put in a lower amount to start with.

"What percentage shares did this Bruno have?" Carrie asked, clearly as sharp as a tack when it came to financials, and on the same page as Stella when looking at the size of the payout.

"I'm not sure," Terri said. "It was before my time, unfortunately."

Carrie frowned at the page again. "This amount seems rather low," she insisted. "Would you know anything about that?"

"I never questioned it," Terri said. She smiled regretfully. "I wish now that I had asked Mr. Coleridge about it. He just mentioned to me that there had originally been a second shareholder."

"Do you have the payment details?" Carrie asked.

"Yes, I do." Swinging her chair around to face the laptop, Terri tapped keys.

"Mr. F. Bruno. The payment was made into Banco BPM in Lombardy, Italy."

"Do you have any contact details for Mr. Bruno?" Stella queried.

"Let me see what I have here," Terri said. Her fingers rattled over more keys. "I have an Italian street address," she said apologetically. "No other details.

"Okay," Stella said. Investigating a five-year-old street address could be done, but it would take a couple of days, since it seemed as if Mr. Bruno had gone back to Italy.

"Did he keep in touch, or have any further dealings with Mr. Coleridge, to your knowledge?" Stella said, looking to confirm this.

"Not to my knowledge, no," Terri explained. "I definitely never heard him mentioned or saw anything further from this name or account."

Stella glanced at Carrie, who was still reading through the statements, looking dubious. Stella was sure the size of the payout was still uppermost in her mind. She'd seen how intensely she'd scrutinized it. Perhaps this had caused Carrie to rethink her original opinion of Patrick and she was now having doubts.

Like Maxwell, it seemed Carrie would change her mind not on gut feel alone, but only when cold, hard evidence led the way.

At the door, Harriet was now hovering, looking expectant.

"I have some time freed up if you'd like to confirm anything or ask any further questions."

They left Terri's office and took the elevator downstairs again. Harriet gestured to the armchairs at the far side of the reception area.

"Let's sit," she invited.

Stella and Carrie took a chair on either side of her.

Carrie had clearly decided to go in with a tougher approach.

"Ma'am, we have a situation here. Mr. Coleridge was murdered in a violent way. It was not a robbery gone wrong. Someone must have had a motive. Is there anything – anything at all in this organization, which might have triggered something like this? Perhaps there was a client that decided not to invest? A staff member who left on bad terms? Did the original co-investor feel cheated or leave under a cloud? Please, think back and tell us."

Harriet placed an elbow on her slender knee, tapping her chin with her finger as she thought.

"Honestly, nothing. That's what has always made this such a pleasant workplace. There really has been no friction. No fights. Most definitely, no unhappy clients. And no staff leaving on bad terms. We've had a couple of people move on, but I think it's always been due to relocating, as Mr. Coleridge paid good salaries. I never really dealt with the original investor, but given the rest of the dealings I've experienced, I don't believe there would have been any problems there."

"What percentage shareholder was Mr. Bruno?" Carrie asked.

"Fifty-fifty," Harriet said, and Carrie's eyebrows shot up.

"You're clearly wondering about the size of that payout," Harriet continued. "The company started out small. Mr. Coleridge was the one who built it."

"Where is Mr. Bruno now?" Now that she'd been convinced the payout was problematic, Carrie was like a dog with a bone, Stella thought, with a flash of admiration.

"I'm sorry, I have no idea. The payment was made into his Italian account," Harriet said, confirming what they already knew – but Stella wondered if it was everything she knew.

"Did they leave on good terms? Why is he no longer in contact with Mr. Coleridge?" Carrie asked.

Harriet shook her head. "There was no reason for them to be. I've worked in finance my whole life, and believe me, this is normal. They did business together, and then moved on once their business partnership had ended," she said in factual tones.

But Patrick Coleridge had been everyone's best friend, so breaking off contact with an ex-partner didn't make sense, Stella thought. She looked over at Carrie again. Carrie was clearly as frustrated by these non-answers as she was, but she suspected they'd get no more information from Harriet.

"You worked closely with Mr. Coleridge," Stella said. "What about his personal life? Anything that might be problematic there?"

Now, Harriet stared at her with a touch of coldness in her gaze.

"There were no personal issues that I was aware of," she said firmly. "Mr. Coleridge kept his work life and personal life very cleanly separated. He was a devoted family man."

"Thank you," Stella said.

They stood up and walked to the basement elevator.

It was clear that they were going to make no further progress by questioning the personnel at Zenith Capital. They were unanimous in praise of their boss, and their insistence that absolutely nothing irregular had taken place.

Stella felt more and more convinced that they were hiding something, and her main suspicions were focused on the original shareholder payout.

There were a lot of reasons why the staff might be downplaying a historic problem. For a start, the company's reputation was now critical. Presumably, with the owner deceased, Zenith Capital would be sold or taken over. As such, the staff would need to ensure everything was squeaky clean. After all, their own jobs and bonuses depended on it.

But it meant they were coming up against a stone wall in every direction.

The elevator swooped down to the basement. Stepping out, Stella heard a clatter of footsteps on the stairs.

It was the male worker she'd noticed earlier in the office adjoining Terri's. He was hurrying down the stairs toward them. Running an errand, she guessed – but then she rethought. There was something about the way he was looking at them that told Stella he had orchestrated this meeting.

Her suspicions were confirmed when he looked back at the stairway, as if checking the coast was clear, and then walked over to them with purpose in his stride.

"Hi there. You're the FBI, right? I was listening to the conversation earlier." The man was dark haired and looked to be in his late thirties. He spoke in a soft, rapid voice.

"We are. What's your name?" she asked.

"I'm Luke Molteno," he said. "I'm a contract worker here."

"How long have you been here?" Stella asked.

"On and off, ever since the company started. They use me at busy times to keep the books current. The company stays lean in terms of staff. They don't carry excess weight, is what Mr. Coleridge told me. So they rather outsource, and they've used me periodically. I mean, there's enough work for a full-time job. But I'm fast, and I have other clients also," he explained, looking serious.

That was interesting. So Luke was a temporary worker, not permanent. And despite the veneer of extreme wealth and this luxurious building, Patrick Coleridge had been unwilling to invest in staff members outside of the basic core team.

This surprisingly cheap attitude was a deviation from the paragon of goodness they'd been sold.

"So you heard what was said earlier?" Stella confirmed, as Luke glanced behind him again. He was making sure nobody else was there, she thought, with a flare of excitement.

"That's right, ma'am."

"Are you wanting to correct something?" Carrie asked.

"I do want to correct something," Luke stepped closer and lowered his voice even more. "I didn't overhear everything that was said in there, but it didn't sound accurate to me."

"What?" Carrie challenged him.

"You asked about the initial lump sum payment made to Mr. Bruno," he said.

Now Stella felt even more excited. That was the one discord she'd noted in the otherwise perfect harmony.

"Yes?" she said.

"I was working here at the time, and I know that Mr. Bruno was forced out. There was some legal issue that wasn't properly addressed in the contract. Mr. Coleridge wanted to take over, so he enforced it. Look, I think there were personal problems between them as well. But to me, at the time, that payment was way below the company's market value."

Stella heard Carrie gasp. Finally, they had incontrovertible proof that Patrick Coleridge was not a saint.

"Was Mr. Bruno angry?" Stella asked, thinking he must surely have been.

"Oh, yes. He was furious. There was a big flare-up for a few days, but in the end, I think the contract held up and he couldn't fight it. I might be the only person who remembers that whole drama apart from Harriet, and Harriet won't say anything that might affect the company's value. I heard them speaking earlier about reputation management. But I mean, you guys are investigating a murder, and you ought to know."

Stella glanced at Carrie excitedly, but Carrie's face was red, and she looked away.

"So you knew Mr. Bruno?" Stella hoped that this man might provide the link to him they needed.

"Yes, I actually saw him a few times."

"Did he go back to Italy?"

"To Italy? No, he didn't do that as far as I know. I think he still lives here. At any rate, he owns a home in Greenwich. I remember the address because I collected documents from there once," Luke said, casually dropping the bombshell. "His name's Franco Bruno, and his house is in Quayside Close, near one of the yacht clubs."

At that moment, the pieces of information slotted into place for Stella.

Franco Bruno was one of the names on the list of patrons that the South Sands yacht club manager had provided, although Stella recalled he was one of the few with no social or business links to Patrick.

He hadn't gone back to Italy. Although he presumably owned properties in both countries, he was still residing right here, in Greenwich.

He'd been forced out of a company now worth multi millions, and he'd been at the club on Friday evening. Stella recalled that he had left an hour before Patrick Coleridge had been murdered.

There was no time to waste in tracking down this strong suspect.

CHAPTER ELEVEN

Carrie climbed in the car, feeling conflicted about this new lead as they headed for Franco Bruno's home.

She simply couldn't believe that Stella Fall had been right all along. Patrick Coleridge was not the icon of respectability everyone thought him to be. Carrie had been sure that Fall was biased against him because of her own prejudice. Now Patrick had proved to be unethical, a man who'd sneakily used a contract clause to force his partner out of a growing business, compensating him with nothing more than a meager payout.

How had Fall known? Was it just luck that she'd taken that stance, Carrie wondered for a hopeful moment. She had a feeling it wasn't luck, and now felt ashamed as she remembered how vehemently she'd opposed Fall, believing that her attitude might send the investigation off on the wrong tangent.

Now, Carrie had to face the uncomfortable truth that her own attitude could easily have done the same. It was due to Fall's persistence that they'd uncovered this background. Carrie felt as if she'd personally failed, as if she'd not been insightful enough, and as if she was a useless agent.

The older financial records had led the way to this discovery. Would Carrie have requested those earlier records from Zenith Capital if Fall hadn't been there?

Carrie squirmed inwardly as she forced herself to confront this difficult question. Truthfully, she was not sure. She hoped she would have done so, but now she'd never know.

Worse still, Fall had been the one who'd put two and two together and had realized Franco Bruno had been on the list of members present at the club that night.

It didn't mean Franco was the killer, Carrie told herself anxiously. This all happened a long time ago.

"He has a strong motive," Fall said, looking intent as she keyed the address into her phone. "Leaving an hour before Patrick arrived is significant in terms of timing. You turn right at the light and then join the main road."

Carrie shrugged. In her confusion and embarrassment, she was not going to allow herself to get excited and was going to continue to play devil's advocate.

"Remember, this took place years ago. Soon after the company's inception. This is not a recent event, Fall. If he'd been furious enough to do something, why wouldn't he have done it then?" she argued.

"I know. A lot of time has passed. But something could have happened to re-trigger the anger. Perhaps it was even seeing him at the club," Fall suggested. "Having a big personality like that, taking all the limelight, making all the friends, networking for new business after he'd screwed his ex-partner over – it might have made Franco Bruno reach a breaking point. Go left here, then right at the next cross street."

As Carrie drove, she wasn't thinking only about Franco's motives. Part of her mind was also on the short, messaged conversation that she'd discreetly replied to while taking a bathroom break early this morning.

The message had been from her friend – the one who knew the Marshalls.

"Hey C, hope ur well! We need to talk urgently."

"Sure, what's up?"

"G needs your help. He's shattered by his wife's death. He's looking to get S removed from the Bureau."

Carrie knew who G was. Gordon Marshall. And S stood for Stella, Carrie had picked up, feeling suddenly motivated.

"Let's speak later today. I'm on a case with her now," she'd replied.

On a case where Fall had just uncovered critical information, proving Carrie's theory wrong.

What if Fall went back to Roth and told him this? Carrie would have done so if the tables had been turned. She felt breathless with anxiety that Roth might consider her to be an incapable agent.

Getting Fall removed from the case, and from the FBI, felt like a lifeline. It would pre-empt Fall's ability to do her any damage. She imagined Roth's praise, and her father's pride, when the news broke that she had single-handedly solved her very first murder case, despite her partner having to withdraw halfway through.

Carrie had deleted the message in case it proved incriminating, or in case Fall ended up peeking at her phone. She had no idea what the Marshalls could use to get this done. Proof of incompetence, she guessed, but that might be hard to provide. She'd been reluctantly impressed by Fall's competence so far.

Of course, it might be possible to create a situation where Stella Fall was shown up to be incompetent through circumstances, Carrie mused briefly. This case had shown her in the most brutal way that people could make mistakes during the course of an investigation.

She didn't want to be unfair to Fall, though. That would be wrong. What could she do…?

"It's here," Fall's voice interrupted her thoughts, jerking her back to the present so suddenly that she jumped.

"This house up ahead?"

"That's the one. With the big, wrought-iron gates."

They were in a nice neighborhood, Carrie saw. Enormous mansions set in spacious grounds. Clearly, Franco was not lacking for money. Again, this detracted from his possible motive, she reassured herself.

Luckily the gates to Franco's magnificent home were standing open. They drove in, up the blacktop driveway that wound between gracious oak trees. Trying to put her angst about the case aside, Carrie checked the time. It was almost nine a.m. She wondered if Franco had a family, and if so, whether they would be home. It was a Saturday, after all. Would it be easier or more difficult to get the truth from him if his family was there?

As they approached the house, she saw a sleek black Lexus sedan outside the quadruple garages in the east wing of the sumptuous home. The door opened and a young woman who looked to be in her twenties climbed out. She wore blue jeans and a pink down jacket, and her brown hair was tied back in a ponytail.

Carrie guessed this was the au pair or nanny, who must have taken the children somewhere.

The woman looked curiously around when she saw the unmarked approach and hurried over.

"Good morning," Carrie said, taking the lead as she climbed out of the driver's seat. "FBI agents Potts and Fall. We're here to interview Mr. Franco Bruno."

The au pair's eyes widened in consternation.

"Um, I – I'm not sure if he's available."

Then her expression melted into relief as the scrunch of wheels sounded from behind them.

Carrie spun around, to see a massive black Range Rover powering up the driveway.

It swept past them and stopped next to the Lexus.

The tinted windows offered no clue as to who might be inside. Was this Franco? Carrie hoped so.

The door opened, and a blond woman climbed out.

She was tall, slim, extremely attractive, and dressed in a yoga outfit, over which she'd slipped a fleece jacket. The massive diamond ring on her wedding finger provided the final clue that this must be Mrs. Bruno.

"Good morning," she said, sounding surprised. "Who are these people?" Her question was directed at the au pair, which Carrie considered rather rude, and as if this blond princess was relying on her minions to protect her from unwanted arrivals. At any rate, before the au pair could answer, she did.

"FBI agents. We're here to speak to Franco Bruno," she said firmly to the blonde.

The blonde made a rueful face.

"He's unfortunately not home yet. Perhaps you can come back this afternoon?"

She nodded at the au pair. It was clearly a gesture of dismissal, because the young woman left the group and headed into the house.

"Are you his wife? Where is he? We need to ask him some questions," Fall asked.

Mrs. Bruno folded her arms. "I am his wife. Why do you need him so badly?"

"It's in connection with the murder of his previous business partner," Carrie said.

A tiny frown creased Mrs. Bruno's flawless forehead.

"Who? Which partner?" she asked, sounding confused and curious.

"Mr. Coleridge. Patrick Coleridge," Carrie enlightened her.

She took a moment to absorb this, her hazel eyes widening.

"Mr. Coleridge has been murdered? Are you sure? There's been nothing on the news about it."

"It happened last night at the South Sands yacht club," Fall explained. "Your husband was there yesterday, so we need to interview him."

Mrs. Bruno shrugged.

"He had nothing to do with the murder. He and Mr. Coleridge parted ways ages ago."

Carrie couldn't tell from the wife's tone if she knew there had been animosity between them. Maybe she didn't care. Another thought occurred to her. Perhaps Patrick and Franco had put their earlier conflict aside.

"They attend the same yacht club," Carrie countered. "They must surely have associated with each other. Do you know if your husband was friendly with him? Or were you aware of any problems between them?"

Mrs. Bruno shrugged again. "No."

She reached into the car and took a slim, silver phone out of her purse. She dialed.

"Nope, his phone's turned off. He's not back from the club yet, and I've no idea where he is," she said.

"Not back from going out last night?" Carrie couldn't keep the incredulity out of her voice at this matter-of-fact tone. Wasn't she worried that something had gone wrong? And why was Franco Bruno not yet home? His absence was highly suspicious. She saw Fall's eyes narrow – the closest she ever got to showing emotion – and knew she shared her feelings.

"He met two of his friends there. They were meeting to discuss a new business venture," Mrs. Bruno explained. "It's likely he had too much to drink and slept at the club. They have couches in the side rooms. He sometimes stays there for the night."

Carrie exchanged a surprised glance with Stella.

There were definitely no sleeping people unaccounted for in the club after the disaster that had played out last night. It was extremely unlikely that Franco had managed to disappear into a quiet side room, especially since the manager had said he'd left earlier.

Carrie decided this whole situation was weird. It did sound as if there was more to this than she'd first thought. They urgently needed to track Franco's movements. In particular, the fact he was not yet home was suspicious. Was he already on the run?

"You're not worried?" Carrie probed.

"Not at all," Mrs. Bruno said firmly, but Carrie wasn't sure if she was just saying this to protect her husband, who even if he was innocent, certainly seemed to conduct his life in unusual ways.

"Please give us his phone number, and the details of his car," Carrie said. "And also a photo of him, so we know who to look out for. You must have one available?"

"Sure," she agreed. She pressed buttons on her phone, sending the information through to Carrie.

"Who was he meeting?" Fall asked.

“Stefan Macmillan and Gary – Gary someone. I don’t know his last name. They were going to discuss importing a new brand of golf equipment. Stefan is a golfing friend. He and Franco play together every couple of weeks.”

“Where can we get hold of Stefan?” Carrie asked. “Which golf club does he belong to?”

“Greenwich. And he actually lives opposite the golf club. I’m not sure of the house number, but it has gold pillars so it’s quite distinctive.”

“Thank you,” Carrie said.

The wife had no more information to give. That was clear. If she knew more, she wasn’t telling. In any case, there was nothing to be gained by questioning her further. They needed to confirm the whereabouts, and test the alibi, of her elusive husband.

Carrie had been wrong earlier. She had made a mistake. Now the pressure was on for her to redeem herself by solving this case.

“We’re coming for you, Franco. You can run, but you can’t hide,” Carrie muttered to herself, as she climbed into the car again.

CHAPTER TWELVE

Stella and Carrie drove straight to Stefan Macmillan's home. Stella hoped he would be there, and not out on the golf course. As they neared the grand front entrance of the golf club, she saw the house opposite that Mrs. Bruno had referred to.

The mansion was painted blinding white and had a huge entrance porch with four tall pillars. These were painted in actual gold, as was the gate. They gleamed brightly in the watery morning sun.

Stella glanced at Carrie, interested to know what her feelings were about this unusual home. Carrie's face was deliberately expressionless as she gazed through the garish gates, and even at this tense time, Stella couldn't suppress a smile at her careful lack of reaction.

Maxwell would have rolled his eyes and uttered a few choice words about how money couldn't buy good taste.

Her amusement was immediately overshadowed by the seriousness of this mission. They were hot on the tail of a strong murder suspect and needed to find him as fast as possible.

Carrie rang the gate buzzer.

"FBI," she said into the intercom. "We're here to interview Mr. Macmillan. Is he at home?"

"Yes, he is." The female voice sounded surprised. Stella had no idea whether this was a housemaid or a relative of Stefan's. At any rate, a moment later, the gate swung open.

As they drove in, she glimpsed a security guard with a gun, patrolling the grounds.

It created an immediate, fearful flashback to the days after her fiancé's murder, when Gordon Marshall had hired a guard, ostensibly for 'security', but in fact to harass and intimidate Stella.

They parked near the house. Stella saw the security guard was already walking purposefully in their direction. The front door swung open, and a housemaid appeared.

"Good morning," she said, hurrying over to them. "You say you are the FBI? Mr. Macmillan has asked if you can identify yourselves."

Stella glanced behind her. The guard was waiting, watching them intently.

"Sure," Carrie said. She showed her badge. Hastily, dragging her focus away from the armed guard, Stella did the same.

The housemaid scrutinized the IDs very carefully. Stella had the impression this was not just a box-check exercise. Most likely, her job was on the line if she made a mistake. Or perhaps more. This house was weird. This entire setup was bizarre and not what she was expecting at all.

"Okay. Please come with me," the maid said, obviously reassured of their credentials.

They headed into the ornate hallway that featured a huge black-and-gold chandelier, and the maid then led them into a modern lounge with angular, black furniture and fluffy white rugs.

As they sat down, a short, stocky man who looked to be in his forties, hurried in.

In contrast to the immaculately decorated home, he looked underdressed, and Stella thought they'd definitely caught him by surprise. He was wearing blue jeans and a golf shirt, paired with leather slippers. His spiky brown hair looked unbrushed.

"Hi. You're the FBI?" he asked, sounding annoyed and speaking rapidly.

"That's correct. Are you Stefan Macmillan?" Stella asked politely. When he nodded, she continued. "We have some questions about Patrick Coleridge's murder."

"What do you want to ask?" he said. "I heard about it early this morning. It's shocking, of course, but I wasn't even there at the time. I'd left the club before then."

"You were at the club with friends. Who were they?" Carrie challenged.

"Franco and Gary. We were discussing importing some golf gear," Stefan said, confirming what Mrs. Bruno had told them.

"Was that the reason for the meeting?" Stella asked.

Stefan nodded. "Yes. We're golf friends. We play regularly and often discuss business ideas. I'm in gold," he explained, and Stella nodded, now understanding the priority on security, as well as the unusual home decor. "I have shares in a few gold mines, I own a few stores, but I'm always keen to diversify and invest. The other two guys are big entrepreneurs."

"When did you organize the meeting?" Stella wondered if the timeline was significant.

"Franco set it up about a week ago."

"How long have you known these two men?" Carrie asked.

"I've been friends with Gary since school. Franco, I met about two years ago when he joined our golf club."

"Why did you meet at the yacht club, not the golf club?" Carrie then challenged, which Stella thought was a relevant question.

"It was Franco's meeting, and he likes the South Sands club. He's invited us there once before," Stefan said. His brow crinkled. "What's the reason for these questions? I don't want to rain on your parade, ladies, but they seem pointless. Are any of us suspects?"

Stella was interested that Stefan was being rude and critical. To her, it was an adult form of acting out – being obnoxious in the hope that they would leave. It was all the more reason to stay, and keep asking, she thought, glancing at Carrie.

"We're gathering information, and will ask you questions until we're satisfied that we've obtained it," Carrie told him coldly, clearly triggered once again by the use of the word 'ladies.' "What time did you leave the club?"

"At about seven-thirty," Stefan said.

"Was your business concluded?"

As Carrie asked the question, Stella picked up on definite pointers of unease. Stefan was not happy about the direction this was going.

"Yes. We'd had a good discussion," he said.

"Where did you go to from there?" Stella asked.

"I went home," Stefan said.

"Can you provide proof you arrived home?"

Stefan looked surprised. "I – er – well, my wife was home. My twins were home. We all sat down and had dinner. I guess they're family, so you won't believe them." He thought for a moment. "The camera footage at the gate records everything. It goes straight through to our security firm. That will show my car arriving back. It's a short drive from the yacht club. Ten minutes, maybe? As soon as we're done here, I can call them and authorize them to send you the footage."

"That will be great," Stella said.

Stefan was clearly trying to help, but Stella was still not sure why he had looked so worried.

What had she missed, Stella thought quickly. What was she not picking up on? Why had Stefan's demeanor changed when she'd mentioned them leaving?

Had the others left? That was the key point, she decided. He'd gone home and had an alibi. But perhaps the others had been planning something that he didn't want the FBI to know about

"What about your two friends? Did Franco and Gary stay there?"

"No. We all left at the same time. The wait staff there can confirm it, I'm sure."

He sounded confident, but again, Stefan's body language was betraying him. He glanced down at the floor, and then at the door – a tell that he wanted to leave, or for them to leave and stop asking him these questions.

Stella exchanged a glance with Carrie, wondering if she, too, had picked up on this. She was staring at Stefan intently, aware of his unease.

"Where did they go?" Carrie asked.

Stefano smiled. The expression was wobbly and looked out of place. He hadn't smiled since they had arrived.

"You'd have to ask them. Probably home, I'm sure," Stefan said.

Stella exchanged a meaningful look with Carrie. They didn't have time for this evasion. And after an almost sleepless night, she didn't have the patience for it, either.

"Mr. Macmillan, I believe you are well aware of where they went. We are in a hurry to catch a killer and need full background information. If you can't provide us with it here, we'll have to take you to the police department and continue the interview there," Carrie said.

Stefan's eyes flew wide.

"Are you threatening me? It sounds like you're threatening me. I'm not involved in this, so stop insinuating that I'm to blame for any of it. I'm an innocent guy, but if you're going to waste my time, I'm going to get my lawyer involved. Right now!" he snapped. "Then we'll see whose time gets wasted!"

For a moment, Stella saw the ruthless side that lurked under his likeable, guy-next-door persona, as aggressive as a dragon guarding its hoard.

"It's not a threat," Stella said in a quiet voice. She desperately wanted to manage the situation and get him back on the right track. "And we don't suspect you, Mr. Macmillan. We're just explaining the protocols we follow during an interview. They are standard practice. All we need to know is where your friends went. Perhaps they mentioned it?"

She gazed at him calmly, hoping this approach would turn the situation around. She didn't want to end up going head-to-head with the tempestuous Stefan. That would get his ego involved, and the resulting flare-up would waste time they didn't have.

Luckily, the quieter approach worked. Stefan's anger subsided. He made a rueful face.

"I didn't want to be the one to tell you this. They wanted to go on to a club. That's not really my thing, so I headed home."

"Which club?"

"Sinsations. It's out of town, to the west."

"And what is Sinsations?"

"It's a strip club," Stefan admitted.

"So they were going straight there? Nowhere else first?"

"They usually go straight there, I think."

"So Franco does this often?"

"Yeah," Stefan shrugged. "Not my scene, but I can't tell anyone else how to live their life. If they enjoy it, no harm, right?"

"Understood," Stella agreed.

There was nothing else to say. The information that Stefan had given them would hopefully lead them on to the next step to tracking down Franco.

In a strip club environment, it would have been easy for him to melt into the crowds, lose Gary, sneak away and return to the yacht club to wait for Patrick to arrive.

Their next step would be to visit Sinsations and from there, track Franco's movements that night.

Stella had a feeling this investigation was finally starting to get somewhere.

CHAPTER THIRTEEN

Half an hour later, Stella and Carrie arrived at Sinsations.

It was in a neighboring town, at the end of a street filled with restaurants and bars. They'd started off at the top end of the street, which was upmarket and well kept, but Stella observed that as they drove down the long road, the places started looking gradually seedier and more run-down. Sinsations was on the far side of a crossroad – a large building that she guessed must be massive inside.

The neon sign that topped the building was turned off, but at night, the pink and green lettering would be a huge beacon, garish and unmissable.

The detritus of the night before was still visible. At half past ten, a cleaner was at work outside, picking up bottles and litter by hand, while another cleaner swept and scrubbed.

As Stella gazed around, she saw a large parking lot on the opposite side of the street. There were three cars still in it.

She checked the details they'd been given. Sure enough, one of the luxury cars now bathed in the weak morning sun, was a black Range Rover, with the number plate that Mrs. Bruno had provided. Clearly, it was Franco's preferred model and color of car, since he and his wife drove identical ones.

"That's his car there?" Carrie asked in tones of outrage.

"Yes. So where did he go? He must have taken a cab – somewhere?" Stella's mind boggled as to where. Had he gone on to a hotel with one of the strippers? Had he gone home with his friend Gary? There was no telling when he'd decide to come and get his car, and he might not even do so personally.

At this critical time, the witness they needed was providing to be elusive. Was there an outside chance that somebody at the club had seen him leave, or knew something?

Turning back in the direction of the club, she walked up to the main door, hoping there would be a manager on duty. But, as she approached, she noticed someone who was potentially an even better witness.

A woman with tawny brown hair, wearing black leggings and a pink leather jacket, pushed open the door, wheeling out an empty beer keg.

She must be a member of the bar staff, Stella thought. Bar staff would surely know who was who and might have had a better chance to see when Franco had left, and with whom.

"Hello!" she called.

The woman looked up, surprised. Then her expression changed as she clocked Stella's and Carrie's outfits, and their guns. Law enforcement was never going to be welcome at such an establishment and must always spell trouble.

"What do you want?" she asked nervously.

"We're looking for information on Franco Bruno's whereabouts," Stella explained, walking closer. "We're FBI agents investigating a murder. We believe he's a regular here."

Carrie opened her phone and showed the woman the picture that Franco's wife had sent through.

The woman peered at it, still looking suspicious. She was extremely attractive, Stella noted, and probably in her early twenties. Definitely, she would get attention and tips from the patrons at the bar.

She nodded.

"Yeah, I know that guy. He's a regular. He's a good customer, and never caused any problems," she added hastily.

"Does he usually come in on Fridays?" Stella asked.

The woman frowned, thinking.

"Yes. I've often seen him on a Friday. Sometimes, Saturdays."

"He was here last night, I believe?" Stella said.

The woman shrugged. "I wasn't working last night. I'm on the early shift today. Eleven a.m. to eleven p.m. The bar's open longer hours. The club only opens in the afternoon."

"Who was working last night?" Carrie pressured.

Stella felt impatient and hopeful as she waited for the barmaid's reply. They urgently needed to track Franco's movements. When had he arrived? Had anyone seen him leave? Had he deliberately tried to create an alibi through his presence at the club? And where had he gone afterwards, so that they could personally question this prime suspect.

"Ilana worked the late shift, but she'll be asleep now. Her phone will be off," the barmaid said.

"Who might know what time Franco arrived, and when he left?" Stella asked.

"When the bar's busy you can't see when people arrive, because you can't see past the customers waiting for drinks," the woman explained. "As far as leaving goes, from past experience, Franco likes to stay late. He usually leaves at three, four in the morning."

"I see his car's in the parking lot. Does he usually call a cab? Is there a motel nearby he checks into?" Stella said.

Light dawned. The woman smiled.

"If his car's here, it means he is, too. He doesn't like to take cabs. He passes out right there in his vehicle and drives it away when he wakes up."

Stella and Carrie exchanged glances.

He was in the car? Neither of them had thought he'd do that. They had assumed he'd have gone somewhere more comfortable, and that a multi-millionaire wouldn't choose to sleep in his own vehicle. Well, they'd been wrong.

Questioning him would be quicker, and easier, than they'd thought.

"Thank you," Stella said, as they turned and rushed to the parking lot.

Stella led the way, keeping in front through sheer determination, as they hurtled toward the black Range Rover.

She couldn't see through the mirrored windows, but when she went around and took a look through the windscreen, there he was. The seat was cranked all the way back and the dark-haired man was reclined in it, his face turned to the car's roof, his mouth open in slumber.

"Well!" Carrie said, sounding shocked.

Moving to the side of the car, she knocked sharply on the driver's window.

Franco woke with a massive startle. His eyes flew open, his mouth snapped shut. He sat bolt upright. His head jerked around to the window, and he stared at Carrie, appalled.

Carrie tried the door handle, but Franco had obviously locked it before passing out. She knocked a second time.

"FBI," she said loudly.

She took her badge out and showed it to him through the window.

Franco's face tautened in panic. The next moment, the car's engine revved with a roar.

"Hey!" Carrie yelled, irate, as the Range Rover reversed in a screech of rubber, leaving her standing open-mouthed.

It accelerated to the parking lot's entrance and Franco sped out.

"We have to chase him!" Stella said.

They raced for the unmarked. Carrie was clearly furious that her suspect had gotten away when she was less than an arm's length from him. She jumped into the driver's seat and started the car up with a roar that rivaled the Range Rover's.

Stella barely had time to fasten her belt before Carrie accelerated at such a speed Stella was flattened against her seat.

"He turned here. Go right," Stella pointed.

Tires wailed as Carrie fishtailed the unmarked in that direction. She snapped on the siren and its screaming tone filled the car.

A discordant blare of horns ahead signaled that Franco had met up with some traffic in his panicked departure. That might give them a chance to see which way he went at the intersection.

Sure enough, there was chaos at the light. Franco had wedged the Range Rover into the oncoming lane. He was veering hard left now, trying to weave the heavy vehicle in between an irate Mini Cooper driver and an equally maddened Porsche driver.

With a squeal of wheels, he made it.

"Go after him!" Stella clutched her seat, feeling guiltily relieved that she wasn't driving. She hadn't had years of experience behind the wheel. She'd moved into town as soon as she'd gotten free from her mother's clutches and had walked or used public transport. She had passed her driver's test only at nineteen, after finally being able to afford enough lessons. The car she had now was the first one she'd owned. When she'd occasionally needed wheels in Chicago, she'd borrowed or rented.

Carrie, on the other hand, had clearly been behind the wheel as soon as she'd celebrated her sixteenth birthday. Stella was reluctantly admiring of the coordination, judgment. and muscle memory she showed as she whipped the unmarked through the exact route Franco had taken.

"You're not getting away," Carrie muttered, sounding livid.

Grabbing the dashboard as she overtook an oncoming car in a swift, risky maneuver, Stella had her doubts, and they were nothing to do with Carrie's skill. Franco was in a far larger and more powerful car. The Range Rover could go double the speed of the mid-range sedan Carrie was driving.

With narrowed eyes, she tried to assess their progress as Franco sped ahead, tires smoking as he squeaked through a yellow light.

Pressing her foot on the accelerator, Carrie followed.

Flinching as she watched the cars to the right screech to a halt, Stella started wondering if they and the unmarked would escape this ordeal without serious damage. It was most definitely thanks to a skilled driver that they were keeping pace with him, but Carrie was taking serious risks.

Franco veered the Range Rover hard to the left, crossing just in front of oncoming traffic. Swearing, Carrie hit the brakes. The cross-traffic was going too fast. Even with the siren, a left turn would have caused an accident for sure. The car stopped so suddenly Stella nearly bit her tongue. Her bracing hand against the dashboard was proving useful.

Carrie didn't wait for green. The moment the speeding bus and two cars had passed, she flattened her foot and flew across the intersection.

"He's there," Stella said breathlessly.

Even as Franco swerved desperately into the oncoming lane to pass a slow-moving row of cars, Carrie accelerated closer. Her hands gripped the wheel. Her face was intent, one hundred percent focused on her goal.

"You are so not going to escape us," she muttered.

They couldn't let him get away. But how were they going to catch him? He would easily outpace them when he had passed this traffic snarl-up. Fleeing from law enforcement was a clear sign of guilt. But if he fled successfully, it could take days before they caught up with him. Having resources and contacts would allow him to hide.

Stella nearly swallowed her heart as Carrie swerved around the clustered line of cars. She was going too fast, and there was a sharp bend in the road ahead. She was going to lose control. Stella felt the back of the car start to slip. The wheels start to slide. As if in slow motion, she saw the trajectory of where the skid would take them. Right under the wheels of an oncoming truck. Now the blare of horns competed with the wail of the sirens and Stella saw the truck driver's face, drawn in horror as he, too, saw what would happen.

And then Carrie pulled out of the skid, carefully guiding the car back into the correct lane. The wheels found purchase on the road and the car roared ahead, engine howling.

Stella's heart was lodged firmly in her mouth. This crazy chase was meaning risk after risk. Every attempt to get closer landed them in a life-or-death situation and they had not yet made any headway in catching up with Franco.

Looking at the signs for the highway ahead, Stella realized with a thud of despair that he was gaining ground on them again. He was going to turn onto the highway and from there, he'd outpace them.

"I'm not giving up," Carrie hissed, leaning forward in her seat as if urging the unmarked to higher speeds, the siren howling as the car's engine raced into the red.

And then – it happened.

Perhaps it was caused by a moment's inattention, a loss of focus, a fearful glance behind him, but Stella watched in horror as the Range Rover lost control.

The car spun across the road, leaving huge, dark slashes of rubber on the blacktop.

Just as she thought it was going to roll, it righted itself, but it was too late. Franco couldn't steer. He couldn't stop. The car's own momentum kept it spinning, across the thankfully clear road, up onto the sidewalk, and finally – terminally – colliding with a lamp post.

The impact took only a moment, but to Stella, it felt as if she was watching it in vivid slow motion.

Metal screamed, and the car rocked to a stop as the hood buckled and the lamp post tipped sideways.

Steam billowed from the damaged Range Rover's engine as Carrie slowed, looking calmly satisfied, and indicated left.

"That was helpful of him," she said in tones that told Stella she was very pleased with herself for her aggressive pursuit.

"Great driving," Stella praised. She had to be honest; if she'd been driving, Franco would have gotten so far ahead he'd never have heard the siren behind him and would never have panicked and lost control. Carrie might be an unpleasant person and far too competitive for her own good, but she was dynamite behind the wheel.

"Thanks," Carrie said, sounding surprised as she deactivated the siren.

She stopped the car near the damaged Range Rover, and they climbed out. Stella felt lightheaded with the adrenaline rush. Her hands were unsteady, her palms cold and damp. But here they were. They'd chased down a fleeing suspect. He seemed unhurt. At any rate, through the cracked windscreen, Stella could see him staring around in consternation, and struggling to open the door, which appeared to be wedged shut due to the damage.

Now they urgently needed to take two critical actions. Firstly, search his car for the weapon and forensic evidence that would hopefully incriminate him. And secondly, question him and find out the reasons for his guilty actions.

CHAPTER FOURTEEN

Opening the door to the interview room at the Greenwich police station, Stella took stock of her suspect.

Franco had his hands cuffed in front of him. He was wearing a leather jacket, chinos, and an expensive dress shirt. One of his well-manicured hands had a graze on the back of it. He had a minor abrasion on his cheek.

He was dark haired and sallow skinned; a tall, rangy guy. His dark eyes looked shifty. Stella guessed he would use his intelligence and cunning to try and evade questioning. But he was at a disadvantage because he'd run. She needed to capitalize on this clear sign of guilt, and not let him wiggle out of his predicament.

Stella was doing this interview solo, because Carrie had opted to search Franco's car for the crucial evidence that would make or break the case. Stella was glad she'd chosen to do that, working together with a forensic expert from the local pathology lab that she knew from other cases. If there was a weapon in there, or any trace of blood on the wheel or the door handles or anywhere inside, Stella was certain that the determined Carrie would find it. And if Franco was carrying any illegal items or contraband, she'd find those, too.

Stella felt her skills were better suited to questioning the man himself, trying to crack open the shield of lies she felt sure he would use in his defense.

"Mr. Bruno, why did you flee when you saw us at your window?" Stella asked in accusatory tones.

Franco shrugged. "I had no idea you were FBI. I was deeply asleep and when I woke, I thought it was an attempted carjacking." His voice was deep and Italian-accented.

"From two women?" The disbelief was audible in Stella's voice and Franco looked momentarily abashed.

"I am an innocent citizen," he protested. "You gave chase and frightened me. Now my car is a write-off and I am injured. My face is cut. I may have a permanent scar. I need a cigarette."

Stella ignored his irrelevant complaints, which she knew were nothing more than an attempt at distraction.

"Your blood alcohol level was tested at 0.16 after the crash. You should not have been driving. You were way over the limit. Why were you driving and why did you flee from law enforcement?" Stella pressured him.

Franco shook his head. "I just woke up. I felt sober. What were you even doing at my car window? It was like a dream!" he pleaded.

"We arrived at your car to question you about a murder," she said. She watched for his reaction.

A small frown added itself to the faint network of lines that characterized Franco's face.

"A murder?" he asked. "Who was murdered?"

Stella fixed him with a cynical stare.

"Patrick Coleridge," she said.

Franco went very still. Only his eyes were moving, his gaze darting around the room. Stella noted that the knuckles on his folded hands whitened, as if his grip had intensified.

The air in the room felt as if it was crackling with tension.

There was silence for the count of five. The count of ten.

And then, Franco let out a bellow of humorless laughter.

"Well, he had it coming!" he said. "He got what he deserved!"

Stella felt punched in the gut by this admission that Patrick was less than perfect. Finally, they had someone willing to acknowledge his other side. She now needed to find out whether Franco had taken matters into his own hands.

"That's why I'm questioning you now," she said.

Franco's eyes narrowed.

"Okay. You believe I did it," he said.

"You are a suspect. You have a motive."

Franco nodded. "Yes. He forced me out of his company a few years ago. My lawyer was Italian. He didn't pick up on the full meaning of a certain clause in the contract. The wording of that clause allowed Patrick to do what he did. He was – how can I say? – a real gentleman about it. Laughing in that way he had, like everyone must share the joke. Saying that there were irreconcilable differences with our partnership, and he was so sorry to invoke the clause."

"Did you go back to Italy?" Stella asked. "The payment was made into an Italian account."

Franco shook his head. "That was for tax reasons. Once he'd forced me out, Patrick was all friendly and helpful. As if he was kissing me after screwing me," he said scornfully. "He organized the money to be wired internationally. Perhaps he expected me to go back. But he didn't know that I had other investments here. I partnered with more ethical people and my other businesses were doing well, so I stayed."

"You had a grudge against him," Stella insisted.

Franco nodded. "Of course."

"Did you kill him?"

"I don't even know how he died. How did he die?" Franco asked impatiently. "I don't know anything about this. Are you going to give me a clue, and tell me how you think I killed him?"

He stared at Stella with a cunning expression in his eyes that told her he was more than capable of thinking on his feet.

Well, one of them had to state the cause of death if this interview was going to continue, and Franco was too sharp to be tricked into a confession. He was crafty enough to lie and deny, all the way down to the wire. Also, he was frustratingly unreadable. From his body language, she still had no idea if he was the killer.

"He was stabbed outside the yacht club yesterday evening," Stella said. "You could have done it. You could have driven back from Sinsations and arrived there and waited for him."

Franco shook his head firmly. "I didn't. If I had wanted to kill him, I would have done so at the time and not waited for five years. That is not my style, to wait. I am an impatient man. But I am also not a killer. Certainly, I could not have stabbed a man, and then – I presume – you think I went back to Sinsations and carried on with my evening pretending everything was normal? That is not my character. Once I arrived at Sinsations, I did not leave again. I stayed there in the company of my friend Gary until we went our separate ways later in the evening, for some private dances."

"Why did you flee from us this morning, then?" Stella pressured.

Franco sighed. "Truthfully, I thought the club had been raided. I am not naïve. I know that there is drug dealing that takes place in there. I know some of the women probably do not have legal papers. The type of place it is, one expects this. I thought I was going to be arrested and that it could have a negative consequence, so I made a bad decision, to run."

"Did you return to the yacht club after you left yesterday evening? How can we confirm the timeline of your movements?" Stella asked. She wasn't going to tell him what time the murder had occurred – yet.

Franco thought for a while, moving his hands restlessly in the cuffs.

"That parking behind Sinsations, it costs money to get in because the club is so busy. They charge ten dollars for parking. The attendant there can tell you when I arrived, and paid him his ten dollars, which would have been soon after eight."

Stella nodded. "Any other proof?" A parking attendant was not a reliable witness.

"I stopped on the way to get gas and draw cash. I can tell you where I went. I imagine there would be cameras in both places. Gary can confirm he waited for me outside the club. We walked in to Sinsations together and I bought a bottle of champagne. Expensive French champagne called Louis Roederer. They do not sell much of it so you should be able to pick that sale up easily on the records. That would have been at about quarter past eight. I paid cash for it and left a big tip. We stayed in the bar for a couple of hours. We sat at the table in the corner, talked some business, spoke to a few friends. I can name the friends. We spoke to the barmaid when I ordered a second bottle, an hour or two later. Then we went through to the club, probably close to midnight. We stayed there a couple of hours, spoke with the ladies, had some fun with them. Gary left after his private dance. I returned to the bar and carried on drinking until the place closed."

At that moment, the interview room door opened. Carrie looked meaningfully at Stella.

She got up and hurried out.

"There's nothing evident in his car," Carrie muttered, as soon as she'd closed the door. "No blood spatters, no blood traces. Not on the wheel, not on the door handles, nowhere. No weapon. No drugs. No contraband." She sounded frustrated.

"I'm getting the same from him. He left the club. Stopped for gas. Stopped to draw cash. There'll be camera footage in both places. He paid for private parking and bought expensive champagne at Sinsations which will reflect on the bar records. It's all sounding legit. Too many details, too many contacts who would remember him. We can check out the timeline, but it's an outside chance at this stage that he could have done it."

Carrie made a face. "We must hold him anyway. He tried to flee and drove under the influence."

"Agreed," Stella said. "Let's confirm his story. We can ask the detectives here at Greenwich to check up on his movements. We do have enough cause to keep him detained meanwhile."

She headed back into the interview room.

“Am I free to go?” Franco asked hopefully.

“No. Not yet. We’re holding you a while longer, while we check out your alibi. You should not have tried to evade us. That is highly suspicious.”

Franco shrugged. “I admit. I frequented dodgy clubs and now, I have paid the price.” A sly expression crossed his face. “But I was not the only one.”

Stella’s eyes widened.

“Are you saying…?” she began.

Franco nodded, looking satisfied.

“Your victim, Patrick Coleridge, he too liked to visit such clubs. He liked to get up to mischief there. He did not associate with good people, even though everyone praises his reputation so much. Maybe you should broaden your thinking, agent?”

He smiled at her. Stella didn’t like the expression at all.

CHAPTER FIFTEEN

Stepping out of the interview room, Stella felt as if this case was increasing in complexity with every hour that passed. Finally, they were breaking through the shiny veneer that had seemed so blindingly perfect. And under it, they were discovering that Patrick Coleridge had been a very different person from that genial, good guy front he presented to the world. The icon's feet of clay were being exposed.

Had he really frequented strip clubs? Franco had clammed up, pleading ignorance and refusing to give any more details, so it was possible he was dangling a red herring to send them off in the wrong direction.

She needed to confirm this for herself, but as she walked down the corridor with Carrie, her phone rang. It was an unfamiliar number.

"Hello?" she said.

"Stella?" The woman's voice on the line was tense, abrupt, and strangely familiar.

"Speaking. Who's that?" she asked.

"It's Viv. You might remember me. I'm a family friend of the Marshalls."

Stella felt utterly shocked. Viv was calling her? This was not simply a social touch-base. This meant something serious was afoot.

"Give me a moment," she said. She turned to Carrie. "I'll be back now," she said.

With anxiety surging inside her, she hurried to the police department's main entrance. As she rushed through the lobby, she vividly recalled how she'd asked Viv for help, while at the Marshalls', alone and traumatized after Vaughn's murder.

Viv had taken pity on her and had invited her to ride along while she headed into town. During that short journey, Viv had explained that the Marshalls were involved in irregularities. It had confirmed what Stella had suspected. Eventually, it had brought them down.

Stella reached the door and hurried out. She didn't want to have this conversation in front of anyone, particularly Carrie.

"I can talk now," she said.

She paced along the sidewalk, moving away from the police department's main entrance, wondering what this was about.

She remembered Viv clearly. She'd been slim, blonde, beautiful, and assured. Except, when she spoke again, Stella didn't pick up the same confidence in her voice that she remembered from before. Viv sounded stressed, her voice low, and she spoke rapidly.

"Stella, I'm calling to warn you. You need to be careful," Viv said, and Stella felt her stomach clench.

"Why is that?" she asked, even though she knew why it must be.

"You know what happened to Cecilia, right?" Viv asked. "She passed away recently. Overdosed."

"Yes. Yes, I do know."

"I don't know what's going on. Since that happened, everything's become completely weird. It's like the whole family has gone off the rails. It's beyond anything I've ever known them do. Gordon, Kathy – they're enraged. They blame you for causing the family's downfall. They're talking about destroying you. There are other things going on, too. Things I can't understand, but I'm trying to find them out."

"Are they talking in front of you?" Stella asked. Would they really discuss such a thing openly?

"No. I've been listening in and picking up snippets. They stop talking when they see me. And I'm scared. It's like – I've known them for so many years, and only now do I see how they behave when the gloves are off. I don't know how far they will take this. I am terrified of what they might do."

"I see," Stella said. Her mouth felt dry.

"I don't dare associate with them anymore," Viv said, now speaking even softer. "Being around them has become like walking a tightrope. They know I know, and they suspect I told you things. I feel they're waiting to catch me out or do something worse."

Stella swallowed. Viv's kindness to Stella was coming back to bite her.

"Why do they suspect you?" she asked.

"There was that day when we left the house at the same time. That was when you rode into town with me. Kathy remembered that we'd left together. She interrogated me about it on Thursday. There's no proof. Nobody else saw us leave. But it feels like there's a witch hunt going on."

Stella felt her anxiety multiplying. "If you stop seeing them, it's going to make it even worse for you, Viv. They might take that as proof you are complicit in this whole mess."

"I'm sure they will. But I'm damned if I do, and damned if I don't," Viv said sadly. "Yesterday was Grace's birthday. I'm her godmother, so I had to attend the party. I heard them speaking about it. I was listening outside the door. Kathy and Gordon are planning something, I'm sure of it. I heard your name mentioned, and like I said, other, weird stuff as well that I couldn't make sense of. Then, when I walked in, they both stopped speaking. They looked at me as if they knew I must have overheard. I felt sick about what they might be going to do to you, and then it got even worse."

"Worse how?" Stella's stomach was churning now.

"They gave me these big fake smiles and Kathy said, in that really poisonous way she has, that it's strange how things always get uncovered eventually. I know she was talking about you and me. Insinuating that I'd helped you. Then Gordon smiled in an even worse way, and he told me to be careful. He said there had been a lot of random crimes near where I live recently, and he would hate for me to get hurt. I wish it was just a threat. But the way he said it, it was a warning."

Stella felt horrified that the woman who'd helped her was now also at serious risk. History and friendship would mean nothing to the Marshalls. The fact that Viv was Grace's godmother would be irrelevant. Even the fact that Vaughn could have told Stella about the family himself would be ignored if they suspected Viv had been disloyal.

"Please, Viv, be careful," she implored. "I'm worried for you."

And for herself as well, she thought.

"I'm doing my best," Viv said. "But I'll admit, Stella, I am scared. Terrified, in fact. I've never lived like this. I don't know how to handle it. I can't pretend everything is normal. I was supposed to meet with Kathy and Helena today, but I canceled. I just can't anymore." Her voice shook.

"Can you leave town for a while? Go elsewhere?"

"No," Viv said ruefully. "There's a major charity event here next weekend and I have to organize it, and attend. I'm the charity's chairperson. Besides, how long do I leave for? I'll have to come back sometime."

"Can you hire private security?"

Viv sighed. "I thought of that, but the Marshalls have links to the two main firms in town. I don't know about the other, smaller firms, but I don't trust them. It might make things worse."

"Please try and protect yourself, however you can," Stella said again. "Detective Bradshaw, from the Greenwich police department, knows about this whole situation. Get in touch with him. He can make sure that if you call, you get help fast."

"I'll do that," Viv said. "And please, take care of yourself. Watch your back."

She disconnected abruptly.

Walking back toward the police precinct, Stella didn't feel safe anymore. After Viv's disturbing call, she felt exposed, as if there were unfriendly eyes watching her. She had no idea how to manage this potential disaster. Desperately, she considered the possibilities.

Contacting the Marshalls herself and sorting things out with them personally was out of the question. They were not the type of people who would be open to that, and in any case the situation had gone way too far. Anything she would say or do to them would make things worse.

Could she tell Roth about it and ask for his help, Stella wondered, feeling frantic.

She toyed with the idea for a few moments before discarding it. She couldn't ask Roth for any help. These problems predated her joining the FBI and were not linked to her job in any way. It would be wrong to place an additional burden on Roth's shoulders.

She could do nothing, Stella realized, feeling fear curdle inside her and wondering if her father had felt the same before he'd so inexplicably disappeared. At least Stella had no family that the Marshalls could threaten, she realized, imagining how she would feel if someone she loved was at risk because of her.

She had to keep doing her job. This case was urgent, and they were under pressure to solve it. At least she had a partner, even if she didn't trust Carrie completely, and she had a firearm. That wasn't much, but it would have to do.

She headed inside, to where Carrie was waiting impatiently in the lobby.

"Oh, there you are," she said to Stella. "Where did you disappear to?"

"I had to take a call," Stella said briefly.

“Stefan sent through the footage showing him arriving home, at the time he gave us,” Carrie said. “Also, Zenith Capital has sent through the list of clients that Patrick saw this week. There are seven clients on the list. All their portfolios show good growth. We could start working our way through them, but my personal feeling is that we should go back to Liane Coleridge. We got nowhere at Zenith Capital. They probably wouldn’t give us the name of any client who had a problem, seeing they’re so invested in this whole reputation management. So if there is such a client, we’ll need to find them another way.”

Stella nodded. “Agreed,” she said.

“I think we need to pressure Liane now, and find out more about her husband’s social life,” Carrie elaborated. “Find out if he really was going to strip clubs and involved in that world. Maybe this time, she’ll tell us the truth. Or give us the names of friends who might know.”

Stella nodded. Going back to Mrs. Coleridge was a logical move now that they knew more about her husband’s darker side.

“Let’s head there now,” she agreed.

CHAPTER SIXTEEN

Patrick Coleridge's elegant mansion looked even more exquisite when bathed in mid-morning light. Stella appreciated how the sunlight brought out the warmth of the stone cladding around the front door, and made the bright, white paint around the windows look pristine and immaculate.

There were two other luxury cars parked outside, and Stella recognized one of them from last night. It was Liane's sister's car. That hopefully meant Liane was home.

She knocked on the door, and a minute later, a butler opened it.

"FBI, here to re-interview Mrs. Coleridge," Carrie said firmly, edging in front of Stella.

"Please come in," the solemn, uniformed man said.

Stella heard subdued voices from the lounge, but the butler didn't lead them that way. Instead, he headed further down the corridor and showed them into the home's library. Tall shelves lined the walls, filled with books, many of which looked like collector's items. In the center of the room, four leather armchairs were placed around a coffee table.

Stella sat down on one of the chairs. Just as Carrie sat on the other, Liane arrived.

She looked immaculately made up and haunted by grief. Her eyes were artfully shadowed, her hair hung loose over her shoulders. Her full lips had only the faintest sheen of gloss. She wore a charcoal dress and a black cashmere coat.

"Good morning, agents," she said softly. "How can I help you?"

She perched on the edge of the chair closest to the door. Stella couldn't help but feel drawn in by her beauty, and by the sense of bereavement she exuded.

"We need to know more about your husband's social activities, as well as any family connections" Carrie said. "We're looking to get a better picture of his life."

Carrie made the question sound matter-of-fact, as if they hadn't just learned that Patrick Coleridge probably frequented dodgy strip clubs.

"Of course, I understand," Liane said. "Family will be difficult, as Patrick was an only child. His parents are in Southampton, in England. He had no close family over here."

"Friends, then?" Carrie said.

Liane shook her head. "So many of those! As I said, Patrick played so many sports, and he socialized continually."

As Liane spoke those words, something about them piqued Stella's curiosity. She felt there was something missing. Something omitted. Before she could explore her instinct further, Carrie moved briskly on with the questioning.

"Who were his closest friends?" she asked. "People he socialized the most with, went out with? Especially in the past couple of weeks?"

Liane looked surprised. "I guess you must have a reason for asking this?"

"We're looking for possible links with any third party who might have wanted to harm your husband. Perhaps a friend of a friend," Carrie replied smoothly.

"Oh, I see," Liane said. "In that case, I would definitely say Michael Yelverton. Michael is also a member of the yacht club, and Patrick mentioned seeing him a few times in the past few weeks. They have known each other ever since Patrick first moved here."

"Is that so?" Carrie asked, in a tone that encouraged Liane to talk more about the relationship, which she seemed willing to do.

"They used to be next-door neighbors. Michael showed him around when he first moved here, and introduced him to all the area's best places, as well as to many future clients. They were such good friends. His 'partner in crime' was how Patrick referred to him," Liane remembered with a sad smile.

"Thank you," Stella said. This felt like a lead filled with potential and she was sure that Michael, being so close to Patrick, would know a lot about his private life. "Anyone else?"

"Kenny Gorman. He and Kenny got together almost every weekend, but Kenny went on an overseas vacation last week, and he's only back in January."

Michael Yelverton it was, then. Stella felt eager to visit the 'partner in crime' and see what secrets, or hidden information, he might hold.

"Do you have his number?" Stella asked.

Liane shook her head. "I don't have it, but he owns a Range Rover dealership outside Greenwich. It's called Yelverton Auto."

"Ma'am, I know we've asked you this question before," Stella said. "I'm asking you again, because you might have had a chance to think more about it. Was there anything unusual you noticed in the past few days? Anything that was bothering your husband? Perhaps he seemed upset after coming home, even if you are not sure why? Perhaps he had an angry conversation or mentioned there were problems with someone?"

Liane sighed. "I feel so unhelpful not being able to give you any details, but nothing seemed wrong. I have racked my brains for anything I might have missed. I guess it didn't help that Patrick was extremely busy. Near the end of the year is always such a social time, and also there was a lot to wrap up in his work."

"Do you know where he socialized? Did he ever mention where he was at night? Did you see any evidence of where he went?" Carrie said, opening the door as far as possible for Liane to explain if she knew anything about his extramarital activities.

Liane shook her head sadly. "A man as busy as Patrick, seeing so many clients, and with all his sporting activities, it would have been a full-time job keeping up with him. I didn't even try."

Finally, the connection she'd been seeking earlier clicked in Stella's brain.

"What sporting and leisure activities did he enjoy most?" she asked.

"Cycling and golf were his biggest passions. And tennis. He also hiked regularly," Liane said, with a small, sad smile.

Stella nodded. This was interesting and aligned with what she'd just realized. She decided to file this information away and keep adding to it where she could. Perhaps it might even have a bearing on the case.

*

The Range Rover dealership, Yelverton Auto, was a hive of activity when Stella and Carrie arrived there at lunch time. Gleaming, glass-fronted windows showed off the latest models, polished to a blinding shine. Salesmen dressed in smart suits rushed around, catering for clients who were treating themselves to an expensive pre-Christmas purchase.

As soon as they walked in, their shoes squeaking on the polished tiles, a salesman rushed up. He was young and blond, with exactly the right mixture of friendliness, professionalism, and a keen desire to earn a hefty commission.

"Good morning, ladies. How can I assist you?" he beamed.

"You can take us to Michael Yelverton's office," Carrie said, bursting his bubble as she showed her FBI badge.

"Um, okay. Sure."

He hesitated. Stella suspected there were strict rules about unannounced visitors. But they were the FBI, so he bravely forced another smile, and said, "Follow me."

They wove their way through the showroom, with Stella breathing in the scent of leather and polish and squeaky-clean tires. The salesman led them to a glass elevator at the back of the building. They rode up to the top floor, walked along a short corridor, and he tapped on the door at the end.

"What is it?" an impatient voice called.

The salesperson cleared his throat.

"Mr. Yelverton, the FBI is here," he called back.

There was a short pause. Then the door was flung open. They came face to face with a genial, beaming man with close-cropped brown hair, wearing a turquoise dress shirt and gold-framed spectacles.

"FBI. This doesn't happen every day. Thank you for keeping our country secure," Michael praised. "Please come in. I assume this is in connection with the tragedy of Patrick's death?"

Stella guessed that you didn't get to be the owner of a massively successful luxury car dealership without being able to dispense fake charm in shed loads. And since there was no way Michael could be so delighted about their arrival, fake charm it definitely was.

Since he was starting the interview off on such a false note, Stella warned herself to look out for the lies that might follow. She was sure that despite this beaming, talkative front, Michael would be reluctant to share any details that might get Patrick, or himself, into trouble.

He led the way into a gray and chrome office with a wrap-around window offering a spectacular view over Greenwich.

"Sit, sit." He gestured to a steel gray sofa before perching on a chair opposite. "How can I help you?"

"Mr. Yelverton, you weren't at the yacht club on the night of the murder?"

Michael shook his head. "No. I do try to connect with Patrick on Fridays, but it was my mother's birthday. Family takes priority," he smiled.

"We heard from Mrs. Coleridge that you did 'connect' with her husband a couple of times, shortly before his death," Carrie then pressed. Stella liked how she emphasized the word 'connect.' It certainly caused a shadow of unease to pass over Michael's face.

"Yes. I hope that's not going to land me in trouble. We did socialize regularly, being good friends."

"Where did you socialize?" Carrie asked pointedly.

Michael fidgeted slightly a motion Stella picked up instantly.

"Um, we would go to restaurants. Bars. We enjoyed discovering Greenwich's latest and greatest eateries," he began, but the sureness was gone from his tone.

Stella decided it was time for her to increase the pressure.

"We heard that you frequented strip clubs."

There was a shocked silence. Michael's face turned brick red. His mouth opened and closed like a fish out of water.

"No, no. Absolutely not. Who even told you that?" he said incredulously. "I'm a family man!"

"Are you willing to go on the record, and state that you and Mr. Coleridge never attended a strip club?" Stella said.

As Michael began nodding enthusiastically, she held up a hand.

"Remember that you are speaking to federal law enforcement agents, who are investigating a criminal case. If you lie, you are committing a crime, and if we find out you lied, we will prosecute you for it."

There was a long silence in the room. Michael was looking cornered.

Eventually, he nodded. "Look, it wasn't a big thing. It was harmless fun, that's all."

"Which club?" Carrie asked.

"Um," Michael began.

"We already have certain information," Carrie added, in a voice that could have cut steel. "You'd better make sure your version aligns with what we have been told."

"Okay. Okay. We liked to go to a very exclusive place. Discreet and upmarket, you understand?" Michael looked at them anxiously.

"Upmarket," Carrie echoed, with a hint of triumph in her voice. "Please give us the details of this place."

"Its name is Treasures, but you won't find any details in the public domain. It's members only. Not open to general visitors. It's a very private establishment," Michael insisted, clinging to this line of argument as if this somehow made it more acceptable for a family man.

"The address," Carrie said sternly.

Stella watched as Michael capitulated.

He wrote it down, scribbling the words on a piece of thick bond paper with the Yelverton Auto logo at the top.

"Thank you," Carrie said.

"Any other places?" Stella added, because she didn't want Michael to have gone halfway in giving them information, while more might still be hidden.

"No. That was the only place," he said.

Stella nodded.

"We may have further questions later. Please keep your phone with you, in case," she warned him.

As she stood up, she had a sudden thought, "Actually, I have one more question about your sport and leisure activities. What do you take part in?"

"Um," Michael seemed thrown by the question. "We have a home gym. I do a lot of my fitness work there. Then I do trail running with my eldest son. And birding with my daughter. I didn't do any sporting activities with Patrick, if that's what you're implying. And I assure you, we are a close, loving family. I'd appreciate it if you did not share the information that I – er –occasionally socialized with him at Treasures."

He stared at them in guilty appeal.

They turned and left, taking the elevator down and walking back through the bustling, festive atmosphere of the showroom.

"Why are you asking pointless and irrelevant questions?" Carrie whispered. "Are you just looking to rile people? Annoy them? Are you conducting some kind of a side-hustle survey? What on earth's your issue?"

"Gathering information. I'll tell you when I know more," Stella said.

For the time being, they had a solid lead, and a real clue to what Patrick had been involved in. Stella couldn't wait to learn more about this ultra-discreet, members-only club, and what goings-on might have taken place behind its unmarked doors.

CHAPTER SEVENTEEN

When she and Carrie reached the address Michael Yelverton had given them, Stella was interested to see that Treasures was much like she had imagined it. It was in a majestic three-story building in a financial and commercial area of town, with mirrored windows and basement parking that she was sure was private. There was no visible signage, and Stella guessed that being so ultra-discreet, there had been no expense spared in soundproofing the interior so that not even the neighboring tenants could hear what took place inside.

The problem was that the club's ornate front door was firmly closed.

After ringing the bell repeatedly, Stella walked around to take a closer look at the basement parking entrance. It, too, was locked up, with a barred gate. Beyond, she thought she could see a booth, where a guard or attendant must sit, but there was nobody in it now.

"They can't be open yet," she said. "They must only open in the evening."

Carrie nodded. "I guess so."

Stella took stock of their situation.

After the practically sleepless night, and a long morning's work, she was beginning to feel like a zombie. She didn't think she could carry on for the remainder of the day, and probably well into the night, without some rest.

"There's a hotel down the street," she said. "What do you say we check in, and get a few hours of sleep while we wait for this place to open?"

Carrie looked down the main street, and then looked back at Stella again.

Stella's heart sank as she feared her partner might veto the idea and insist on pushing on. Perhaps Carrie was one of those rare individuals who didn't need much sleep, Stella thought, feeling overwhelmed at the thought of continuing. Her exhausted thoughts were scattering in every direction.

"Great idea," she said after a pause.

Stella felt dizzy with relief that Carrie was on the same page. They drove straight down the road and parked outside the hotel.

It was a small boutique hotel that looked well-equipped and comfortable, Stella was glad to see. She hoped there were some available rooms.

"You're an hour early. Our check-in time is usually only three p.m.," the receptionist said.

"We're FBI agents busy with a case. We need rest, now, and we'd appreciate your help," Carrie pressured her.

Checking again, the receptionist said, "I see we do have two rooms on the first floor that have just been made up, if you don't mind street-level. Rooms three and four, if that's okay?"

"That's fine," Stella said.

Within a couple of minutes, they had the keys to rooms three and four.

"Shall we meet at six?" Carrie asked.

"Good idea. Six p.m., in the lobby," Stella said. She was sure, by then, the club would be open.

She went into her room, breathing a sigh of relief as she locked the door.

Over the months she'd been working on cases, Stella had learned to always stow a basic change of clothes in her laptop bag. She took out a fresh top and underwear and hung it up in the postage-stamp sized cupboard.

The room was neat and clean. Quiet and peaceful. Warm and cozy. After a day of weak sunshine, a light drizzle was now spattering the window. Stella pulled on her spare T-shirt and climbed gratefully between the sheets.

Her mind was spinning. She had so much to think about. So many worries to process. Plugging her phone in to charge, she saw Maxwell had tried to call her again. She didn't return his call. Not right now, she decided. The detective from the Leavenworth precinct in Kansas had sent through the disclaimer. Quickly, Stella e-signed it and sent it back.

Then she climbed into bed. She thought it would take time for her to unwind, but as soon as her head touched the pillow, she was fast asleep.

*

"I'm here. Stella, can you see me? Can you feel me?"

The voice was as soft as breath, tinged with evil glee. The smell of blood soaked into her nostrils, prickling her senses with terrible fear.

Stella sat up – and there he was. Vaughn's face was gray, leeched of blood, but there was a devilish light in his eyes.

"I've been waiting for you," he whispered, grabbing her arm with a bony hand. There was an unrelenting strength in his grip.

"You're not real," she insisted, in a voice ragged with fright.

She had this nightmare repeatedly. Usually, saying that worked, and Vaughn's specter would dissipate, leaving nothing more than chilly fingerprints ingrained in her flesh.

But this time, he laughed.

"Oh, I'm real, Stella Fall. I'm real, babes," he hissed, using the endearment jeeringly. "My family sent me. They want you to join me. Together, forever. I can't wait!"

Finally, screaming in terror, she managed to break free.

She sat up, breathing hard, reassuring herself that she was in the hotel room. The familiar scents of fabric softener and carpet shampoo surrounded her. It was fully dark, but ambient light from the street outside brightened the curtains. Stella had been too tired to close the blackout blinds.

It was a horrible nightmare. That was all. Most probably, it had been triggered by Viv's call earlier. Sweat was trickling down her temples.

She climbed out of bed and went through to the bathroom, still feeling the last vestiges of her dream clutching at her, like wiry tendrils, refusing to let go.

Turning on the cold tap in the sink, Stella splashed her face. The water was icy, refreshing. She glanced up, seeing her face, pale and drawn.

And movement behind her.

The shower curtain, pulled back. A dark figure, leaping out.

Stella's scream was cut off before it could leave her mouth. Rough hands yanked a rope over her throat.

This couldn't be happening. It couldn't. It must be still a dream. It couldn't be real, Stella's terrified brain insisted. But the rope was pulled tight, ruthlessly and without hesitation. The physical reality of her predicament smashed through her denial.

Someone was strangling her, brutally and efficiently. The rope burned her throat, even as her hands instinctively shot to her neck, in a movement she knew was pointless. Doing that wouldn't save her now. Not when this cord was already lodged deep in her flesh.

This faceless attacker was going to murder her. Straining for breath, she heard nothing more than a guttural choking. Blood pounded in her head.

She must not panic, Stella told herself, even though panic was surging red-hot inside her. She must overcome the shock and the fear, because there were only a few moments now in which she could act before she would pass out and it would all be over.

Remembering her combat training, Stella kicked back with all the force she had, but she was barefoot, straight out of bed. Her heels made bruising contact with the assassin's shins. She heard a startled grunt, but that was all.

She jabbed her hands behind her, looking to make contact with his eyes. She sensed that he ducked, but he didn't let go. Now her throat was burning agony. There was no breath to be had, and she needed air. Her thoughts were jamming in her mind. Her vision was blurring.

The experience she'd had three weeks ago flooded back. There was no escaping her fate. She'd saved herself then, but now she was going to die in the most terrifying way.

In a last-ditch attempt to get free, Stella drew her feet back and slammed them against the wall. Hopefully, she could knock the assassin off his feet and struggle out of his grasp. But he was too strong. The impact made him stagger, but his grip held firm.

However, Stella was surprised by the noise it made. It was a loud, resounding thud, and she guessed that the rooms were separated only by flimsy dry-wall.

Carrie was next door. Perhaps the sound would wake her.

Stella pulled her feet back and tried again, slamming her heels into the wall as hard as she could.

Choking pain overwhelmed her as the assassin tried to drag her away, but Stella managed one last, despairing kick.

It was all over. She'd failed. There was no more air. She'd cheated death the last time, but it had come back to find her again.

And then, just as the dark vortex was swallowing her, she heard a massive crash.

For a moment, her attacker lost focus. The cord loosened and Stella sucked in a huge breath of air, twisting in his grasp, clawing blindly at where she hoped his eyes were.

He let go of her and she collapsed on the chilly tiles. She heard the stamp of feet and Carrie's astonished yell.

"Hey! Stop! What the hell?"

Then the window rattled, and he was gone.

Her head was pounding. Her lungs burned, and she coughed hoarsely.

Carrie burst into the bathroom, brandishing her gun.

"What the hell? What's happened here? You okay? You okay? Stella, are you alright? Just breathe. Can you breathe?" Her voice was a high, shocked shriek.

Stella choked in air, voiceless for the moment.

"Can you breathe? Do I need to do CPR? Lift your hand if you are okay," Carrie gabbled.

She was looking down at the twisted cord that had fallen away from Stella's throat. Regarding it as if it was a snake.

"I – I'm okay." Barely able to cough out the words, Stella raised her hand. It was trembling violently.

Carrie glanced toward the window, taking a deep breath, seeming finally to gather herself.

"Asshole's long gone. Did you get a look at him? I only saw him as he ran."

Stella shook her head. "He – was – behind me. Never – got a look."

"How did this happen?" Carrie sounded confused, as if she was thinking back over the activity of the past day. "Who could have put this guy onto you? Did someone track us here?"

Stella didn't know what to say, but at that moment, she heard concerned voices approaching from outside.

"Is everything okay? Oh, no! No! Look at the door! What's happened here?"

A moment later, the receptionist arrived at the bathroom door, followed by an anxious-looking guest.

"What happened?" the receptionist asked, sounding terrified by the visible aftermath of violence. "Has there been a fight?"

"Call 911," Carrie ordered. "Someone broke in and attacked this guest. I smashed the door to save her."

Looking pale, the receptionist rushed out into the corridor and Stella heard her speaking rapidly on the phone.

"How did he get in?" Carrie sounded incredulous. "That receptionist must have given out our room numbers to someone."

Stella shook her head. She coughed, painfully. Talking was still too sore. Her throat felt raw. Her heels were throbbing from the impact with the wall.

"You don't think so?"

Carrie took her arm. Helped her up off the floor. Practically carried her through to the bedroom and sat her down on the bed. Then she prowled across the room, looking as closely as she could without touching anything.

"Looks like he forced the window from outside. The frame's damaged."

She turned to face Stella.

"What's going on? How did anyone know where we were? Who did you tell? No way was that just a random break-in. Why is someone trying to kill you while we are busy with an investigation?" she said loudly, glancing at the receptionist who was now hovering again in the doorway.

The pain in Stella's throat was subsiding. She was scared to reply to Carrie. Scared to say anything at all.

She'd told nobody she was at this hotel, and she didn't think they had been followed inside. And yet, someone had managed to track her here.

There was only one person who could have given out this information. Only one person who could have leaked her whereabouts to a hired killer.

She stared at Carrie, overwhelmed by horror as she reached the inevitable conclusion.

CHAPTER EIGHTEEN

Stella collapsed on the bed. Hunching her shoulders, she gasped painfully, each breath burning its way into her injured throat. At least she was breathing. She had so narrowly escaped death.

This attack was not related to the case. She was convinced of it, especially after Viv's warning earlier. The Marshalls had hired someone to kill her.

Stella's mind reeled as she battled to take in this horrific reality. She'd had a hit on her. An actual hit.

It had been done so professionally and with careful forethought. Why had he hidden away in the shower cubicle? Perhaps so that he could strike while she would be at her most vulnerable, unarmed, and unsuspecting. Or else, so that he could dump her body in the shower and turn it on before he left, buying time before anyone found her, she thought with a chill.

Around her, there was a chorus of voices and activity. The manager gently placed a blanket around her shoulders.

"Thank you," Stella mouthed the words. Then she glanced up, checking her surroundings, suddenly fearful that in the chaos, with so many strangers walking in and out, the assassin might try to come back and complete his job.

How had this man known where she was? Had they been followed, despite today's random route with all the different destinations, and the stop-starts they'd done?

She had been followed before. She always checked. But she had to admit that this morning, with being so sleep-deprived and navigating the unfamiliar roads, there had been stretches of time where she hadn't checked.

But surely Carrie, as the driver, would have noticed a tail in the rearview mirror?

Suspicious all over again, Stella stared at Carrie, who was waiting by the door for the police to arrive. Her partner looked worried as she peered out into the corridor. As she glanced back toward her, Carrie also looked distinctly guilty.

It must have been her. Stella knew Carrie was connected to people who knew the Marshalls. She must have given them Stella's location.

Feeling horrified by this betrayal, Stella battled to think the situation through logically. Surely it couldn't have come to that. Would Carrie have done such a thing deliberately, knowing it would endanger her partner and even compromise the case?

Perhaps she'd done so unknowingly, and they had somehow used her, Stella thought. After all, Carrie had rushed in to save her. She might not have known what the Marshalls intended to do or that they would go so far. They might have deceived her. But even so, as an FBI agent, how could she have given away her partner's whereabouts, when there was any possibility that the people who were asking for it wished her harm?

And talking of harm, she had to warn Viv. Immediately!

With shaking hands, Stella grabbed her phone from the bedside table and keyed in a message.

"Viv, be careful. Someone just tried to kill me. Youre now in serious danger. Please, move out of state for awhile. The charity event is not worth your life. Don't let them know where you well be."

Only after sending it did she see all the typos and mistakes that her hasty, shaking hands had fumbled into the script, and her shocked brain hadn't noticed. She hoped Viv would understand and take action.

Carrie paced back to the bed.

"Police are on their way. Fall, what is this all about?" she asked again, sounding as wound up as Stella felt.

But now she had no idea whether it was through genuine concern, through guilt, or through a mixture of the two.

She shook her head. She wasn't ready to talk. Particularly not to Carrie.

"Someone tried to kill you. This could be related to the case? If not, tell me what it is? Fall, it's only fair. If this happens again, we could both be in danger. I need to know." Carrie was sounding anxious.

Too anxious?

Stella shook her head. She could not risk speaking about this to Carrie now. Even if she had known where to begin, she didn't trust her enough.

With an angry sigh, Carrie turned away. She stomped to the bathroom. Stella heard the tap run. A moment later, to her surprise, Carrie brought her back a glass of water.

"Here. You need this, I'm sure," she said.

Sipping it gratefully, Stella heard faraway voices grew louder, and a moment later, two policemen entered the room. She recognized the redheaded detective who'd attended the murder scene at the yacht club. He was accompanied by another police officer that Stella hadn't seen before.

"This is where it happened," the manager explained.

The detective stared at Stella in surprise.

"Agent Fall? This was an attempted murder?"

Stella nodded.

The policeman paused for a moment. Then he held out his hand to Stella

Still clutching the blanket around her, as she was shivering violently, she stood up.

"Are you okay to walk me through what happened?" he said gently.

"Sure," Stella said. She passed the water back to Carrie. Even after drinking, her voice sounded awful. She was sure her throat looked terrible, too, as he was glancing at it in concern.

Summoning her mental strength, she walked slowly to the bathroom to point out the site of the attack.

"I'd been in bed. I got up after a bad dream. I came in here, and I was splashing my face at the sink when he attacked me. He'd been hiding in the shower."

"What time was this?"

It was almost six p.m. now, so she guessed she'd woken at half past five. Thinking back, she wondered if the sound of him breaking in had alerted her, causing the nightmare.

"About half an hour ago."

"So he surprised you? What happened then? Did you get a look at him?"

"I tried to fight him off, but he was too strong. And I didn't get a look at him. He was a professional, for sure," Stella touched her throat and winced. It was swollen and painful. "I was able to kick the wall and agent Potts next door heard. She broke the door down. When he heard her, he fled to the window and jumped out. The window is damaged, so he must have gotten in that way."

"I think he had gloves on," Carrie said. Stella realized she had been standing close behind them, listening. "I remember dark gloves."

Stella nodded. She'd be surprised if he hadn't been wearing gloves. For sure, this man was no amateur. He hadn't hesitated. His movements had been brutal and confident. She'd been prey, in the inexorable grasp of a predator.

"Any other identifying features?" the detective asked.

The radio crackled in the background as his partner communicated with HQ. Cold air blustered in through the window, billowing the curtains and causing Stella to shiver.

"I don't remember any other identifying features. He had his back to me as he fled," Carrie said, sounding frustrated. "Dark hair, I think. Dark clothing. Average height, maybe five-nine, five-ten. Fit build. Strong looking guy. And fast."

"Okay. Thank you."

The detectives moved over to the window.

Carrie bustled around the room, grabbing Stella's clothes and her belongings.

"If you're done with agent Fall, I'm taking her next door," she told the police. "You still look cold," she said to Stella. "You can get changed in my room. Get warm. Shower if you need to."

With Carrie grasping her possessions, Stella took her gun belt out of the bedside drawer and hustled through to the next-door room.

"I guess you're going to the hospital once you've gotten dressed?" Carrie asked.

Stella looked at her as if she was mad.

"Hospital? Why would I do that? We're in the middle of a case!"

Hoarse and damaged as her voice was, she could hear the resolve in her own tone.

Carrie blinked, looking astounded.

"Because you're injured. You need to be checked out and rest up. You can't carry on now!" She paused. "Can you?" she asked more uncertainly.

"I'm not that badly injured," Stella snarled. "It's just a graze!"

There was no need for hospital if she could breathe. She could even talk, although she sounded weird. These minor setbacks were not going to derail her focus from the case. Quitting would ultimately mean that the assassin, and the Marshalls, had won.

Stella knew she couldn't let them win. Any step back, any admission of weakness, any show of fear, and they would have achieved their aims. Worse still, they would know she could easily be stopped. No matter how she felt, she had to continue with the case. She knew she'd have to deal with the Marshalls later, because this threat was not going away anytime soon, but for now there was no option but to ignore the danger and press on.

Treasures must be open by now. They needed to get there as fast as possible, and find out who Patrick had been close to, and what he had done, at this secretive, word-of-mouth strip club.

CHAPTER NINETEEN

At six-thirty p.m., Stella and Carrie approached the club's front door. This time, Stella noted, the basement parking was unlocked, and the booth was lit. Treasures was open for business. She felt hopeful about what its interior would reveal, and that this visit would progress the case.

She'd bought a scarf on the way out of the hotel, because her neck was reddened and bruised, and had a raw graze where the rough cord had bitten in. The fabric rubbed painfully against the open wound, but it was better than having a visible injury. That would be a show of weakness right now.

Stella glanced back at the small white unmarked they were now using. The red-haired detective had suggested they should take over the car he'd been driving. He'd offered to take their unmarked back to Greenwich police department and lock it in the basement parking, where they could collect it in a day or two. That was good, because if the assassin had been following their car, they had now broken the link. The detectives were still working in the hotel room, but Stella doubted they would find any forensic evidence from such a professional killer.

She and Carrie had checked out of the hotel. If they worked late again, it would be safer to check in somewhere completely different. If the case wasn't solved, they would have to do that. But she hoped that they would find the answers here.

Walking up to Treasures' ornate entrance door, Stella tried the handle. It swung open and she stepped into a small, plush lobby.

A red-shaded standard lamp in the corner cast a ruddy glow. Just inside the door stood a doorman who she guessed doubled as a bouncer in the case of any trouble. Wearing a smart black suit, he was tough looking, shaven-headed, and solidly built.

When he saw them, his face darkened into suspicion, and he stepped immediately toward them.

Beyond him, Stella saw a young woman wearing immaculate make-up and a glittering evening gown. Tawny hair cascaded over her shoulders. She was standing behind the mahogany counter at the far end of the lobby and she, too, was looking anxiously in their direction.

"Evening," the doorman said tersely, moving to stand in front of them. Stella guessed he'd pegged them as wives, who'd somehow followed their husbands here wanting to find out more. She didn't think a wife had any chance of getting further into this place, or finding out more, so it was with some satisfaction that she showed her badge as Carrie spoke.

"FBI," Carrie said. "We're gathering information on a murder. We need to interview some of your staff."

The doorman did a classic double take, looking alarmed. This was clearly an unprecedented situation. He pressed his lips together, not wanting to let them in, but realizing he was unable to stop them.

He glanced at the receptionist who gave a small, reluctant shrug.

"I'll call the manager," she said.

At that moment, the entrance door opened again, and two men walked in. One wore a gray suit; the other wore chinos with a smart jacket. From the look of their clothing and their demeanor, Stella pegged them as being from the same wealthy echelon as Patrick. They were talking together, clearly discussing something important, as they barely glanced at Stella and Carrie.

"Good evening, gents," the receptionist welcomed them. "Please, go through."

The bouncer opened the side door and Stella peeked interestedly in as the two men headed inside. She saw a glimpse of dark carpet, muted lighting, and the polished curve of a bar counter, and picked up the throb of rock music. Then the door closed again, shutting out the music and the view.

A few moments later, it swung open and a heavily made up, glamorously coiffed woman wearing a turquoise evening gown walked out. She looked to be in her early thirties and possessed an air of calm authority.

"I understand you are from the FBI?" the woman said as Carrie stepped forward.

"That's correct, ma'am. We are investigating a murder. The victim was a client here."

The manager hesitated. "His name?" she asked.

"Patrick Coleridge," Carrie replied.

Stella had expected recognition. Perhaps shock. More likely, some sort of commiseration. But the manager looked entirely blank. After a moment, she shook her head.

"I don't recall that name," she said.

Stella stared at Carrie. Now they were the ones looking shocked.

Michael Yelverton had specifically stated that he and Patrick had attended this place. It had sounded as if they'd done so recently. Now, Stella wished she'd pinned him down with dates, but she hadn't thought there would be a need.

"How long have you worked here?" Carrie challenged the manager.

"Three years," the woman replied confidently.

Carrie took out her phone, scrolled through, and turned the screen in the woman's direction.

"This is him. This gentleman."

The manager shook her head. "He's definitely not familiar to me," she said.

Stella personally thought she hadn't looked at the screen for long enough to make out his face. She was wondering if this evasion was part of the policy at this club. She could see Carrie was thinking furiously, just like she was. Her partner was scrolling through her phone again, clearly intent on trying a different angle.

"How about this individual?" she said, flashing up a picture of Michael Yelverton, their most recent interview. "His name's Michael Yelverton."

The receptionist's eyes widened. She knew that name, for sure. But the manager maintained her poker face.

"That gentleman is not familiar to me either," she said regretfully.

Angry, appalled and frustrated at this blatant lie, Stella saw her own feelings reflected in Carrie's expression as she stared at the manager menacingly.

"Do you have a list of members?" Carrie challenged. "Show us the list."

The manager paused.

"Membership is completed online. Once members are paid up, they receive a card that they can print out or display. This allows them access. So no, we don't have a list of names and nor do we need one. The site is managed separately from the club and under top security, to ensure discretion."

"Those men who just walked in didn't show a card," Carrie accused.

"They are regulars who we know by sight," the manager explained.

"And you don't know the regulars we are talking about?" Carrie now sounded incredulous.

"Unfortunately not," the manager shook her head.

Stella seethed inwardly, knowing the manager knew, but wasn't telling. She decided to pressure her further. Clearing her throat, she stepped forward.

"We need access to this club, and to interview your hostesses. One of them must know the victim."

"Sure," the manager paused. "I doubt that they will know anything, but of course I cannot stop you speaking to them. You are the FBI after all."

Stella nodded, suspecting another 'but' was going to follow, and wondering what it would be.

"However, please could you make this as discreet as possible," the manager said. "Would you be willing to work with me on this? Having a visible police presence in the building will be problematic. Our clients pay a lot of money to be here, and we guarantee them a relaxed, discreet environment. If they complain, then our jobs will be on the line," she explained, with the first smile she'd shown so far.

Stella nodded again, feeling cynical. She didn't want to cooperate with a woman she strongly suspected of having lied from the start. But perhaps, given the levels of discretion at this expensive club, the manager's job might also be on the line if she admitted to knowing the victim.

"We can work with you," she said reluctantly, clearing her throat painfully once again as she spoke.

"I think it will be best if you wait in one of our private lounges. We have ten hostesses working tonight and I can send them in to you one by one."

"That sounds fair." Stella was eager to get beyond that highly polished and firmly closed side door. She felt sure that once they were inside, they'd have far more chance of finding out exactly what Patrick Coleridge had been up to. Someone must surely be willing to tell the truth.

Feeling so curious she barely noticed the throbbing roughness in her throat, she followed the manager to the side door. Her footsteps were soundless on the carpet, and her feet sank into the thick pile.

The manager led the way through.

Inside, Stella saw a large, exquisitely crafted wooden bar along the right-hand wall. Plush red stools stood at intervals along its curved length. The bar was a serious showpiece. Hundreds of bottles gleamed behind the counter. Crystal glasses glittered on shelves. A pretty blonde barmaid stared at them from behind the counter, looking taken aback at their presence here.

The lounge beyond was enormous – a dimly lit, darkly carpeted expanse dotted with leather furniture that looked immaculate and expensive, although Stella noted no chairs for one. All the couches were big enough for two or more. She saw a few doors in the far wall, presumably leading to the private lounges that the manager had talked about, and near the back, to her surprise, she spotted a poker table.

Inside this sumptuous space, commercial rock music boomed from the speakers at a volume that surely encouraged up-close-and-personal conversation. Fascinated, Stella stared around.

There were a couple of patrons at the far end of the bar, wearing suit jackets and dress shirts. They looked disapproving and defensive when they saw two women, who were clearly not hostesses, walking into this space.

They picked up their drinks and moved away, heading to the lounge area beyond. There, two women wearing exquisite and revealing evening gowns materialized as if by magic, escorting each of the gents to a couch.

"Please, follow me," the manager said.

She led the way across the club. As Stella followed, she breathed in a mixture of aromas. Cigar smoke, the whiff of cognac, and hints of men's cologne.

She guessed that in this club, the hostesses refrained from using perfume, as it would surely lead to questions once the customers got back home.

The manager led them all the way to the back, where she pushed open the door to one of the private lounges. It was a small space, big enough for two double-seater couches facing each other and a couple of drinks tables. There was a window looking out onto the main lounge, but Stella remembered seeing a mirror from the other side. So this was one-way glass, to ensure the privacy of those inside.

"I'm going to call someone for you straight away," the manager said. "A couple of our girls are free now."

She left the room.

"Classy place," Carrie observed cynically. "Not for the low spenders, I'm sure. I wonder how much this 'private membership' costs? And what they pay for a dance? And the average tips?"

"I'm sure it's top-end," Stella agreed, but she feared that the levels of discretion would equate with the pricing scale. Nobody working here would want to bite the hands that were feeding them so generously.

The door opened and a young, beautiful hostess stalked in, balancing perfectly on six-inch stiletto heels. She wore a thigh-length, sequined sheath of a gown that showed off her tanned, perfect legs. Shiny brunette hair cascaded down her back.

"Hi," she said. "I understand you need to speak to us? I'm Crystal."

"Please, sit, Crystal," Stella said.

Crystal perched on the couch opposite them.

Through the one-way glass, Stella saw more men arrive. Two headed straight for the bar. The other one went over to the poker table, greeting the two men already there.

"How long have you worked here, Crystal?" Carrie asked.

"A year," Crystal replied.

"How many nights a week?"

"Four to five nights. Usually four," Crystal said with a smile.

"Did you know either of these men?" Carrie turned her phone in Crystal's direction and swiped between the two photos. Carrie had clearly decided to improve her chances of any recognition, by showing both pictures.

"Patrick Coleridge and Michael Yelverton are their names," Carrie explained. "We believe they were regulars here and would probably have come in together. Patrick Coleridge was recently murdered, and this is the reason why we are here."

"I don't think I've seen either of them," Crystal said, sounding hesitant now.

Stella felt frustration surge inside her at the obstructive behavior of the pretty, fake Crystal. This was a murder investigation! Why were they not cooperating?

This stonewalling was extremely suspicious, Stella decided, and she wasn't going to give up until she had answers.

"How does this place work?" Stella asked. "Do all the hostesses circulate, or what happens when a client walks in?"

"We do circulate, but if a certain client likes our company, we stay with that gentleman," Crystal said demurely. "Some of us work in the upper lounges and some on the lobby floor."

"So this evening, will you see all the clients who come in?"

Crystal shook her head. "That's very unlikely. I will welcome a few of them and spend time with three or four."

"Who's your favorite regular?" Stella challenged.

"I have a few regulars. Mark and John are my two best regulars."

Stella regarded her cynically at the mention of these extremely common names.

"Would you recognize them by sight?"

"Of course," Crystal responded innocently.

This was getting nowhere, Stella decided, trying to clamp down on her anger. They needed to come up with a new strategy for the next interview.

"Do you have any other questions for her?" she asked Carrie.

Carrie shook her head.

"Please send in the next hostess," Stella said.

As soon as Crystal had closed the door, Carrie sighed impatiently.

"These people are lying to us, Fall. Blatantly. It's unacceptable in a murder investigation."

Stella nodded. "They've clearly been trained to do exactly what they are doing."

"Trained to say a lot of words that don't mean anything at all," Carrie snapped. "Mark and John. I never heard anything so ridiculous. Let me guess, their last names were Smith and Brown?"

Stella couldn't suppress a flicker of amusement at Carrie's wry, but accurate, observation.

"I think we should be tougher on the next one. Give her a hard time," Carrie insisted.

"Sure," Stella agreed. "Let's try that."

"I think doing that will work." Carrie said, her confidence returning. "They know, and they're not telling, so we need to bully the information out of them. I'm not being nice to any of these girls, anymore. We're being lied to every way we turn, and it has to stop. They clearly know information that's important to the case, and I'm going to force it out of them. Now!"

Carrie sounded determined as she stared angrily at the door, waiting for the next hostess to appear.

CHAPTER TWENTY

Soon after Carrie uttered her dire threat, Stella saw the door swing open. The throb of music from outside swelled as another woman walked in. She was tall and slim, with huge, dark eyes and waist-length dark hair.

"Hi. I'm Storm," she said.

Carrie had been telling the truth about no more nice guy, Stella noted. Clearly, her partner had lost patience entirely.

"Storm? Is that your birth name? Show me your ID," Carrie snapped.

The woman's eyes flew even wider open. "I – we don't use our real names here. My real name's Mandy Bowen," she stammered.

"Mandy, do you recognize this man, Patrick Coleridge? He was murdered. We are looking for background information. Keep in mind that withholding information from an officer of the law is a federal crime," Carrie said, shoving her phone at Mandy.

Mandy blinked. Stella thought she looked apprehensive as she glanced down. But Stella also thought she didn't look as afraid as she would have liked her to. Stella had the impression that working in this environment, Mandy had already seen lots of people breaking lots of laws. This threat wasn't scaring her as much as it needed to.

"I can't say I remember him," Mandy said, and Carrie let out an exasperated sigh.

"Perhaps a few hours in a police station interview room will help your memory?" Stella asked meaningfully. "We can do that, you know. We could take you in for questioning, right now."

Now Mandy looked hunted.

"I hope you won't do that, because I'd hate to waste your time," she said in a small, but determined voice. "I don't recall this man. I usually work on the second floor. I don't see everyone who comes in."

Feeling annoyed beyond words, Stella looked through the one-way glass window, needing to reestablish her self-control before speaking again. In the lounge, another hostess in a black dress with a plunging neckline was welcoming a new arrival and leading him across the floor.

The poker game was still ongoing, she saw, but the participants in it seemed to have changed. There were two new players sitting there, as well as one guy who'd been there all along. Wearing a black fedora hat and sunglasses, he looked like he was dealing all the cards.

They could take Mandy in. They could sit her down and bully her for hours. And Stella had the feeling that she still would not talk.

These hostesses had been very well trained, and they'd been taught that they didn't need to say anything, because the club was set up in a way that protected them from having to say anything. From the registration to the entry to the circulating among floors, it was all done in a way that ensured anonymity – or at any rate, enough of it to pass the buck when law enforcement arrived. No one hostess could be proven to be liable.

How could they get past this, Stella wondered.

Everyone knew. She was certain. But this was a conspiracy of silence, where nobody was saying what they knew. She'd got Mandy's real name because that was a concrete detail that could be easily confirmed. But the presence of guests at the club was far more difficult to keep track of, thanks to the club's setup.

Stella imagined what might happen if she stepped out of this mirrored lounge and walked over to speak to some of the male clients. She was tempted to try, just so that she could tick that box, but she guessed it would also be a waste of time, and that she wouldn't get anything out of them. Most likely, they'd be offended by the questioning and leave immediately. Or laugh at Stella and Carrie and ask why they would take notice of any other men with such beautiful women around.

How could she pry information out of this unwilling prospect? Perhaps a plan might be to get her talking. Once feeling more confident and relaxed, she could accidentally let something slip, and then they would have her.

"Tell me about the men who come here. Where are they from?" she asked.

"They are mostly from Greenwich, I think," Mandy said.

"What do you talk to them about?"

Mandy shook her head. "We are here to entertain. To bring drinks and offer dances. We don't talk about anything serious. If they want to talk business, they go to the cigar lounge on the second floor. That's an area where the hostesses don't stay around. We bring drinks and leave."

"Do all the men have favorites? Ladies they request more often?"

"Some of the men do, yes. Others prefer a variety. Even the ones who request one hostess, will do so for a while and then move on. We encourage that, also, as it's better for everyone," Mandy explained with a smile.

"Did Patrick have any favorites?" Stella then asked, deciding to slip the curveball in.

She almost got an answer. Mandy actually drew breath and then stopped herself. Stella could practically hear the clash of mental gears.

"I don't know who Patrick is. But like I say, most of our clients prefer a variety," she explained in a voice wobbly with tension.

Stella felt frustrated that she'd gotten so close but hadn't quite managed to distract her attention enough. Now Mandy was on guard again. The opportunity had passed.

"Please send the next hostess in," Stella said.

Mandy smiled. "I will do," she said, getting up and walking out of door on her spiky, ultra-high, bejeweled heels.

"Well, this is going fabulously," Carrie snapped.

Stella shook her head. "These girls – their jobs are on the line if they say anything. Most likely the manager's, too. They're not just unwilling to talk. They are simply not going to talk."

Stella imagined that if you were in the industry, this would be a good place to work. She was sure the tips would be phenomenal. It wasn't a job anyone would want to lose, thanks to a careless mistake like telling an FBI agent you knew a certain client existed.

Even so, she couldn't help feeling puzzled by the level of stonewalling they were getting. All they needed was for one person to say what they knew, but how would they get to that one?

She looked out at the poker table again.

One guy was getting up. Another was sitting down. The dealer, his fedora pulled low, was shuffling the cards. He was sitting sideways to Stella. Faintly, she could make out his profile under the brim.

"This isn't going to work," Carrie said. "I think we should call in the local police to come and help us. Shut this place down and interrogate every single staff member until we get answers."

It was a tempting thought. But Stella wasn't sure if the situation merited doing it. After all, they were simply getting background information. There was no proof at all that Patrick had been murdered by anyone here. An exercise like that would be costly in terms of time and resources. It would blow their investigation all the way into the public eye, and it would show that they were casting around without any meaningful leads. And they would make enemies that way. That was never a wise decision if it could be avoided, and right now, Stella didn't want to make any more enemies. She had enough.

She'd been so close to tricking Mandy into talking. Trickery would be better here, Stella sensed it. Subtlety was needed. Pinpointing the weak spots and honing in on them, rather than barging in with guns blazing.

Trickery and subtlety were her areas of expertise. *What could she do*, Stella wondered, feeling increasingly desperate.

She wasn't getting anything from face-to-face conversations with the hostesses, but perhaps they could sneak out of this lounge and prowl around. Perhaps feet on the ground would allow them to observe or overhear something.

She stared again through the mirrored glass toward the poker table, where there was more activity. One man was standing up, another was sitting down.

Perhaps she didn't even need to prowl around, Stella thought with a spark of insight. What she needed might be right in front of her. In fact, it was now so obvious that it sent prickles down her spine.

"Carrie, there's something weird about that poker setup," she said.

"What's weird? Look, I'm all out of patience. I've sat here long enough. These people are messing around. They're literally inviting us to bring in the Greenwich cops and go full-on."

"Just wait. Don't do anything yet. Look where I'm looking. That's not a real poker game. They're not playing enough hands," Stella said excitedly.

Carrie shrugged. "Well, there are other things to do here, Fall," she observed in sarcastic tones.

"You don't just sit down at a poker table for a few minutes. Even in an environment like this. Poker is addictive. Everyone wants to win. Players stay seated for hours. Or, if it's a tournament, they play until the last man is standing, but this isn't a tournament setup. People are coming and going. And why are there no hostesses bringing drinks?"

Stella felt intrigued.

Since Mandy was clearly dragging her feet about bringing the next hostess in, or perhaps briefing her colleagues on Stella's sneaky questioning technique, she stood up and took an even closer look at the poker table. The one-way glass provided a very convenient viewing portal.

She was looking out for something she already suspected, but even so, she almost missed it. It was done so discreetly she barely picked it up.

A man sat down – dark haired, business-suited, and Stella guessed, freshly arrived at the club. He handed over four hundred dollars.

The dealer handed back a stack of chips.

Then he dealt.

It was only by following his actions closely that Stella saw the white plastic bag that the dealer slid along the table to the newcomer, with the second of the two cards.

That was it. She had him, now! She knew exactly what the next step should be.

In a flash, Stella was on her feet and at the lounge door. Bursting out of the lounge, she marched up to the poker table and grabbed the dealer's arm.

"FBI," she announced. "We're investigating a murder and you're under arrest."

Pandemonium ensued. The client who'd just sat down jumped up again, so suddenly that his heavy wooden chair thudded backward onto the carpet. Abandoning his cards, he fled. A moment later, the other two men at the table did the same. They got up and they raced out of the lounge, heading at speed for the club's exit door.

"Please, please don't –" the dealer stammered. He looked appalled. Under the fedora, she could see his fox-faced features were taut with shock. She'd surprised him so completely that he had no words in his own defense.

Stella turned to Carrie, who had arrived at the poker table looking equally astounded, and as if Stella must have gone mad.

"Handcuff this suspect. Let's get him down to the car and take him in. We can question him at the Greenwich precinct."

Carrie's face spoke volumes. Stella could see in her eyes that she didn't understand anything of what was happening.

But Stella did. At that moment, watching the drug deal take place, she'd realized how she could use it, and how this would give them the advantage they needed.

Since she'd caused chaos in the club, and had deviated way off their mandate, Stella hoped her brainwave would get results. If it didn't, Roth would be rightfully angry, and she was going to have a lot of explaining to do.

CHAPTER TWENTY ONE

Standing outside the Greenwich police precinct interview room, ready to question the drug dealer, Stella checked the time. It was seven-thirty p.m. She felt a flash of anxiety. The evening was wearing on. There were only a few more hours left if they were going to solve this crime today.

So much hinged on this interview. She hoped she hadn't made a terrible mistake.

Her misgivings were not helped by Carrie, who marched down the corridor toward her, hissing out a warning as Stella reached for the door handle.

"Do you really think this is wise?" Carrie seethed. She looked angry, but also fearful, as if Stella's reckless actions might compromise the entire investigation. "We're filling up this building with people who don't have any direct link to the crime! Franco Bruno is still in a holding cell while they check up on his movements. Now we've dragged in a drug dealer who has no obvious connection to this murder and Roth is going to want answers on why we're doing this."

Carrie stopped and thought. "Why *you're* doing it," she amended.

"Come on in," Stella said, deciding that there wasn't time to explain, and it would be better to push on. "Look angry."

That wasn't difficult, as Carrie stomped into the interview room behind her.

Without his fedora, the dealer looked stripped of his character and authority. Stella stared at the narrow-faced man. His jacket was expensive and his shirt a top-of-the-line item. He wore a thick gold ring on his right thumb, and a gold chain around his neck, but his skin was pale and dull, and his hair was overdue for a wash. According to his ID, he was thirty, but the man in front of her looked a few years older.

Drugs got you in the end, Stella reminded herself. One way or another, they ate away at who you were.

"Benjamin Freitas," she said accusingly.

Looking up at her apprehensively, the dealer nodded. "Y – yes, that's me," he said.

"You were dealing drugs. You were in possession of drugs," she said threateningly.

He'd had a hundred grams of cocaine on him, and two thousand dollars in cash. He'd clearly been doing a brisk trade until the FBI had put a spoke in his wheel.

"I – I – are you on a drug bust?" Benjamin sounded sick with fear.

"We're investigating a murder."

Stella didn't think it was possible for the sallow man to turn any paler, but he managed.

"I'm not guilty. I don't know what any of this is about," he said.

"The victim is Patrick Coleridge. Do you know him?" Stella said.

She glanced at Carrie, who quickly pulled out her phone and showed him the photo.

"Yes, I know him," the dealer said. And then he clamped his lips shut, looking horrified.

Stella sat down, noticing that her partner looked both stunned and admiring as she figured out what Stella's successful strategy had been.

"I know this club is big on privacy," Stella said. "I know you've been told not to give out any information on the clients. Correct?"

Looking deeply unhappy, Benjamin nodded.

"We're investigating a serious crime. We need information. So you now have a choice. Either you tell us what you know, and we release you, or else we charge you with drug possession and drug dealing. That's significant jail time and you will go down for it, without any doubt."

Benjamin nodded. Stella could see he was having an internal battle with himself. It didn't last long. Stella suspected that he was not a seasoned criminal, but rather someone who'd gotten sucked into this well-paying gig and was raking in a profit at the top end of the drug dealing spectrum.

"He came in regularly. Sometimes with a friend, sometimes on his own," the dealer said.

Stella felt vast relief that her strategy had worked. This key individual at Treasures was talking. Now, hopefully, they could get some answers that would lead them further in this challenging case.

"How long have you worked there?" she asked.

"I've been working for nearly a year. Six days a week. The club's closed on Mondays but I'm there every day otherwise. I didn't officially get hired. I kind of just – just drifted into the role," he explained in a quivering voice, confirming Stella's initial impressions of him.

"And how often did Patrick Coleridge come in?"

"At least twice a week. Sometimes more."

"How did he behave at the club?" Stella asked, wanting to get a feel for what the dynamic had been.

"He was very well liked. He always caused attention when he came in. He was one of the biggest spenders. He'd often buy a case of French champagne for the club, hand out bottles to everyone he saw. Very free with his cash. He bought a lot from me," Benjamin admitted.

"Cocaine?" she confirmed.

"Yes. He'd buy for himself, and also to share."

Stella didn't dare glance at Carrie in case she gave away her feelings about the pillar of the community's behavior as she confirmed, "Is that so?"

"He went overboard, I mean, he used to go wild here. He'd spend the whole night in the club, get private dances, do a few lines, drink a couple of bottles of champagne. That's why it was so important to keep it all discreet. Because obviously the club, and the hostesses, earned a lot from him. He was a top client, without a doubt," Benjamin shared.

"So everyone there knew him?"

"Yes. He was known as Pat. The girls would get excited when they saw him walk in the lobby. They'd call to each other, 'Pat's in tonight!'"

Stella nodded.

"Thank you for explaining in full," she said.

Anxiety flooded back into the dealer's face.

"You said you'd let me go. Are you going to let me go?"

"Not yet. We'll be back," Stella said sternly, wanting to keep his anxiety high. She had an idea of what she wanted to ask him next but needed to discuss the theory with Carrie first.

She got up and walked out, with Carrie following.

"I don't believe Patrick's behavior!" Carrie sounded outraged. "And I seriously don't believe that everyone kept it so secret! It's insane that there was such a – such a conspiracy of silence, and that nobody said anything about the fact he seemingly spent half his life in strip clubs and lived on a diet of cocaine and champagne!"

"It's unbelievable. It shows how money talks," Stella agreed. When it came down to it, this was what it was. Money. Vested interests powerful enough to create an unspoken network of silence.

“The problem is that we still don’t have any suspects,” Carrie complained.

Stella nodded. “We’re getting there. We know more about who he was. There’s every chance – in fact, I’d say it’s a certainty – that his hidden side caused his murder.”

“Yes. His actions would make that likely,” Carrie said. “So now we know what he was doing. How do we look for a motive? How do we sift through all of this to find the connection to who got angry enough? It could well have been someone working at Treasures.”

“Perhaps one of the hostesses,” Stella theorized. “You know how it could play out in that environment.”

“They see a rich guy, get all friendly, and then start getting too involved with him?” Carrie said.

“Perhaps he made promises, or the relationship went further.”

“And that’s where the expectations went overboard?” Carrie nodded. “That could be a motive for murder. Someone he got too close to.”

“Yes.” Stella could imagine such a scenario playing out. “So that’s the important question we need to ask now. We need to know who was close to Patrick, because the relationship, or the expectations, might have been why he got killed. I’ll go back in and ask.”

She turned and walked back into the interview room to where Benjamin was miserably waiting.

“I have one more question. Were there any hostesses that Patrick was particularly friendly with?”

Benjamin thought. Stella could see he was thinking hard. She sensed that he was trying hard to give good information. Benjamin really didn’t want things to go the way she’d threatened. He was scared and regretting his life choices big-time.

“There was one. Her stage name is Cyndi, and her real name is Katie Robinson. Patrick loved Cyndi. He always used to request her when she was available.” He paused, and then spoke again, sounding anxious. “What’s happening now? Are you going to keep your word and let me go?”

“Firstly, give me the manager’s phone number so I can locate Cyndi,” Stella said.

“It’s on my phone.”

Stella handed him his phone. Hesitantly, he scrolled through and read out the number.

“Thanks,” Stella said. “You can go. But your file will be kept on record as an incomplete docket. Should you be arrested again for any related charge, this will be added to it, and you will go inside for a long time. Plus, my friends in the Greenwich police precinct will be stopping by the club in the future and looking out for you. They’d better not find you there again. Ever.”

“I – I’ll make big life changes. They won’t find me there again. I promise.”

Stella added, scathingly, “You don’t need to do this! You can make better choices. A month from now, you could be restarting your life. Or you could be in a far, far worse place. I can’t help you make that choice. But I won’t have to face the consequences either. You will. What’s obvious is that this is going one of two ways. Up or down. You decide. I’ll send the police in to process you now.”

She turned and walked out.

“We’ve got a name,” she said to Carrie. “There was a preferred hostess. Katie Robinson. Let’s get her address and find out more about her relationship with Patrick Coleridge.”

*

Katie Robinson lived in an upmarket neighborhood in downtown Greenwich. As she and Carrie pulled up outside, Stella saw the homes were large, double-story, with spacious yards. She wondered if the crimson Alfa Romeo parked outside the garage also belonged to Katie. If so, then lap dancing was a more profitable gig than she’d realized.

“Nice wheels.” Carrie sounded surprised and Stella guessed that yet again, they’d reached the same conclusion at the same time.

At this time, thinking along the same lines as her partner felt disturbing. She had to work with Carrie, but she still had no idea if she had been the reason that a killer arrived at the hotel.

That fearful, sick suspicion kept surfacing in her mind over and over. Yet again, Stella tried to push it aside. Now was not the time for distractions. She walked up to the front door and rang the bell, wondering if Katie would be home.

She was. Footsteps trod to the door and a moment later, a young woman opened it.

The slender, dark haired woman had large eyes and features that looked beautiful even without a speck of make-up. She was dressed in skinny jeans and a knit top. Immediately, Stella was reminded of Liane.

If Patrick Coleridge had a preferred type, this was definitely it, she thought.

Katie seemed surprised to see them outside. She raised an eyebrow questioningly.

"Can I help?" she asked.

"You're Katie Robinson?" Stella confirmed. "We're FBI. You work at Treasures?"

For a moment, Katie looked utterly appalled. Stella could see the clash of mental gears as she realized that, with the cops on her doorstep, it had gone way past the stage of upholding the club's standards of discretion.

"I work there, yes," she admitted.

"We're investigating Patrick Coleridge's murder," Carrie said firmly. "We know he was a member of the club. The dealer told us everything. The manager gave us your address. We don't have time for any lies or for anyone pretending they don't know who he is. We need clear answers from you, and fast."

Katie's face fell. Now that her initial shock was over, her demeanor was charming again.

"I will answer as best I can. And I'll be glad to do so, because I'm appalled by this news. It's so tragic. Do you want to speak inside? It's cold out." She wrapped her arms around herself theatrically. "Please come in."

They followed Katie in.

At least she'd admitted to knowing Patrick and agreed to talk openly, Stella thought. But that didn't mean that Katie would be truthful down the line. Especially if she'd had a closer relationship with Patrick, she would not want the FBI to know about it.

Stella was impressed by the size and scale of the beautifully decorated home. Katie's lounge was furnished in elegant gray and blue, with a few paintings on the wall that added a splash of color.

"We understand Mr. Coleridge requested you often at the club," Stella said, as they sat down.

Katie nodded. "Yes. He often used to request me. He was definitely one of my best customers."

"What did your relationship involve?" Stella asked.

"I would spend time with him, serve him drinks, and then take him for a private dance. He tipped very well, and was a real gentleman," she said.

"How often did he request you?" Stella asked.

“He’d request me when I was working and available. Look, if I wasn’t available, he’d choose one of the other girls. But I do think I was his favorite. He even sent gifts to the club for me.” Katie smoothed back a stray lock of her shiny hair.

“What gifts?” Stella asked, wondering why Katie was volunteering this information. Perhaps it was to prove that she was not a suspect and had no reason to kill him.

“Perfume, the one time. A gold bracelet, another time. Flowers, as well. So yes, he was – I guess, a caring, fun person would be the best way to describe it,” she said thoughtfully.

“Was sending gifts unusual?” Stella asked.

Katie shook her head. “It’s quite normal for us hostesses to receive treats and thank-you presents from clients. You know, if you dance well and you do a good job, make the customer happy, they remember you and think about you.”

“And how did you feel about him?” Carrie said.

“He was a wonderful client. I am shattered that he’s no longer here. I was totally shocked when he heard. I can’t believe it, in fact.”

“Did you have any relationship outside of the club?” Carrie pressured.

Katie shook her head. “We don’t do that. There are very strict rules about it. It’s a good job and we would be fired instantly if we had affairs with clients. Besides, why complicate things? Who wants that? Not the customers, that much I know. We’re an hour’s entertainment for them. Nothing more, and that’s how it should be.” She gave them a rueful grin before her serious expression resumed.

“Did Patrick ever ask you for anything different from what you were allowed? Did he hint about taking things further? Did you ever ask him for favors or extra money?” Stella asked, wanting to rule out any possibility.

“Absolutely not,” Katie declared.

Stella wasn’t sure if she believed her, but since Katie clearly wouldn’t admit to any of these misdoings, she’d need to find another way of proving if they existed.

But for the moment, there was a more important place to go.

She hadn’t realized Patrick Coleridge had gone so overboard when it came to his extramarital activities. He’d purchased expensive gifts for his favorite hostess. He’d been a massive, reckless spender at the club.

Was it really possible his wife had known nothing about all of this? Had she not wondered where the money was going? Or where her husband was? She remembered Liane had said Patrick came home at midnight on Fridays. But Benjamin had said he'd spend the whole night at the club. That was another inconsistency that needed to be questioned.

"That's all we need from you for now," Stella said. "Thanks for your time, Ms. Robinson."

They turned and headed back to the car, walking briskly in the cold, blustery night.

"Are you thinking what I'm thinking?" Carrie asked as they climbed inside.

Stella said, "I'm wondering if Liane Coleridge knew what he was up to."

"That's exactly what I was thinking," Carrie agreed decisively.

With her hypnotic personality, Liane was no pushover, but a strong and forceful woman. If she found out what Patrick had been getting up to, Stella imagined she might be angry.

Perhaps furious enough to do something in the heat of the moment, and then coldly intelligent enough to play the part of the grieving widow afterward. Stella hadn't trusted that performance and had suspected it might be fake.

It was time to go back to Liane Coleridge, for the third time, and drill down further into what she knew.

CHAPTER TWENTY TWO

It was after eight in the evening by the time Stella and Carrie returned to Liane's sumptuous home. Stella felt frustrated that they'd worked the whole day on this case without concluding it. In fact, the more they uncovered, the more complex it was becoming. With any luck, this visit would shed more light on Patrick's hidden activities, and the real relationship between him and Liane.

She rang the bell, and a few moments later, Liane's sister opened it. She looked taken aback to see the FBI there once more.

"Um, good evening," she said. "You'll be wanting to talk to my sister again?" She slightly emphasized the word 'again,' as if she personally thought the FBI had outstayed their welcome at Liane's home.

"Yes. Is she available?" Stella asked politely.

"She's already in bed. But I'll ask her to get up. Come through."

The sister beckoned them into the lounge where they'd sat the first time. A minute later, Liane walked in.

She was wrapped in a black satin dressing gown, and her hair hung loose around her shoulders.

"Good evening, agents. I apologize. I was preparing for an early night," she murmured.

"We need more information from you," Stella said.

"I so appreciate the hard work and long hours you are clearly putting in," Liane praised, in a soft, sad voice. "I hope it's going to provide closure soon. I am finding the stress and uncertainty to be emotionally exhausting."

"Unfortunately, a murder investigation can be a time-consuming process," Stella explained, thinking that these words were a subtle message from Liane that she'd had enough of them coming back with more questions.

"What can I help you with?" Liane asked.

"Your finances. Your bank accounts. Did you and your husband bank jointly?" Carrie probed.

"We had a shared account. We each had a credit card that we used as we needed." Liane seemed untroubled by the question.

"So you were open about your finances with each other?" Stella asked.

"Oh, yes. There was no need to hide anything. We were fortunate that Patrick's business was doing very well, so we could buy whatever we needed, within reason, without worrying, or having to ask the other."

"Do you have a recent bank statement available?" Stella asked.

Liane hesitated. Now she seemed taken aback. Stella wondered if she'd assumed the agents would take her word for it, and not need to dig further.

"I never looked at the bank statements."

"You didn't?" Stella queried.

Liane shrugged apologetically. "That was Patrick's department. I just used my card when needed. But he kept the statements in his study."

"We need to see them."

"Sure. Come this way."

Liane's momentary hesitancy had vanished, so much that Stella wondered if she'd imagined it. She didn't yet know what to make of Liane, or how much she knew. Stella hoped the evidence itself would provide more clues.

Liane stood up. She turned and walked out, with Stella and Carrie following. She walked up the carpeted staircase and stopped at the first door on the right.

"Here we are," Liane said.

She pushed open the door and snapped on the light. Stella and Carrie walked into the wood-and-leather enclave that Stella had expected to see.

A comfortably upholstered leather chair stood behind a heavy wooden desk. One of the side walls was lined with wooden filing cabinets. A large TV was mounted on the wall near the door and there were two laptops on the desk, both closed up.

On the walls were framed photos of Patrick's office building, taken from different angles. He was clearly proud of the modern architecture.

A couple of bottles of fine cognac and single-malt whisky stood on an antique table near the window. Stella could imagine Patrick walking into this space. Settling himself at the desk with a sigh, leaning back in that comfortable chair. Reaching over to pour cognac into one of the crystal balloon glasses. Sipping.

Smiling to himself, perhaps. She could visualize him smiling, but somehow, she couldn't make the expression seem warm.

What would he have been thinking, Stella wondered, wishing she could tune into the secret thoughts that must have gone through his mind as he sat here.

"The bank statements are in here somewhere," Liane said, pointing to a cabinet. "You're welcome to look."

Opening the cabinet, Stella spotted a folder labeled 'Statements.'

She took it out and paged through.

The most recent bank statement was on the top. It was dated just a week previously. Given that Patrick had frequented Treasures so often, Stella knew that there should be some evidence, in the past few months, of what had happened there.

She hoped to see some large cash withdrawals. Perhaps credit card swipes with vague references that matched up to one of the big nights.

But as she and Carrie paged through, Carrie gazing at the entries with the intensity of a bloodhound, Stella had to admit that she wasn't seeing the big amounts.

There were payments to beauty salons and home décor stores from the card that clearly belonged to Liane. On Patrick's card, there were petrol swipes and parking payments, restaurant expenses and a few cash withdrawals, but there was nothing on the scale that Benjamin had described. Stella wasn't picking up on the reckless spending that she knew must be somewhere.

Truthfully, she hadn't expected to find the evidence so easily. Because it was much more likely that Patrick had kept his activities concealed.

"You say this is the only account?" Carrie asked, sounding confused.

"That's correct," Liane said. She was hovering in the doorway, looking anxious.

Carrie ran a finger down the list of figures.

"I'm sure there's more," she muttered. "This account receives a monthly salary from Zenith Capital. Where are the bonuses? Where are the dividends and profit share? There's a lot more that should surely be here." She paged back through the statements, frowning.

"May we take a look at the other files?" she asked.

"Sure, but I don't see why, because that's the only banking file," Liane said.

Stella and Carrie went methodically through the cabinet, lifting out every one of the folders. Liane was now watching in concern.

"This one is business expenses." Even so, Carrie paged through carefully, clearly not trusting that other paperwork could be stashed further back. "And this one is a property portfolio."

"Everything is in the banking file," Liane explained, sounding anxious now.

"That's possible, ma'am. What we're doing now is trying to ensure every expense matches up."

"They should all do that." Now Liane had a defensive tone to her voice that Stella hadn't heard before. She thought that was interesting.

"Here's another folder. Historic Accounts." Carrie opened it and paged through. "Oh, wait," she said, with a note of triumph in her voice. "Not just historic accounts. Look here, Fall. There's another lot of bank statements at the back!"

Excitement flared in Stella. Could this, at last, be what they needed?

"Those must be old statements," Liane faltered. She stepped into the room and edged closer.

"Ma'am, they're a current set. Same as your other ones. Did you know your husband had an account with Bank of America?"

Liane shook her head. She looked innocent and confused as she replied, "He doesn't bank there. We've always banked with Citibank."

"This account is not brand new. It goes back a few years. The balance is currently at a couple of hundred thousand dollars. Do you know anything about it?"

Liane had gone pale, Stella saw.

"I know nothing about it. Are you sure this is correct?" she asked.

"Look!" Carrie pounced on an entry. "Treasures Limited. There. And there again."

Head-to-head, they peered down at the pages.

The credit card swipes were regular, and the amounts were phenomenal. Patrick truly had thrown money around while at this club. There were also large cash withdrawals. Regular amounts landed in the account. Big bonuses, every three to four months. And they were clearly spent on recreational activities. She saw credit card swipes from shoe stores, jewelry stores. Probably those would have been gifts for his preferred hostesses and not for his wife.

"What's Treasures?" Liane asked.

Carrie stared at her impassively. "Ma'am, I'm sorry. Treasures is a private gentlemens' club in the Greenwich financial district. Your husband was a big spender there."

Liane's eyes widened in horror. She clapped a hand over her mouth and took a step back, staring at them wordlessly.

"You can't be serious," she whispered. "You cannot be serious? Is this some kind of a setup? Patrick would never do such a thing. Never!"

"It's here. In black and white. Unfortunately, your husband did spend a lot of time at this club. He supported it well," Carrie said. "Were you aware of this at all? Apparently, he'd often stay there until the early morning. Did he really get home at midnight after going out?"

"He came back at midnight from the club!" Liane insisted. "He would sometimes stay overnight at work if there was a lot to do. I was not aware of anything else. I honestly can't believe it! You must be wrong. Patrick was a good man, a faithful husband. He was a loving father. A family man!"

Her eyes, wide and horrified, were brimming with tears.

Real or fake? Stella couldn't tell. Liane was visibly distressed, but then, if she admitted to knowing, it would mean much of what she'd told them so far had been lies. Stella knew how freely crocodile tears could flow when a person's interests and reputation were at stake. Had she really thought it was an all-nighter at the office, when he staggered home in the early morning, reeking of cognac and champagne?

If she had been innocent though, Liane was learning the truth in a cruel and devastating way. Having had no option but to use that shock factor, Stella was uneasily reminded of how ruthless she needed to be as an FBI agent in pursuit of justice.

Hearing Liane's voice raised, her sister rushed into the study. She, too, was now wearing a fluffy dressing gown.

"What is it, Lee?" she asked.

"They're saying that Patrick had another account. That he used it for clubs and – and strippers, and things I never dreamed of. This is a nightmare! My life has turned into an absolute nightmare!" Liane sobbed.

"I don't believe this!" her sister snapped, glaring at Stella and Carrie as if they had personally caused this catastrophe.

"Nor do I. I need to go to bed now. I can't deal with this any longer. I can't look at these people and hear them telling these, these –"

"These lies," the sister seethed, giving Stella another dagger-like look before putting a protective arm around Liane and leading her away.

Stella hoped she didn't get too comfortable in bed, because there was a good chance that they would need to call her back for yet more questions.

But then Carrie said, "Look here! Take a look at this, Fall!"

She sounded excited. Quickly, Stella turned back to where Carrie was still poring over the pages.

"I've found something interesting. There's a wire transfer that has been going out of this account on the first of every month. Same amount, and it goes to the same account. Except at the beginning of this month, it wasn't paid."

Stella looked and raised her eyebrows.

Every month up till now, Patrick Coleridge had been wiring money to an account with another bank. This transaction was helpfully described on the statement.

"Internet Pmt to Katie Robinson."

"Now that is interesting," Stella said slowly.

Liane might or might not have been lying to them, but Katie had blatantly lied. Patrick hadn't just been a good client and hadn't just sent her gifts. In fact, he'd been paying her substantial sums every month, going back – Stella checked – nearly a year.

What had this money been for? Had their relationship gone further? And the most important questions of all: why had the payments stopped, and had Katie been angry about that?

They needed to put Liane's questioning on hold, and hurry back to the attractive hostess who'd hidden the truth so skillfully the first time.

*

When Stella and Carrie knocked on Katie Robinson's door again at half past nine, it took her a long time to answer. When she finally opened the door, she didn't look thrilled to see them at all.

"Is anything wrong?" she asked.

She didn't just look surprised, Stella thought. She also looked apprehensive.

"We read through Patrick Coleridge's bank statements," Stella said bluntly, getting to the gist of the matter without any introduction.

Katie stared at them in horror. Her eyes were wide. She stood very still but Stella could see she was thinking furiously.

"You – so what are you doing here?" she asked in a trembling voice, clearly choosing to try and bluff this out.

"Payments were made on the first of the month, every month, from him into your account. Until this month, when they stopped. Why were they made, and why did they stop?" Carrie pressured her.

"I – I –" Katie began.

Then she capitulated. Her face crumpled. Her head bowed. She stared at the floor for a few moments, her shoulders shaking. When she looked up at the agents again, her eyes were brimming with tears.

"I loved him," she confessed. "I loved him, and I think he loved me, too. Please, I can't say more."

"We need more explanation," Stella said, feeling like a real hard-ass, having to pressure the facts out of this sobbing woman, but reminding herself that if Katie had honestly disclosed the facts in the first place, they wouldn't be back here again, watching her cry.

Carrie rummaged in her purse and handed Katie a Kleenex.

She wiped her eyes and sniffed hard. "This is so difficult," she said in a quivering voice.

Stella waited until Katie had pulled herself together enough to continue.

"It – it was a while ago now. Back in January, I mentioned it had been a bad month, and that I was feeling depressed. He asked me about my life, and I explained that I support some of my family members, that things had been tough recently. My brother lost his job last year after being injured in a car accident, and he had major medical bills that he was struggling with. And Patrick – he said he cared for me deeply. And that he'd like to do more for me. He asked me for my bank account details."

"How did you feel about that? Are you allowed to give those details out?" Stella asked.

"No. We're not allowed to, and I could have gotten into a lot of trouble. I knew I shouldn't have done it, but I was desperate. It wasn't an easy decision. I was risking my job, and more than that, it felt humiliating to ask for help, but he insisted."

"Did he say how much he would pay you?"

"No. He just said he'd like to help. When I saw the amount, I was stunned. I cried for a whole day. I knew that what we had was special."

She raised her head and stared at Stella, tears streaming from her eyes.

"Did your relationship ever go beyond the club?" Stella asked.

"No," Katie said. "I – I wouldn't have minded, but Patrick said it would be wrong to do that, and that he wanted to help me with no complications or strings. And that's why they stopped. It was because I asked him to stop them. I didn't want him to feel I was leeching off him. December is always a good month at the club, so I decided it was time. I told him I was so grateful, but that I was in a better situation now."

Stella took that information with a hefty pinch of salt. There must have been more to it. And she was sure that Katie was still holding something back. This version sounded too Hollywood. Too good to be true.

How could she prove this? What information was this cunning, desperate woman still trying so hard to hide?

"Please, I – I need to wash my face." Katie turned and stumbled back into her home.

"Are we done here?" Carrie asked in a low voice.

"No. We're not done," Stella replied.

Stella didn't trust Katie at all. There was nothing uncalculated about her response. Katie had years of experience in tuning into her audience and exploiting their reaction. Tears or not, there hadn't been one moment where she had truly lost control. Her sob story about the brother and hard times was even less believable when you looked at her luxury home and pricey set of wheels.

At that moment, Stella realized how skillfully they had been misled, and why letting Katie go back inside to 'wash her face' was a bad idea.

She rushed into the house after her.

"Fall! Where are you going now?" After a short, astounded pause, she heard the quick thud of Carrie's footsteps behind.

Stella hurried past the conveniently located guest bathroom near the hallway, where Katie could easily have detoured to wash her face. Then she passed the master bedroom with its door half open revealing another bathroom beyond.

Stella finally caught up with Katie at the entrance to the second bedroom at the end of the corridor. Katie was making a beeline for the desk on the far side of the room, looking determined.

“Katie Robinson, you are under arrest,” Stella announced, as the hostess turned to face her in panic. “We are taking you into custody, on suspicion of the murder of Patrick Coleridge.”

CHAPTER TWENTY THREE

Carrie felt totally confused as Fall marched the protesting Katie Robinson to the car.

"You can't arrest me! I've done nothing wrong!" the leggy brunette pleaded, now sobbing with stress. Carrie couldn't help feeling sorry for her, especially since she, too, had no idea why this was all happening.

"I'll get in beside her," Fall said. "You drive. Let's take her to Greenwich. We can process the arrest and question her there."

Carrie shook her head. At this moment, Fall's decision making was beyond her ability to understand. Yet again, Carrie worried she was derailing the case, making a move that would delay them at best, and get them in trouble with Roth at worst.

She wasn't going to say anything, though. Because Fall had been right the last time, when Carrie had thought she'd gone all the way off the rails. So this time, she was going to give her respect, Carrie decided. She'd earned it.

That thought jolted her. She'd never thought she would have that mindset about Fall.

Carrie climbed into the driver's seat. Fall got into the back, next to Katie.

Katie was still crying loudly. "Please, this can't be happening! Let me out! You can't just arrest me! Surely I have rights? I need a lawyer!"

"You do have rights," Fall said in level, if slightly hoarse, tones. "We will read them to you at the Greenwich police department."

The calm formality with which she spoke quelled Katie's protests and she lapsed into silence. Behind her, Carrie heard nothing more than an occasional muted sniff.

As she drove, Carrie realized the silence in the car felt unfamiliar. They'd spoken a lot during the previous trips around town. Apart from the first time they'd gotten into the car at New Haven to drive to the scene of the crime when, Carrie had to admit, the atmosphere had been decidedly frosty.

But since then, they'd been discussing the case, or else Fall had been helpfully directing her. Again, Carrie felt surprised to remember how the conversation had flowed in a cooperative way between them.

Now, there was no need for directions because she knew the way to the Greenwich police department, which was close by, and the five-minute drive would give her a chance to think.

Immediately, her mind flashed back to that panicked moment in the hotel room. She'd heard the thud on the wall and had known, instantly, that something must be wrong.

Perhaps she'd been expecting it.

She'd jumped out of bed, thankful that she'd been too tired to undress and had simply passed out with exhaustion the minute her head had touched the pillow.

She'd never forget the shocking sight of that man, storming out of the window as Fall coughed and choked, fighting for breath after she'd fought for her life.

Indicating right to turn onto the main road, Carrie wondered again: who had wanted to kill Fall?

She felt guilt crush her as she thought about her actions earlier in the day.

She could have prevented this. But she hadn't. She might be to blame for having actually caused it. But how could she tell Fall that she'd failed her partner?

Could she even do so?

For an agonized minute, Carrie battled with this impossible decision. She felt relieved when the police department came into sight and she could put it out of her mind, for now at least.

She parked right outside the entrance. Fall got out and hustled inside with Katie Robinson. Then Carrie drove off to find parking around the back. At this late hour, that was easy. It was freezing cold, and snow was threatening again. Picking the space closest to the building, she climbed out and rushed around to the entrance, ducking her head to avoid the stinging sleet.

Inside the police station, one of the officers was escorting Katie to an interview room. Fall had taken Detective Bradshaw to one side and was speaking to him in a low voice. As Carrie walked in, Bradshaw nodded and hustled purposefully out of the door.

"Let's go and question Katie," Fall said to her.

They walked to the interview room, where Katie was now seated behind the table. She stared at them apprehensively as they walked in. Her hair was mussed and her cheeks tear stained.

She sure was upset, Carrie thought, wondering again why Fall had made such a sudden decision to bring her in, and whether this tearful reaction indicated guilt. It certainly seemed excessive for an innocent person. Looking back, Katie's story about the payments had been rather Hollywood, Carrie decided, sitting opposite her.

"Ms. Robinson, please will you answer these questions honestly. We need the full truth from you," Fall said sternly.

"I have been truthful!" Katie appealed in shaking tones. "I don't know why you brought me here!"

"When did you meet Mr. Coleridge?" Fall asked.

"When I started at Treasures. I'd been working at another club. I heard there was an opportunity there, so I applied to join."

"How did you hear that?"

"The receptionist is a friend of mine."

"So you moved to Treasures – when?" Fall asked.

"Last year. I – I can tell you the exact month. I'm feeling flustered right now so I can't remember it offhand. It was near the middle of the year."

"Did you get interviewed for the position?"

"Yes, I did."

"Who interviewed you?"

"Maddie. She's the manager there."

"Have you ever met the owner?"

"No – no. I believe he lives in Los Angeles. I mean, he has visited the club. I do know that. I just haven't seen him."

Carrie wondered what the point of these questions was. Fall wasn't getting anywhere new. Try as she might, Carrie could not discern a reason for this particular line of interrogation. Other than upsetting Katie. That, it was certainly doing. As Fall's barrage of questions intensified, Katie was looking more and more panicked. Her anxiety was peaking, although Carrie couldn't see why. It wasn't as if the answers were incriminating her in any way.

"Do you usually work with the same team? Can you choose who you work with?"

"We – we can choose. But I do usually work with the same group."

"Did you fall for Mr. Coleridge as soon as you met him?"

"I – yes. I definitely had feelings for him the first time I saw him."

"Do you think he felt the same?"

"Yes. Yes, I do. I think he thought I was special."

"Do you think he went out of his way to visit the club when you were there?"

"Yes. He would ask me when I would be working next, and that he'd try to see me then."

"And how did that make you feel?"

"I felt pleased. I felt like I mattered to him and that he cared about me," Katie's voice was quivering. Carrie could see she desperately wanted them to believe her.

If she'd had the chance, Carrie was sure she would have jumped to her feet and run right out of the interview room. She was looking hunted.

"I see. Thank you."

Fall glanced at her and stood up. To Carrie's surprise, Fall now left the room. Feeling even more confused, Carrie followed her out.

"Is there any point to these questions?" she hissed, as soon as the interview room door had closed behind them, leaving Katie alone.

"Yes. There is a point."

Fall took her phone out of her jacket pocket. She glanced at it expectantly. Carrie guessed she must have been waiting for it to ring, because at that moment, it rang.

"Detective Bradshaw?" Fall answered.

Carrie heard the other voice crackling over the airwaves but couldn't make out the words.

"That's great," Fall said. She sounded relieved. "Can you send the shots through to me now? Thank you."

She glanced at Carrie with a conspiratorial expression that Carrie still didn't understand.

"Back in we go," she said.

She opened the interview room door, and Carrie noted that Katie visibly jumped.

Confused, Carrie walked in behind Fall, who folded her arms and glared at the other woman.

"As you were arrested as a murder suspect, who would have a motive for destroying evidence, we were legally allowed to search your house without a warrant," Fall told the terrified-looking hostess. "Detectives from this precinct are searching your house now, and have just told me what they found in the second bedroom."

Katie's mouth dropped open.

Carrie had to stop herself doing the same. This was the reason for the prolonged questioning? Fall had been buying time while the police searched. What had they found? And how had Fall guessed there was anything to find at all?

"In a locked desk drawer, the detectives found these photographs."

Fall turned her phone toward Katie. Katie's eyes flew wide. Watching her reaction, Carrie knew that these must be incriminating.

"These photographs would have damaged Mr. Coleridge's reputation if they'd been leaked. They are very compromising, with him being a married man."

Carrie gasped as Fall continued inexorably.

"So it seems that you were blackmailing him. The payments made into your account were not just done out of the goodness of his heart, but because he must have been threatened that these photos would otherwise be made public."

Katie's face had gone brick red. Although her mouth opened and closed, she wasn't saying a word. Carrie guessed that at this moment, there were really no words to say.

She, too, felt speechless at this bombshell.

Blackmail?

Luckily, Fall realized at that point how curious Carrie was about the photos. She turned the phone to Carrie, who stared at them, fascinated, as she scrolled through.

The shots were very clear. Whatever hidden camera had been in place must have been good quality, Carrie thought.

In one, Patrick faced the camera. His features were in perfect focus, as was his bare chest and belly. There was a lascivious expression on his face as he clutched onto the tawny-brown locks of a woman, whose head was at the bottom of the frame and almost out of the shot.

In another one Patrick was seated, again with his face to the camera, his hands clamped greedily over the naked buttocks of the woman on his lap. From the background, Carrie couldn't tell where they were taken. It was interesting that in none of these shots was the woman's face visible. Only Patrick's.

"I wonder how you organized this. Were you working together with other women at the club, so he didn't blame you for it? This seems to me like something you've done before. A nice team effort. You seem practiced in it," Fall's tone was flat and condemning.

Carrie turned to face Katie, wondering how she would respond to this new bombshell. She guessed there would be more tears, but to her amazement, Katie's attitude had changed in a flash. Gone was the sweet, tearful young beauty who'd claimed to have lost her heart to the wealthy tycoon's false promises.

In its place, someone much tougher and more cynical stared back at the FBI agents. Someone who, now that she was all the way up against the ropes, was showing herself for exactly who she was.

Katie nodded.

"Okay. Okay, you're right. I did do that. I'm not dumb enough to think he'd really fall for me. But I did want more than what he tipped me for the dances, and for going further, and doing some other stuff for him which he kind of bullied me into and said I should do it with him if I wanted him to pick me again. So yes, he deserved what he got."

"I'm sure he deserved what he got," Fall continued. "But this means you had a motive to murder him. The payments stopped. Clearly, he'd decided to blow your little racket out of the water. He was going to put an end to the good times and put you at risk in many ways."

Katie shook her head, sounding adamant as she spoke again.

"He never found out I was part of it. He wasn't even that interested. I think he thought it was small-fry. Not worth his time. Just an expense of living his life the way he wanted. That's how rich he was. He could buy what he wanted. Pay people off." She sounded sour and contemptuous as she continued, "I have no idea why he didn't make the last payment. Perhaps he just forgot, or thought that after so long nothing would happen, or maybe he had plans to divorce his wife. How would I know? But I'd gotten a lot out of him. I had no reason to kill him. Why would I kill him when I was still getting good tips and gifts from him at the club?" She stared defiantly at the agents.

"I don't believe you. A man with so many resources could have decided to put a stop to this if it was making him angry or becoming an inconvenience. He could easily have hired someone to trace that bank account and take things further. Ultimately, the situation could have exploded in your face. So, where were you last night?" Stella accused.

Carrie hoped this question would floor Katie and lead to a confession. But to her surprise, the pretty hostess sounded confident as she spoke.

"I was out of town. It was my aunt's fiftieth birthday last night. She lives in Poughkeepsie. I drove there yesterday morning. Booked into the hotel where she had the party, and I stayed there overnight. You're welcome to check; it was at the Hyatt. I drove back after lunch. Got home at six p.m."

Now, Carrie saw that Fall looked nonplussed, as if she had not expected a solid alibi.

"We'll need to check that," she said.

"Sure. Look on my phone. There's a whole family Whatsapp group set up. With hotel bookings, photos, the works. So whoever murdered Patrick, it wasn't me," Katie said, with a brittle assurance to her words.

Carrie didn't realize how far her hopes had been raised until she felt them shatter around her. Fall's intuition had been brilliant, but it had led them nowhere.

They could investigate the blackmail ring and put a stop to that crime. But they were back to square one in terms of finding the killer. Defeat, and her father's scathing criticism, was staring her in the face.

To her astonishment, Carrie found herself hoping that her resourceful partner would have some fresh ideas. Could it really be that she was starting to respect Stella Fall, after twenty-four hours of working with her, Carrie thought, feeling stunned at how her mindset had changed.

Perhaps that would be the deciding factor, Carrie thought. If they didn't work as a team, they wouldn't be able to solve this.

That meant she would have to confess to Fall about her part in what happened earlier. Was she ready to do that, Carrie wondered uneasily as they walked out of the interview room.

CHAPTER TWENTY FOUR

Stella was shaking inwardly as she closed the door behind her. She'd trusted her instinct and taken a gamble and she'd failed. Yes, they'd discovered irrefutable proof of highly criminal activities. But the prime suspect, the woman she'd hoped would go down for murder, had an alibi.

"I'm going to dig further back into that bank account," Carrie said firmly. "And we now have every reason to send the police in to raid that club. Let's see what else, and who else, we can uncover. They probably targeted other guys, too. But first, I need to speak to you about something else." She sounded nervous.

Stella checked her phone. She'd felt it buzzing in her pocket during the interview.

"I see I have a missed call from Roth, so I'd better call him back quickly. We can speak afterwards," Stella said.

Carrie pressed her lips together. Then she shrugged.

"Okay. While you speak to him, I can process Franco's release, if we're ready to let him go? I can check if they've confirmed his movements now." She glanced at Stella questioningly. Stella liked it that they were actually starting to cooperate and collaborate.

She wanted to trust Carrie fully. But the memory of the attempted assassination still loomed in her mind. Her throat was still so painful that talking was difficult.

Could she really trust her partner?

What did Carrie want to tell her? Suddenly, Stella felt scared to know.

"I say we release Franco if his alibi checks out. His crimes were secondary to the investigation. I'm not up for prosecuting him for fleeing us. Not when we still have so much to do," Stella said, feeling stressed all over again about the unsolved case.

"Any other information you need from him before he's released?" Carrie asked her.

Stella thought. "Actually, yes. There is one question you can run past him."

She saw Carrie jump to the correct conclusion before she even spoke.

"Fall, no. Don't make me ask him –" she began angrily.

"What sport and leisure activities he takes part in. I'd like a list. The top five will do."

Carrie was positively fuming now. Stella could see she bitterly regretted asking that question, and that she actually thought she was being played.

"It's for a reason," Stella reassured her.

"I literally can't believe I'm asking these pointless questions on your behalf. Why are you so hell bent on getting these irrelevant answers?" Carrie snapped. She whirled around and stomped back to the police station's main desk.

Stella walked further down the corridor, finding an unoccupied interview room. There, she called Roth back.

He answered immediately, sounding as stressed as she'd ever heard him.

"Fall. What's going on?"

Before she could figure out what exactly he was asking, and how she should answer, Roth steamrollered on.

"I want you off this case," he said.

"What? Why?" Anxiety surged inside her and she knew Roth could hear it in her voice.

Was it because she hadn't found the killer yet and he thought she was dragging her feet? Or had she unknowingly done something else wrong? The one-second pause before he replied felt like an eternity, but when he did respond, the words shocked her to her core.

"Because you've had an attempt on your life! And it damn near succeeded!" Roth shouted down the line.

Stella had to stop her mouth falling open. How had Roth known?

"Did the Greenwich PD say something?" she hazarded. "They didn't have all the facts. It wasn't as bad as it looked."

"They didn't say anything," Roth shot back. "Your partner, Carrie Potts, called and told me. And from what she said, it was worse than it looked!"

Stella gasped in outrage.

"No! I can't believe it. She had no right to do that!" she blurted out as emotions clashed within her.

Carrie had sold her out. She'd gone to Roth and squealed to him. *Had she done so hoping Roth would pull her off the case*, Stella wondered wildly.

She wished Carrie was with her, so that she could kill the call and confront her immediately, to demand the truth about her motives. She'd been right not to trust her. This felt like a sneaky, underhanded stab in the back.

"Fall, calm down," Roth snapped.

His tone derailed her thoughts and yanked her back to reality.

She was an FBI agent on a case. No matter what curveballs came her way, she had to handle them professionally. Bursting out in rage was not in any way professional and Roth was right to tell her off for it.

It took all her self-control to contain the anger and betrayal that surged inside her, but she managed by thinking back to the wise words that Clem, her mentor, had given her while she'd still been at the University of Chicago.

"One thing I learned in the FBI, is that you should never speak in a temper," he'd warned. *"Always be calm. Always think rationally. Over-emotional individuals have no place in the Bureau."*

Remembering this, Stella was able to bite back the words that threatened to spill out of her mouth. Continuing with her behavior would be out of line and would count against her badly.

It was actually correct for Carrie to have told Roth what had gone down, she acknowledged. He needed to know about an event this serious. And it didn't seem like Carrie had asked for Stella to be removed. Roth might have decided on this because he thought she was trapped in a dangerous situation. So first and foremost, Stella needed to reassure and update him.

"I'm sorry, Roth," she said. "Can I explain in more detail?"

"Sure," he said tersely.

"Firstly, I don't think this is related to the case in any way. I think it's the Marshalls. Remember, you recently told me Cecilia Marshall committed suicide after her guilty verdict? I'm sure this is her husband's attempt at payback. So Potts is in no danger. I'm the only one they're going to target."

"Go on?" he snapped.

"It was bad," she admitted. "But the assassin didn't cause me any serious damage, thanks to Potts breaking into the room. Also, we were able to switch vehicles immediately. We're in a different unmarked now, and the other car is parked out of sight. So if they were tracking our car, that would have broken the trail," she said firmly.

"Okay." Roth sounded doubtful now.

"We're moving on with the investigation as fast as we can," Stella continued, hoping to cement her argument. "I'm okay. I can breathe fine. I can speak. I'm not in any immediate danger. And we're watching our backs very carefully. I know I have to try and handle this somehow. But I need to solve the case first, and a personal attempt at revenge shouldn't prevent me. If I do drop this case, they're going to know they have what it takes to stop me and that will compromise my ability to do my job. So I have to push on."

She waited.

Stella knew Roth well enough to know that he would not come back with a reflexive response. He would think about what she'd said and would then make a decision based on the new information she'd provided.

Once he had rethought, it would be impossible for her to change his mind. But she'd said enough, Stella warned herself, even though she wanted to keep on talking, doing everything she could to try and convince him.

Roth didn't need more detail. He had enough. And his decision now was likely to be unchangeable.

The silence felt endless to Stella. She felt nauseous with tension as she waited for him to assess the updated facts.

"All right," he relented. "You can stay on it for now. But if there is anything else – anything at all, Fall, that makes you think this threat is ongoing, you come straight back to New Haven. I need you to promise me that. Otherwise, it'll compromise the investigation."

"I'll do so," Stella promised.

Who knew what the future would bring? But for now, she was able to continue.

"What progress have you made so far?" Roth then asked, which caused Stella's stomach to clench all over again.

It was nearly ten-thirty p.m. on the second day of an unsolved case. They were no closer to finding the killer and the lead she'd had such hopes for had fizzled out completely.

"It's getting more and more complex as we go," Stella admitted to her boss. "Patrick Coleridge was no pillar of the community. He had a secret life that involved strip clubs, hard drugs, and we are still digging into it. It has to be the reason why he was murdered, but there's still a lot we haven't uncovered."

Roth sighed impatiently. "Uncover it as fast as you can, Fall. I'm getting pressure on all fronts to get this wrapped up."

"I will do," she promised Roth, before he disconnected abruptly.

Stella glanced at the closed door of the interview room, wishing that Katie Robinson hadn't had such a firm alibi, and feeling even more stressed as she realized they didn't have any plans about where to go from here.

Feeling as if she had nowhere left to turn, Stella did the only thing she could think of.

She picked up her phone again and called Clem, hoping that he would pick up at this late hour, and that he'd be able to guide her out of what felt like a dead-end street.

CHAPTER TWENTY FIVE

"Well, it's Stella Fall!" Clem sounded pleased as he answered her call, and Stella felt relieved that he was a night owl who usually worked or socialized late into the evening. Then his voice sharpened. "Are you okay? Your hand – is it fully healed yet?"

The last time they'd spoken, Stella had updated him on the outcome of her previous case. At that stage she'd still had the stitches in her hand, and it had been at its most painful.

"It's fully healed, yes," she was glad to reassure him.

"Good. So you're back on active duty again?"

"I'm back in the field and on a case," she said.

"You must be pleased about that." She could hear the smile in Clem's voice. She knew from the stories he'd told her about his time in the FBI, that he felt the same way she did about back-office work.

"I am, but the case feels stalled to me. I need your guidance, Clem," she admitted.

"Stalled? Why's that?"

Stella felt grateful that Clem loved the mental challenge of feeling his way through a problematic case and would willingly spend as many hours as it took to help her.

"A Greenwich finance firm owner was murdered outside a yacht club. He seemed at first to be a pillar of society, but we've been uncovering more and more evidence that he was the opposite."

"That's so?" Clem sounded intrigued.

"He forced his partner out of the business. He went to strip clubs and was getting blackmailed by one of the strippers. He took hard drugs. And that's just what we've uncovered so far."

"Definitely not such a golden boy, then," Clem agreed thoughtfully.

"The problem is that his entire life is wrapped in a shield of lies. And I have never met so many people linked to an individual, who have lied so much. Everyone is trying to protect their interests and stay out of trouble. I don't think anyone we have interviewed has told us the truth yet. And I'm partnered with Carrie Potts – remember, she was with me at the academy?"

Clem knew the past history between the two of them, and she could hear the heaviness in his voice as he said, "Okay, that's not great."

"I don't know if I can trust her. I don't know if the Marshalls are using her. Someone tried to kill me earlier today."

"What?" Clem exclaimed, sounding incredulous. "Stella, this is serious. Are you okay?"

"I got away. I was hurt, but I'm okay. Carrie broke into the hotel room and saved me."

"That must mean she's working on your side," Clem said, but concern still thrummed in his voice. "If it's the Marshalls, have you figured out how they got to you? Are you taking further precautions?"

"I'm watching my back. We switched cars."

"Is that enough?" Clem pressured her.

"I'm hoping so. I can't do more while we're busy on the case. Tracking down this killer is so urgent, and I feel we're making no progress. At the moment I just feel stuck. We've reached a dead end. I don't know how to find a way through this, Clem."

Clem was silent for a while. Stella knew he'd be thinking hard about what she had said and analyzing her words.

Then he spoke.

"You told me you feel this victim's life is wrapped in a shield of lies."

"Correct," Stella said.

"Everyone has a reason to lie. So if you feel everyone on this case is lying to you, then what are the reasons? I think that's where you need to focus."

"Okay?" Stella said, hoping he'd explain further.

"We all have something to hide, if you think about it. We all decide what face to present to the world. Even you," he said ruefully.

Surprised, Stella found herself agreeing. "I guess so," she said.

"It sounds as if in this case, one lie has led to another."

"Yes, it's felt like a domino effect," Stella said.

"So, if it's a domino effect, what do you need to do?"

Now that Clem was drilling down to the core of the issue, it was easier for Stella to reason her way through.

"I think I need to find the first domino. The starting point."

"Yes," Clem sounded approving. "Exactly. At the moment, you seem to be sifting through quicksand. That's why you're not getting traction. One lie is uncovering the next. If you'd found the truth yet, you'd be further than you are. So work back from your starting point, rather than working forward. Dig deeper. Don't take anyone at face value. Work out why they are lying and what they are trying to protect."

"I'm going to do that. Thank you so much for the advice," Stella said.

"And be careful, please. Check in with me when you're done with the case. I'm worried about you," Clem said.

"I will," she promised.

Disconnecting, Stella felt as if she was seeing the case through new eyes, and from a different perspective. Now, she knew where she needed to go. However, Clem's words had raised an uncomfortable point. How could she expect honesty from other people when she, herself, was hiding away important truths?

As Carrie headed back toward where she was standing, Stella realized that the starting point, the game-changer, lay with her. If this case was going to change direction, she needed to be upfront and honest with her partner.

She took a deep breath.

"I need to explain some things to you," she said.

Carrie looked surprised.

"You do? Go ahead."

"Perhaps we should talk in one of the rooms," Stella decided. There were people passing back and forth along the corridor. It wasn't private. She wanted privacy to explain what she needed to.

Looking curious, Carrie followed her down the passage and into one of the empty interview rooms. Stella closed the door behind them. Only then, in the small, warm, and slightly stuffy room, did she feel ready to speak.

"The Marshalls are the family of my ex-fiancé. He was murdered after I'd been staying with him, on their property, for just a few days. Everyone thought I did it. The family already hated me. They'd sensed that I was going to fight for Vaughn, and not let them control him. They saw I hated how they used their power to get whatever they wanted, regardless of who they hurt or destroyed, and that I was not going to become like them," Stella explained, hoping that Carrie would understand.

"Okay," Carrie said. She sounded doubtful and Stella dreaded again that they might somehow already have corrupted her, or got her onto their side, and her words would be futile.

"Waking up to find my fiancé stabbed to death next to me was – it was the worst thing I'd ever had to deal with."

"I can imagine that!" Carrie looked alarmed.

"I was totally alone. They closed ranks. I didn't have any choice but to try and clear my name, because they didn't care who had done it – they cared that I got the blame."

"Seriously?" Carrie sounded incredulous.

"I found out who the killer was. But while I was doing that, I learned about some of the things the family had done. They'd collaborated with the local police, covered up past crimes. They were basically trafficking the people who worked for them. They were the most evil people I've ever known. When I told the detectives what they were doing, and exposed them, the Marshalls decided to get rid of me. And I mean just that. Get rid of me," Stella said, hoping that the firmness in her tone would distract Carrie from the tremble in her voice as she thought, in horror, of what they had already done, and might do.

Carrie was silent for a while. Stella had no idea what she was thinking.

Then she nodded.

"Okay. I'm understanding a lot more. And I believe you, Fall, by the way. It's making sense. Your version is actually fitting in with things I knew and things I suspected and –" she hesitated. "And things I didn't want to think were true, but I do now."

"I think they sent the killer," Stella said, hoping and wondering if Carrie would take this further. Had she been part of it? Had they used her without her knowing?

What had Carrie wanted to say to her earlier? Would it be different now?

She stared at Carrie wordlessly, hoping that whatever she said, Stella would at least know the truth.

Carrie sighed. She looked down, and then she looked directly at Stella.

"Okay. I need to tell you this and get it off my chest. An acquaintance of mine who knows them contacted me yesterday. She said the Marshalls wanted to get you removed from the FBI. She hinted that they wanted to discuss it with me," Carrie said.

She sounded ashamed, and something else, too. Unsure?

"What did you do?" Stella asked, feeling sick with dread.

"I admit, for a moment I wondered what it would be like to solve this case on my own," Carrie confessed, sounding mortified. "My father is a top criminal lawyer who owns a very successful firm. He puts pressure on me to be the best. To be the only one who wins. I've had a lot of pressure from the time I was young. He didn't want me to join the FBI but when I did, he then gave me a hard time about it. He expected me to be the best. To be the winner. To be the only."

Stella nodded. Now, a lot about Carrie's mindset and behavior was making sense.

"Some things he said I should do didn't fit in with the FBI's ethos. I guess joining has changed me in a way. It's helped me think differently from how he's always told me to think."

Now she stared at Stella with all of the former defiance in her gaze.

"I'm sure you believe I had something to do with that attempt on your life. Well, I didn't."

Relief crashed around Stella as Carrie continued in a resolute voice.

"I thought about it, and I didn't call my acquaintance back. I knew it would be wrong to even speak to her about such a topic, because even speaking to her could damage my career. I'm not stupid. What if I had to investigate her one day and she tried to use this against me, to blackmail me?"

Stella made a face. "You made a wise call there," she said briefly.

"Yeah. But I did mention to her that I was on a case with you. I don't know if that helped them track us down, or if people were already following us. I didn't disclose any details at all. But I also wasn't aware enough, and that's the other thing I need to tell you. I made a mistake. I was careless and I feel terrible about it. I did notice a gray SUV behind us, once or twice, during the day today. I saw it for a moment and then thought it was too far back, and it didn't look like it was tailing us. But now I think it was. It was a very professional tail. If I hadn't been so brain-dead and tired after working all night, I might have been more alert to it. And that's taught me something, too," Carrie said.

"It was probably easy to miss. That man was not an amateur," Stella agreed. "And it's my fault, also. If I'd explained my situation to you before now, you would have known to look out for any signs, even small ones. I should have told you I might be targeted. You're my investigation partner, after all."

"And I should have told you about that woman messaging me," Carrie admitted. "I think subconsciously, I felt worried about the situation. The whole thing rang alarm bells, and I had this feeling something was wrong. And that's why I got to you so fast, when you bashed your feet on the wall. In a way, I was anticipating it."

"I am so glad about that," Stella said. "And I really am relieved you didn't decide to give any details to your friend."

Carrie shrugged. "She's not my friend. I'm not speaking to her again. I've blocked her. I don't appreciate being used," she said.

"Yeah. Not a nice feeling," Stella agreed.

She felt a moment's surprise. Never had she thought she'd be standing with Carrie Potts, discussing their backgrounds openly and, weirder still, agreeing with her. This case had taught her that there was no such thing as a dead end where relationships were concerned. They could always change.

Starting out from a bad standpoint, she had believed Carrie would be a lifelong enemy. Now, they were not exactly friends, but there was a lot more harmony between them than there had been at the start. And she understood the burdens and pressure that Carrie was dealing with, which had shaped her, just as Stella's had done.

"We've cracked a blackmail and extortion ring. But we're no further with the case," Carrie said, bringing the conversation all the way back to the present moment. "Where to from here, Fall? What angle is there left to try?"

"I was speaking to my mentor just now," Stella explained. "In the discussion, we talked about lies. That's actually why I wanted to tell you the truth now. I feel like I'm all done with lies and holding information back. We've had far too much of it happening to us in this case and it's why we're not making progress."

"I was thinking that there isn't a single person who's been truthful with us," Carrie agreed. "Usually, one or two witnesses tell the truth? But here, it feels like that hasn't happened. We've been going back and forth between Katie and Liane, getting different versions and new surprises every time. Why do I still think there's more to find out?"

"I don't think we've got anywhere near the real story, and I think when we do, we'll start figuring out this case better," Stella said. "My feeling is that we need to go back to Liane. But first, I want to confirm her alibi, because what if that was her very first lie?"

"Good point. She said she was out with a friend. We never confirmed that, and we should have," Carrie said.

"It's too late to interview anyone now, but we can start again first thing tomorrow," Stella decided. "Let's get some rest, and in the morning, question this friend to see if Liane was really with her, and where she claimed to be, on the night of the murder."

CHAPTER TWENTY SIX

Stella felt nervous but determined as she climbed out of the car and headed to the gracious home where Liane's friend Amelia Engels resided. At seven a.m., the light was still gray, but the sky was clear, and the air felt fresh and cool.

Today, they might solve this case, Stella hoped.

Then she hastily corrected her own thinking, glancing at Carrie as they walked up the stairs to the smart front door with its gold knocker. Today, they must solve this case, or the delay would have serious consequences for both of them.

"Let's see if Mrs. Engels is at home," Carrie murmured to her. "She should be in, right?"

According to their research, Amelia was married to one of the area's leading estate agents, Bob Engels, and had two teenage children.

Carrie knocked sharply on the door.

After a short pause, they heard hurried footsteps approaching. The door was opened by a slim girl of about fourteen, who stared at them curiously.

"FBI," Carrie showed her badge. "We need to speak to Mrs. Engels."

The teen's mouth dropped open in amazement. She turned and yelled into the house, "Mom!"

Dressed in an attractive floral dressing gown, a slim brunette hurried down the stairs and padded barefooted to the door. Despite the early hour and being surprised while in her bedroom attire, Amelia looked composed and together.

"Good morning," she greeted them. "You're the FBI? What is this about?" She smiled at them, looking innocent and questioning all at once.

"It's in connection with Patrick Coleridge's murder," Stella said. Her voice sounded hoarse after yesterday's attack. She hoped it would warm up as the day went on, so that speaking became easier. As she spoke, she watched Amelia intently.

"I don't know anything about that," Amelia said, sounding confused.

Intentionally confused perhaps, Stella wondered. She didn't seem like such a naïve woman. There was shrewd intelligence in her eyes.

"We're confirming his wife's alibi," Carrie retorted.

"Oh! Oh, of course. Poor Liane. Yes, I guess you have to do that. We were out together that night. We went to Gio's Prawns."

"How did you get there?" Carrie asked.

Amelia blinked, as if she hadn't expected that question at all.

"I drove myself there. I didn't take a cab, if that's what you are asking. I don't drink."

"And Liane?"

"She drove, too."

"Where did you sit in the restaurant?"

Now Amelia's eyes narrowed thoughtfully. She gave an apologetic smile.

"I don't remember," she said.

Stella stayed quiet. She liked Carrie's questioning technique. The rapid questions were simple and should be easy to answer. Each one that wasn't answered represented a red flag. Already, they had one flag.

"No problem, ma'am," Carrie said politely. "How did you pay?"

"We split the bill," Amelia said.

Now, she was showing signs of impatience, shifting from foot to foot, tugging her robe tighter around her. Or maybe that was unease, Stella thought. Either she was being truthful and was just getting anxious about her morning being delayed, or she was worried there would be too many holes in her answers if this continued.

"That's great, ma'am, but I asked how you paid," Carrie repeated.

"Cash," Amelia said firmly.

"What did you eat?"

"Prawns, of course," Amelia said with a smile.

"And Liane?"

"The same."

"Did you book?" Carrie asked.

"Did we book? Um, I think Liane booked."

"Who arrived first?" Carrie asked.

"Liane," Amelia said, but she didn't sound sure.

"Where did you park?"

"Outside the restaurant."

"Is it paid parking?"

"Yes. Yes, it is paid parking."

"How do you pay?"

"You go through a booth and pay the attendant."

"Who served you at the restaurant?"

Amelia's eyebrows raised. "Who – um, I didn't get their name."

"A description?" Carrie asked. "Male, female? Hair color?"

Now Amelia glowered defensively. "Look, I was there to see my friend. I didn't take note of our server."

Again, Carrie asked, "Did you sit downstairs or was there also an upstairs section? Were you near the front or back of the restaurant?"

Amelia pressed her lips together. Her face was flushed, and Stella could see a visible pulse beating in her slender neck. Her stress levels were rocketing because she was lying. This dinner had been just two days ago. So recent that anybody would be able to remember whereabouts in a restaurant they had sat, as well as the basic details of the server.

"Ma'am, lying to an officer of the law is a federal offense. It carries jail time. Lying to confirm a false alibi is even more serious. We are going to have to bring you in, and we are then going to hold you in an interrogation room while we contact Gio's Prawns and confirm all the details. I imagine they have cameras at the parking booth. We'll need your car's number plate and the approximate time of your arrival. Then we'll ask the restaurant if they served you and your friend. I hope they remember you, better than you remember them," Carrie said meaningfully.

Amelia stared at her in horror.

"Of course, you might have misremembered, and gone there on another night. It would be an easy mistake to make with the stress of the murder and everything that happened since," Carrie said. "If you have misremembered, you can retract your entire version now and it will not count against you. We will walk away. But if we end up disproving your story, there will be serious consequences."

Amelia was now clamping her lips so tightly together they looked blue-white. Stella could see she was thinking furiously. Should she carry on with her bluff? Was it going to be worth it when there would be such trouble ahead and the agents facing her had already said they knew she was lying?

She let out a resigned sigh. Her shoulders slumped.

"I might have misremembered," she muttered.

With satisfaction radiating from her, Carrie nodded. Stella was filled with admiration for the efficient way she'd broken this woman's fake story in the shortest time.

"It happens, ma'am. We'll need to record a short statement from you correcting the information." She rummaged in her purse. "You can start with your full name and date of birth. Then please tell us, truthfully, where you were on Friday night."

She drew a tape recorder from her purse, pressed Record, and held it out to Amelia.

*

At a quarter to eight, armed with the recording they would need to use as their trump card, Stella and Carrie hurried up to the door of Liane's residence. They'd rushed there as fast as possible. Stella felt glad the two friends lived so close to each other. She hoped that given the circumstances, and her betrayal of her friend, Amelia would not yet have called Liane to warn her. She guessed she would still be processing her own guilt and shock after that catastrophic interview.

The pressure was weighing heavy on Stella. At any moment she expected Roth to follow up with them, angrily asking when they planned to get results and stop spinning their wheels.

There was a gardener on duty this morning, carefully trimming the topiary hedges that surrounded the ornamental pond near the home's front gate. And, almost as soon as they knocked, a housemaid opened the door.

"Good morning," she said.

"Is Mrs. Coleridge in?" Stella asked.

"Yes, but she's heading out," the maid said nervously.

Liane appeared as she spoke, smartly dressed in dark pants and a taupe jacket. She had a purse slung over her shoulder and looked ready for a day of shopping on the high street. Stella was interested to note her brisk, businesslike demeanor. It looked very different from the grief-stricken persona that had so powerfully impressed both of them on the previous visits.

When she saw Stella and Carrie standing outside the door, she stopped dead and stared at them.

"You're here? Again?" The surprised words blurted out of her before she managed to gather herself.

Clearly, she hadn't been warned, Stella thought.

Liane took a deep breath. In a calmer voice, she continued. "I'm sorry. I haven't even greeted you. I felt completely undone after you uncovered those details last night. I feel like my world has fallen apart.

This whole tragedy has made me very stressed. I feel brittle," she shared.

Now the sad smile Stella remembered was back, but this time, she didn't trust it at all.

"Perhaps, before you head out, we could sit in the lounge for a moment?" Stella suggested.

"Will this take long? As I have an appointment."

"I'm not sure how long it's going to take," Stella said, wondering what the appointment was.

Liane looked uneasy. A frown briefly darkened her face.

"Can I make a call?"

"Sure," Stella said.

Liane walked quickly back down the passage. Stella kept alert, because she didn't want this important witness trying to flee the premises, but in a few moments, she heard her speaking in a low voice.

Whoever she was calling, Liane kept the conversation very short. Not even a minute later, she rushed back.

"Please, sit," she said.

Stella sat. Carrie took a chair opposite, and Liane finally sat down on the couch between the two agents.

"I understand you must have been very shocked when we uncovered those details last night," Stella began.

"Agents!" Now Liane had summoned her theatrical demeanor again. "I still can't believe it. Are you sure it's true?"

"It's true," Stella said shortly. "And I don't think you had any trouble believing it. I think you knew about it all along."

Liane looked appalled. She stared at Stella for a long, horrified moment.

"Are you calling me a liar?" she said eventually, in a hard voice. "You are slandering my name, and I will not hesitate to take this further."

Stella shook her head. "You were shocked that we found out. You weren't shocked it was happening," she retorted.

Carrie added, "Mrs. Coleridge, you are an intelligent woman. That money was not exactly well hidden. The bank statements were mailed to your home address! You would have seen them arrive. That 'secret' account was pretty much an open secret. You knew about it. You knew he was going to strip clubs. Did you really think he pulled so many all-nighters at work? On weekends? With alcohol involved? You knew what he was doing. You most likely knew about the drugs, too. You probably even knew he was being blackmailed."

Now Liane sat very still. She was facing Carrie. Stella felt sure she was projecting the entire force of her personality onto her.

"Do you honestly think that if I knew about something like that, I would have ignored it?" she flashed back.

"Well, ma'am, that's the question we've been asking ourselves, too," Stella said.

Liane spun around to face her, and Stella was shocked by the fury in her eyes.

"What?" she spat out.

"Where were you on the night of your husband's murder?" Stella asked.

Liane clutched at the seat of the chair with her perfectly manicured nails. Stella was sure that she would rather have leaped up and clawed her with them. That was how furious she looked.

"You are seriously questioning my integrity? I told you where I was!"

"No, ma'am. We checked with Amelia. We met her at her home early this morning. She never saw you on Friday. She told us she'd misremembered, and that she'd spent the evening at home with her husband and family. We have a recording of her version."

Liane's eyes flew open in shock.

"So, you are calling me a liar?" she whispered.

"Where were you on Friday evening?"

Pressing her lips together, Liane glowered at Stella.

She glared right back. She'd had enough of people who believed they were above the law.

"We're arresting you on suspicion of the murder of your husband," she said.

At that, Liane let out a cry of wrath. The carefully controlled façade she'd presented to them shattered as she leaped to her feet, turning to face Stella with fury blazing from her eyes.

"You are deliberately framing me for this! You just want to destroy my life. I never had anything to do with this and if you think I did, then you're a fool!" she yelled.

Clearly done with the drama, Carrie grasped her hands from behind and propelled her toward the door.

"Let go of me!" Liane's voice rose to a shriek.

"You are under arrest," Carrie growled.

A horrified shout from down the corridor caused Stella to turn around. Liane's sister was rushing toward them.

"Where are you taking Liane? What is happening?"

"We're arresting her on suspicion of murder. She'll be taken to the Greenwich police precinct."

Stella felt grim satisfaction as she provided the facts to Liane's sister, whose mouth fell open in shock.

"Call my lawyer!" Liane entreated, sounding on the point of tears.

"I will. Don't worry, honey, I will," her sister called back.

Stella hustled along behind Carrie, who was roughly escorting the now-sobbing woman to the car. She hoped that in the stark confines of the police interview room, with her alibi destroyed, they would be able to prove that this skillful liar had cold-bloodedly murdered her husband.

CHAPTER TWENTY SEVEN

Half an hour later, Stella stood outside the interview room, preparing herself before walking in. This would be a critical session. Liane was sneaky, she was entitled, and with her back against the ropes, Stella suspected she'd stop at nothing to defend herself. With everything to lose if they didn't succeed, Stella would have to use all of her hard-won skills to cut down to the bare bones of the truth.

She opened the door and walked in.

Carrie was already seated, facing Liane and staring her down. They'd decided to begin with the silent treatment. This would hopefully disturb Liane, creating a vacuum effect that would encourage her to speak.

Liane looked up at her. She looked furious. Silence resounded in the room and Stella was sure that so far, nobody had said anything.

Stella sat next to Carrie. She waited for another minute before speaking.

Liane stared at them contemptuously. She was too angry to be scared, Stella thought.

"Where were you on Friday evening, Mrs. Coleridge?"

"I was home alone," Liane snapped.

"Why didn't you tell us that?" Carrie asked.

"I was worried you would unfairly blame me for the murder, since you clearly haven't found the killer yet," Liane shot back. "And that I'd end up in exactly this situation."

Stella immediately picked up the major flaw in this argument.

"Home alone is not a bad alibi," she agreed. "But it doesn't work so well when you have household staff. We could interview all of them and find out exactly what time you went out and came back. I don't think you prepared enough to tell your staff to lie for you, did you? Shall we go back and talk to them? Or would you prefer to give us the correct version now."

Liane shot Stella a poisonous glance.

"I went out," she admitted.

"Where?" Carrie asked.

Liane shook her head. "I won't tell you," she insisted.

"To the yacht club?" Carrie pressured her.

"No. Not to the club."

"You wanted to kill him. You were angry."

"I was not!" Liane shot back.

"Don't you get angry, Mrs. Coleridge? Because you seem angry now."

"I'm not!" Liane spat.

"You seem furious. You fought me when I was taking you to the car. I felt how you were struggling. You're strong and you're determined. Strong and determined enough to stab your husband when you realized how his behavior was escalating."

"I did no such thing!" Liane entreated. Now she seemed on the point of tears again, but this time, Stella thought they were tears of frustration.

"Then prove it!" Carrie retaliated.

Liane was breathing hard, and her gaze was flickering from side to side. Stella guessed she was reviewing her options. Liane was like a chess player. She would think through the consequences of everything she said, and if she didn't like what they were, she would lie. Only, Stella got the impression they were now ripping through Liane's options, and she didn't have many left. She sensed that Liane would have to capitulate.

They would then see the true person, the one who lurked behind those wide appealing eyes.

"You went to the club. You knew about your husband's hobbies, his reckless spending, his extramarital activities. You were angry and you wanted to kill him." Stella stared stonily at Liane.

With a sigh, Liane opened her hands and placed them, palms up, on the desk.

"Look, if you want the truth, the honest truth, then let me give it to you."

"Go ahead," Stella said. She felt a flare of triumph. This would have to be the truth. There was no other choice now.

"I knew about what Patrick was doing. Of course, I knew. He'd been this way for years. It was nothing new. We've been married for twenty years. I know about the clubs. I know about the affairs. Do you honestly believe this behavior only started recently?" Liane queried, and now the assurance was back in her voice. "Do you really think that after twenty years of living with the same person, whom I knew well, in a very comfortable life, I would bother to kill him?"

Stella was taken aback by the raw contempt in Liane's tone.

"Of course not." Liane answered her own question. "Why should I? I didn't care what he did. I also had my fun on the side."

She took a deep breath and, looking from Stella to Carrie's now-stunned face, she explained. "I was having an affair, too. On Friday night, I was seeing my lover. We have a standing arrangement. It's our night, as Patrick is always out carousing."

Stella felt her stomach flip uneasily over in shock. This was all too plausible. What Liane said made sense.

"Prove it," Carrie pressured her.

But now, Liane shook her head.

"I won't prove it. That, I refuse to do. He is also married. None of this was his fault and if I give you his name, it will destroy him. I'm going to wait for my lawyer's advice before I say another word. But this I promise you, agents." Her eyes narrowed vindictively, "I will not be found guilty of murder. I guarantee it."

Stella felt cold inside.

Spoken with entitlement and confidence, she believed Liane's words a lot more than she wanted to.

Suddenly, it felt to Stella as if she was the one with her back against the ropes.

Glancing at Carrie, she got up and walked out of the interview room.

She was aware that Liane was watching them go with a half-smile on her beautiful face. Sitting at the desk, she seemed confident and, once again, fully composed.

"She's got to be guilty," Carrie muttered as soon as the door was closed.

Stella shook her head. "She's looking too sure of herself. And remember the effect she has on people. Unless we can provide concrete, one hundred percent proof that she was at the scene of the crime, she'll be cleared. What jury would convict her when she puts on that act, and opens her eyes wide, and speaks in that sad voice?"

Carrie rolled her eyes. "You're right. And she might have an ace up her sleeve. She won't tell us where she was, but she might have passed by somewhere with cameras. She could get her lawyer to pull footage that clears her, without ever having to disclose where she went."

"This is so frustrating," Stella said.

So often, in a murder like this, it was the spouse. But not this time. Even though Patrick had been a lying, deceiving, cheating husband who'd had affairs and betrayed his wife, the twist was that she didn't care, because she'd been doing the same.

But, as she thought that, Stella stopped herself.

Affairs?

Liane hadn't meant to help them at all. Not one bit. But inadvertently, she just had.

She'd said she knew Patrick had affairs.

"What affairs is she talking about?" she asked Carrie in a low voice and saw her eyes light up as she followed the same train of thought.

"We haven't uncovered any of those so far," her partner agreed.

"Exactly! We have a piece of the puzzle missing," Stella said.

So far, they had no evidence of any actual affairs. Patrick had spent recklessly on the company of hostesses and exotic dancers. He'd used drugs. But Katie hadn't been sleeping with him. She'd been blackmailing him. Where were the affairs Liane had referred to, and how could they find out more about them?

"We need to uncover this," Carrie said. Then she grimaced. "But how? Where do we dig now?"

This was a crucial question that would make or break the case. As Stella considered it, she found her thoughts returning to the place where all this had started.

The South Sands yacht club.

Maybe there was a reason why Patrick had been murdered on that club's doorstep.

That got her thoughts moving in the direction they'd been going before they'd learned about the strip club and the secret bank account.

"Did you ask Franco that question before you processed his release?" she said to Carrie.

Carrie sighed, looking even more frustrated by Stella's insistence on this pointless line of thinking.

"Is that really relevant right now? Yes, I did. I didn't want to because it seemed completely irrelevant. He thought so, too. So much so that he laughed at me when I told him I needed to know." Carrie sounded annoyed, as if being laughed at had been one insult too many.

"What did he say?" Stella probed.

"He said...," Gazing at her partner cynically, Carrie counted on her fingers. "He said he gyms and runs. He owns a small airplane that he flies regularly. He collects vintage cars. And he owns six racehorses."

Stella felt her suspicions start to make sense.

"Did that strike you as odd?"

"No, it didn't," Carrie snapped out. "He's a wealthy guy. He has expensive hobbies. Where are you going with this?"

"Why have none of them mentioned something rather obvious?"

"What have none of them mentioned, Fall? Enlighten me!" Carrie challenged.

"None of them have mentioned sailing."

"Sailing?" Carrie blinked rapidly as she took in this bombshell.

"None of them have said they own a yacht. They're all members of a yacht club, but you wouldn't know it, because nobody we've talked to so far, not one of these guys, has ever mentioned going out on the water. Not even during summer. Not at all. My fiancé's family belonged to a yacht club. Guess what? Everyone there owned super-yachts and hired a team of staff when they felt like sailing them, which was all the time, because they used them for partying and socializing. They were a possession to brag about."

She could see the realization on Carrie's face, the excitement now in her eyes, as she continued. "So, what I want to know is this – what really goes on at the South Sands yacht club?"

"Good point!" Carrie was now nodding vigorously. "It's so obvious that I never picked it up. If none of them sail, what is the purpose of that club?"

"I think Patrick's secrets are being kept there. And the best way to find out will be to go there now, when they're not expecting us, and surprise them," Stella said.

CHAPTER TWENTY EIGHT

Stella and Carrie arrived at the South Sands yacht club half an hour later and parked in the temporary parking. It was ten a.m. on what was turning into a beautiful Sunday morning. The winter sky was cloudless, the sun was shining, and there was no wind.

The sea was calm and blue. It was also notably devoid of yachts, Stella saw, even though it was surely a fine day for sailing, and there were already several luxury vehicles in the temporary parking.

She marched along the walkway, glancing at the construction work in the permanent parking lot as she headed past. The wall was now at head height. The contractors must have spent the whole of Saturay working hard on it.

"A wall," Carrie said, echoing Stella's own suspicions, because once you'd seen what was wrong, you couldn't unsee it. "A wall around a yacht club's parking? Why would they do that? I've never heard of such a thing."

"Me either," Stella agreed.

They reached the club entrance and walked in. The manager was on duty, behind the desk, in conversation with the receptionist. When they walked in, he looked up. He appeared surprised, and then alarmed.

"Good morning, Mr. Perry," Carrie greeted him briskly. Stella remembered how she'd insisted on interviewing him on the night of the crime.

"Good morning. How can I help you?" he said in wary tones.

Stella didn't miss his reflexive move to the side. Why was that?

Instinctively, Mr. Perry was trying to put himself between the FBI agents, and the club's restaurant area beyond. Now that was interesting.

"We need to follow up on some things," Carrie said.

"Of course, of course," Perry explained, speaking rapidly. "Let me take you through to the back office."

He gestured to the door in the right=hand wall. Again, he was deflecting their attention from the restaurant.

"Sure," Stella smiled.

She waited until Perry was all the way over to the right-hand door. Then, she marched through the lobby and into the club itself.

It was just as she remembered it from the time before. The leather chairs and the plush couches. The tables freshly prepared with white cloths, silver cutlery and gleaming crystal. Coffee jugs, champagne bottles, and orange juice carafes lined the sideboard. A few patrons were already seated.

Including one she recognized, who was there with a young and beautiful companion.

It was not her arrival into the club that alerted Michael Yelverton. It was Perry's horrified cry as he rushed in behind her. He was closely followed by Carrie, a look of keen curiosity on her face.

Michael looked up with a stunned expression. The young blonde sitting opposite him turned and stared curiously.

"Good morning," Stella said, noting that Michael had hurriedly moved his hand away from his partner's, which still rested on the starched white tablecloth. Stella further noted there were no rings on this pretty blonde's wedding finger.

"What are you doing here?" Michael looked completely thrown, and he was angry. The veneer of charm he'd shown them at the car dealership was gone.

"What a surprise to find you here, Mr. Yelverton" Stella said politely. "And who is enjoying your company this morning?"

Michael turned bright crimson. "This is Ella. She's – she's a friend."

"That's interesting," Carrie said in the same brisk, businesslike tones she'd used earlier. "As of now, we're separating you two. We're going to take you into different rooms and we're going to question you about your friendship. We're also going to check your phones. Finally, we'll call your families to confirm their knowledge of this friendship."

Stella had never actually seen anyone's blood pressure shoot through the roof before, but Michael was providing ample evidence of his emotional turmoil. He was flushed deep purple, and a vein in his temple was throbbing visibly.

"Please don't do that," he choked out.

"Would you like to explain, then?" Carrie said sweetly.

From behind, Perry cleared his throat.

"Is this interference really necessary?" he asked. He sounded stressed and his voice was weak. Stella knew the words were no more than a token effort to try and protect his customers.

"Was it really necessary to lie to us?" Stella turned to ask.

"It was not a lie. Our customers are free to bring whoever they wish to our yacht club," Perry insisted.

"Your yacht club, where none of the members sail? This is not a yacht club," Stella said angrily.

The blonde was looking appalled. She was shrinking back in her seat as if hoping it would swallow her. Yelverton was puce with fury and fear.

Even though she felt they deserved everything they got, Stella reluctantly decided there was no need to question Michael and his partner further. She had seen what she needed to. Now, with enough ammunition to make sure they could get what they needed it was time to focus on Patrick's activities at this club.

"Let's talk in front," she said.

They returned to the front desk. Perry, too, looked flushed and flustered.

"This is not a yacht club. This is a men's club," Stella accused him. "Your patrons use it to network and socialize, but they also use it as a discreet venue where they can bring their lovers. Your 'side rooms' with couches must come in useful."

"You're wrong. This is not what this is about."

"A seven-foot-high perimeter wall around your parking?" Carrie's voice sounded incredulous. "I've never heard of such a thing being needed in a yacht club. You don't need the wall for security. You need it for privacy. So that your members and their 'good friends' can socialize here without their cars being seen by any watching eyes."

Perry stared angrily down at the polished reception desk.

"Who did Patrick Coleridge bring to this club?" Stella pressured him. "He brought someone. Didn't he? He was having an affair. Wasn't he?"

Still, Perry responded only with silence.

"If you'd told us this on Friday night, we could have solved this case in a couple of hours," Stella pressured him. "This is a criminal investigation. Your club's discretion is already blown out the window. Tell us."

Perry shook his head. Stella could see he was going to take this all the way down to the wire.

From her jacket pocket, she produced a folded piece of paper.

It was actually the release slip that Carrie had obtained after processing Franco Bruno. But Perry didn't know that. Stella just let him see the official Greenwich Police Department crest as she waved it in front of him.

"We brought a search warrant with us. This warrant gives us access to everything in your club. The first thing I'm going to do is seize the footage from your cameras. For the past two weeks, to start. We're going to take a look at every person who's walked in, and who came in with them. And then we will make all the footage public. We'll say it's a PR move and we're appealing to the community for help. Do you think that will be good for the club, Mr. Perry? Do you think the club's owners will be pleased? Or will they be angry with you for escalating the situation all the way to this point, when you could so easily have provided the information that we need. Because I know that you know the names of the people who come in here. You told me the first time that you make it your business to know. And I'm sure part of your service is to send gifts and messages, 'through the club,' so that nobody suspects a thing."

Perry had gone several shades paler, Stella saw, and from the stunned expression on his face, she saw her guess about the gifts was accurate. He was now cornered. The worst-case scenario painted by her words was making any other option seem reasonable. Suddenly, giving out the identity of one person's partner didn't seem so bad anymore.

"I will do that," he gabbled.

"A good decision," Carrie said in smug tones, glancing at Stella with a pleased expression.

"There's only one problem," Perry added, sounding nervous.

"What's the problem?" Stella asked.

"The problem is that during the past three weeks, Mr. Coleridge didn't bring just one woman to the club."

"He brought two?" Carrie asked incredulously.

Perry shook his head. In hesitant tones, as if hoping this bombshell wouldn't bring more trouble down on his head, he said, "He brought three."

Stella felt as shocked as Carrie now looked.

"He was having affairs with three different women?" Carrie asked in tones of disbelief.

"I can't comment on the relationship," Perry said, glancing around and lowering his voice. "But he brought three different women here."

Stella felt encouraged by this information. With multiple affairs now exposed, there was three times the chance that one of the women had found out he was a serial liar and cheater and lost her temper. It made it more likely that one of them must be the killer.

"Let's hope you have a record of who they are," Stella said meaningfully. "Or we will have to seize that footage and make it public."

"No, no, no," Perry gabbled. "I'm absolutely sure we have enough information on each of them."

"Go ahead?" Stella waited as he paged through the visitor book on the reception desk, occasionally glancing at the computer screen.

"The first one is Ursula King. We have her address as we organized her a limo home last week."

"And the second?"

"The second one is Giselle Dittmer. She's divorced, and her husband used to be a member here, so yes, we know her address."

"Okay," Stella said. "Who's the third?"

"The third is Michaela. I don't know her last name."

"Do you know her address?" Carrie pressured him.

Perry bit his lip. "She's only been here twice. The first time – yes." Relief softened the tension she saw around his eyes and mouth. "The first time we delivered flowers to her from Mr. Coleridge. So, I can look up her address."

Stella moved away, close to the entrance door, and Carrie sidled there together with her.

"We need to get to these suspects as fast as possible," Stella said.

"Agreed. You take one, I take the other, and as soon as they've looked up Michaela's address, we could ask the Greenwich detectives to visit her?"

"Yes," Stella said. "That sounds like the best plan. Shall I go to Ursula, you go to Giselle?"

"Okay," Carrie said.

"Here are the addresses," Perry handed over two of the club's business cards, with neatly printed wording on the back.

"I'll ask Detective Bradshaw to call you for Michaela's address as soon as you have it," Stella asked him. "I'll brief him."

There was no time to waste.

Finally, they had come full circle, back to the club, the epicenter of the lies, the place that had shielded and protected Patrick, along with all its other members. This was where these wealthy cheaters had been able to behave as they pleased, all with the utmost discretion.

They had three new suspects. One of the three must surely be the killer. If they were lucky, this case could be solved in the next hour.

Stella rushed to her car, hoping that Ursula King would be at home.

CHAPTER TWENTY NINE

Stella arrived at the home address of Ursula King twenty minutes after leaving the yacht club. Ursula didn't live in one of the wealthier parts of Greenwich. She lived in a more modest, though still beautifully kept, suburban area. The homes along this road all had small, neat, and well-tended front yards.

Ursula had lived the furthest away of the three women, so Stella would be the last to arrive at her interview. She, Carrie, and Bradshaw had agreed to call or message each other as soon as their suspects were struck off the list.

Ursula's house was number twenty, and Stella saw a sporty white Mini parked in the drive. So hopefully Ursula was home.

She rang the doorbell and waited, feeling nervous and hopeful that when it opened, she might come face to face with the killer.

That would be the first step in a dangerous dance, because Stella couldn't hope for an outright confession, and would need to use all her skills to obtain proof. She would only have one chance. And this felt like her last chance.

Her heart banged hard in her throat as she heard footsteps approach. A moment later, the door opened, and Stella stared in surprise at the woman facing her.

She was tall, athletic-looking, but to Stella's surprise, she was not the same glamorous stamp of woman as Liane and Katie. Ursula was pretty in a simple, girl-next-door way. She had thick, brown, bobbed hair tucked behind her ears and a sweet, heart-shaped face. Stella guessed her to be in her late twenties.

"Ms. Ursula King?" she asked.

The other woman nodded, looking equal parts curious and confused.

"That's me. What is this about?" she asked.

"I'm Agent Fall from the FBI. We're investigating the murder of Patrick Coleridge."

"Oh. The murder? And you're here?"

Stella watched her carefully. As she'd expected, a whole series of emotions briefly flitted across Ursula's face. First surprise, then concern, and finally fear.

Since she clearly wasn't going to say anything further, Stella asked, "May I come in? I have some questions for you."

"Questions? Of – of course. I – I have heard about his death. I'm utterly shocked. I don't know how I can help, though, as I barely knew him."

Still unable to conceal how rattled she was, Ursula turned and led the way into the house.

Unlike the calculated Liane and Katie, Stella thought that Ursula's emotions were more on the surface. She was definitely more reactive and less guarded than the other two. Stella wondered if Patrick had been attracted by that openness. It was certainly different from what surrounded him.

She headed into the kitchen, which was compact and pristine, decorated in white and pale blue. A white wooden kitchen table at the far end had four chairs neatly placed around it.

Stella sat down in one of them and Ursula sat opposite.

She stared at Stella. She swallowed, and then bit her lip briefly.

"I'm very nervous," she admitted. "I've never been interviewed by the FBI before. I'm so worried I'm going to do or say something that gets me into trouble. Do you usually find this happens?"

"Everyone is different," Stella said. "If you can answer my questions truthfully and in detail, that will help."

"I'll try my best," Ursula said, her voice twanging with tension.

"I understand you spent time with Mr. Coleridge at the South Sands yacht club," Stella opened the conversation.

Ursula nodded. "Yes, that's right. He was a very friendly, kind man," she gabbled.

Stella wasn't going to allow for any evasion. Interrupting her, she steamrollered over the other woman.

"I know this was not a business meeting or a friendly get-together, ma'am. You arrived with him and were transported home in a limo afterward. This was a romantic assignation, correct?"

Ursula literally gasped, as if she'd been about to deny that there had been any relationship, but Stella had pre-empted her.

"I don't know what to say," she blurted out. "I suppose it was, but please don't think there was anything serious between us."

"Tell me how this happened. How you ended up with him there. How and when did you first meet?"

"Well, I guess I was feeling lonely. Vulnerable. My fiancé had recently broken things off with me," she explained. "Patrick and I got chatting when we were in a store together. It was one of the furniture stores in downtown Greenwich. He saw me shopping and asked for my opinion on some chairs. The way he spoke, I assumed he was a single man."

"You did?" Stella queried.

"Yes. That was the impression I got. We walked out of the store together, and he asked if I'd like to go to lunch with him. I said I would. So we arranged to have lunch at the South Sands club."

"You first met him when?" Stella wanted to get a timeline in place.

Ursula looked up thoughtfully, her gaze fixed on the simple but attractive lampshades in the ceiling light.

"A week or two ago, I think," she said.

That seemed very recent to Stella. And why had Ursula looked up before she spoke? She wondered if they'd known each other for longer. This might be a small lie. Perhaps she was condensing the timeframe to downplay their involvement. That meant Stella might have to go back to it. But for now, she wanted to move forward.

"So you went to the club?" Stella prompted.

"Yes. We had a lovely afternoon." Now Ursula smiled. "I admit, I thought there was a spark between us. But having gone through a bust-up recently, I took it slow."

"Go on?" Stella said.

"We arranged another lunch date for this coming week, but I broke it off with him before then."

"Why did you do that?"

"Because I found out he was married," Ursula said, looking sad.

Stella didn't trust her words or her sad look. Not after her experience with all the other people in Patrick's circles, who had lied so reflexively to protect themselves or their interests.

"You had no idea beforehand?" she asked.

"He told me that he and his wife were estranged. Perhaps I was too innocent, but I believed him. There didn't seem to be a reason not to. I think things would have gone further except I was lucky. The day after our lunch, I got a warning that everything was not as it seemed."

"You did? What warning?"

"One of his friends called me and said to me that he'd seen us at the club and that I should be careful, because he was married."

"How did you feel when you got the call?" Stella asked.

For some reason, this statement was ringing alarm bells. There was something strange about it. She couldn't put her finger on it but hoped her intuition would start to make sense of it.

"I realized I'd been too naïve. I did some research online which confirmed what I'd been told. I decided I wasn't going to waste any more time. I immediately broke it off with Patrick, and said I didn't want to see him again, so that lunch was actually the last time I saw him."

"Were you angry? How did you feel? Did you not want to discuss this with him in person?"

Ursula smiled ruefully. "I guess if things had gone further, I might have ended up being angry, but they didn't. I felt I'd had a lucky save. That I'd ended up being sensible. I mean, I knew when I started dating again, that there would be guys who misrepresent themselves. This won't be the first time," she sighed.

Stella gazed at her consideringly. Overall, the story sounded plausible enough. She couldn't work out what had piqued her attention a few moments ago.

"Where were you on Friday night?" she asked.

"I was home alone. I recently started a new job. I work hard during the days. I was tired," Ursula confessed with a smile.

The lack of an alibi was a potential problem, but Stella acknowledged that people sometimes were home alone, inconvenient as it was for an investigator. Truth was better than a fake story.

At that moment, her phone buzzed in her pocket. Quickly, she checked it.

It was Detective Bradshaw.

"Michaela has an alibi for the night of the crime," his brief message read.

Stella realized with a jolt that Carrie had not yet checked in. Surely she should have, because her interview's address had in fact been closer.

That might have been what was bothering her. Perhaps it had been nothing to do with Ursula's responses, but everything to do with Carrie's lack of response in calling her.

Carrie could be facing up to the killer right now, needing her help.

Stella agonized inwardly.

She was worried about her partner, but she was equally troubled that she was missing a detail here.

She couldn't leave Ursula now. It would give the other woman too much time to dream up more plausible answers to her questions, now that she had a clear idea of their direction.

But, at that moment, she realized to her relief what had been niggling at her mind during this interview. It was a small but important additional piece of information that she needed to ask. Once that was done, she could go.

Since the question was both important and specific, she decided not to make a big issue out of it, but to slip it in as she left. That way, Ursula would be more relaxed. Her guard would be down, and she would hopefully tell the truth.

Stella stood up.

"Thank you so much for your time," she said, walking out of the kitchen and back into the tidy hall.

"No problem," Ursula sounded as relieved as Stella had expected her to as she headed out behind her.

"By the way, which friend was it?" Stella asked, glancing back at her.

"How do you mean, which friend?" Ursula stared at her, puzzled.

"The friend who called you and told you Patrick Coleridge was married," Stella elaborated.

"Michael Yelverton. I saw him at the club when we were there. I know his Range Rover dealership. My ex-fiancé bought a car from him a few months ago so he had our details. Michael told me that I should be careful, and I was very grateful for that information."

Ursula looked sadly down.

This changed everything, Stella thought, feeling her spine prickle.

Ursula had spoken in a very convincing way. Stella hadn't found anything suspicious in the tone of her voice. But the words themselves were ringing huge alarm bells.

In fact, this statement clued Stella that everything so far had been false.

"I don't believe you, Ms. King," she stated coldly, turning to face her.

Ursula's face tautened into an expression of utter shock.

"What do you mean?" she whispered.

"If there's one thing I've learned during this investigation, it's that the guys at this club stick together. It's like a brotherhood. They protect each other and shield one another from anyone knowing what they were doing," Stella explained firmly. "Michael Yelverton would never, ever have betrayed his best friend, his 'partner in crime,' by calling a random acquaintance and warning her against getting involved."

"He – he did –" Ursula whispered.

"I will argue that he did not. I think your version is totally untrue, and that you're lying to me. But let's give you the benefit of the doubt. Give me your phone. Show me the proof of this call that Mr. Yelverton supposedly made to you. You should have it on record. It was recent enough," Stella challenged her.

Stella watched Ursula's face change. Shock replaced the carefully sad expression that had been lodged there. And then, rage replaced both those emotions.

In a split-second, her entire demeanor changed.

"I'm not a liar! How dare you say that? You're the liar!" she screamed.

Her hands curved into claw-like shapes, and her mouth twisted into the ugliest snarl Stella had ever seen. The sweet girl next door was gone. Stella had never seen such rage consume anyone in such a short time. It was like watching someone slip on a second skin and she knew in that instant, that she was facing the killer.

Now she saw that deep psychological problems consumed Ursula. Problems so severe that in her fury she'd stabbed a man, viciously enough to pierce his heart.

Stella wasn't taking any chances and she wasn't going to let this woman put her in danger. Her hand dropped immediately to her gun. But she'd never thought that the other woman would react so fast.

With lightning speed, Ursula lunged forward and grabbed Stella's gun as she drew it from the holster.

CHAPTER THIRTY

Yelling in shock, Stella made a grab for the other woman's wrist, struggling to get her weapon back. The brute force in Ursula's wiry tendons astounded her, even though Stella knew that she shouldn't have been surprised. She should have guessed what it would take to murder a tall, strong man at close quarters, so swiftly and lethally, using only a knife.

Now, she was up against the same changed person. Ursula was attacking without any fear. She had her hand clamped around the butt of Stella's gun, and she was stronger than Stella had thought possible.

Worse still, although the gash in Stella's palm had healed, her hand was still weak. She didn't have the steely strength in her muscles and sinews that she needed to wrench her gun away. Instead, she had to improvise, and fast. She shoved Ursula with her left shoulder, bashing her as hard as she could. She stomped on her feet and Ursula screamed. Her grasp on the gun loosened, but as Stella tried to get her own hands over the grip, Ursula made another grab for the barrel. Shrieking in horror, Stella managed to shove her back again.

The gun clattered to the floor.

As Stella bent to grasp it, she picked up the gleam of metal out of the corner of her eye, and she leaped away. The dagger-like blade of the knife that Ursula had drawn, had missed her by a hair's breadth.

The rush of adrenaline made Stella feel as if this deadly scene was playing out in slow motion.

She knew she was fighting for her life against an opponent who knew no fear at that moment. Battling a level of aggression that she'd never experienced before, Stella made another grab for Ursula's wrist. She missed it the first time, writhing away as the knife flashed toward her again.

Making another desperate lunge, Stella got hold of her wrist. She hung onto it with all her might, because she was up against a spitting, screaming hellfire of an opponent.

"Stop this! Help," she yelled, hoping that someone in a nearby house might hear.

But her voice was ragged and broken. It felt as if razors were slicing into her damaged throat. She couldn't shout again. She didn't even know if she could speak.

She was doing all she could to hold the woman back, but her strength was abnormal. Supernormal. The cutting edge of that lethally sharp knife jerked toward her again and again. Stella's entire focus was on holding that knife back. Every fiber of her body was engaged in the struggle. There wasn't time for anything else. Wasn't time to see if she could grab her gun. She didn't even dare to shift her weight. Couldn't risk any of the street fighting techniques she'd been taught at the academy. Instinctively, she felt they would not work against this woman, because she had no care for her own safety at all.

All she cared about was plunging that knife deep into Stella.

How could she stop her? She was going to run out of strength fighting her, long before the other woman would.

She had to try and get through to her. Behind this explosive fury that had consumed her mind, buried deep, there still had to be coherent thought. If she could somehow calm her down from this terrifying surge of anger, she would stand a chance.

Reasoning with Ursula might allow her to come back from the precipice of fury where her mind had taken her. If she could get this woman to relax, to start thinking with her conscious brain again, she would have more chance of escaping the same fate as Patrick.

Given that Ursula was wrestling to get a knife in her, Stella didn't know if she could achieve this, but she had to try, even though her whole body was trembling with the effort of holding this maddened, struggling woman at arm's length.

And her voice? Could she speak at all? Her throat felt on fire.

If she lost her voice at this point, it would all be over. Imagine if the damage that the assassin had done prevented her from saving her own life now? Horrified by the thought, Stella did her best to force out the words.

"It's okay, Ursula," she managed to say. It sounded cracked and grainy, but at least the words were audible. "You don't need to do this," Stella soothed her breathlessly, wishing she could infuse more calmness into her severely damaged voice.

Talking took energy. Energy she needed to keep this murderer from killing her, but right now she had to invest that energy and hope it would save her.

"Be calm. I know you're feeling angry. Don't be angry. It won't help you now. You've already done what you wanted to do. You achieved it. I'm sure it made you feel good."

Her stomach coiled with tension as Ursula made another desperate lunge. She only just managed to force her back. The blade had been within an inch of her eye. It had been about to sink deep into her brain, and Stella felt sick with fear at the thought.

"You are okay. You don't need to fight," she continued, as persuasively as she could, clinging onto Ursula's wrists while her own arms quivered with exhaustion.

"I know what it's like to be lied to. To be misled. It makes you feel furious and small and filled with anguish. You must have been heartbroken when you found out how he'd cheated you. And how little he cared for you. I've been in that situation too. You feel destroyed, shattered into pieces, and as if there's no way out. But there is a way. You should step back from your desperation now. Don't let it take you any further. You are strong enough to decide differently. I know you are."

At that moment she felt it. The first sign of hesitation. A break in the nonstop onslaught. For one moment, Ursula paused.

Her strategy was working, but whether Stella would be able to get results in time, she didn't know. She was shaking with the effort of holding Ursula back.

"You are safe," Stella reassured her, thinking how bizarre it was that she was saying such a thing, while she was in terrible danger herself. "You don't need to fight. You must be exhausted. You must feel like you're balancing on a precipice. What's the point in carrying on when doing so might destroy you? Rest your arms. Rest your mind. It's all going to be okay."

The words spilled from her. She knew they were meaningless to a logical person. But Ursula was far beyond any logic, and perhaps these simple mantras were doing something to take her back from the edge.

Suddenly, it seemed as if her mind disengaged from the fury that had consumed her. Her arms dropped. She stepped away from Stella, looking unsure and confused, as if she didn't even know what had happened or why she was reacting this way.

Ursula's hands were shaking violently. So were her own. But Ursula was still clinging tightly to the knife.

The hallway was now a mess. Their struggles had knocked several books off the shelf, smashed an ornament on the side table, and crumpled up the colorful rag rug on the floor.

The problem was that Stella's gun was at least two yards behind her and she didn't dare look around. Didn't dare to break eye contact. The tenuous communication she'd managed to get with Ursula was all that was keeping her at bay. If she moved, she would break it. They would be back to where they started.

What was she going to do now? How was she going to contain this woman without triggering this rage again?

Keep her talking, she thought. Keeping her talking might just take her further from the edge.

"Why did you do it?" Stella asked in a conversational tone.

Ursula looked startled, as if the question had jolted her out of her proposed course of action.

"I got angry," she said.

"Why?" Stella asked, in a voice so hoarse she could hardly get out the words.

"He lied. He told me I was the only one. He promised he would look after me, and that we would be together. I believed him, but I couldn't understand why it wasn't happening. I had known him for a few weeks. I thought I loved him, and I wanted more from him. I felt impatient, so I decided to go and speak to him."

"And what did he say?" Stella asked. Undoubtedly, Patrick's own reaction had sealed his fate.

"I knew he'd be at the club. He told me he went there Fridays. He must have just arrived, because I caught up with him on the way in. He was drunk, and I saw a side of him I'd never known. He laughed at me. He said if I'd believed him, I was a fool. That I wasn't the only woman he was messing around with, and that he sure wasn't going to let me coerce him into supporting me."

"How did you feel when he said that?" Stella asked.

"I couldn't believe it. He was totally different from the man I'd thought he was. He was so callus, so cold. He was contemptuous of me. He looked at me like I didn't even exist. How dare he! How dare he do that!" In the moment, Stella saw her anger flare again. She'd bought time, but now Ursula's emotions were keeling all the way back out of control, to where Stella didn't want them.

“I had the knife with me,” she continued, speaking rapidly. “I don’t know why I’d brought it along. I’d never thought I would need to use it, ever, but somehow, having it with me made me feel safer.”

“I understand,” Stella said.

“I think I lost my temper with him. I wanted to destroy him, because he didn’t care if he ruined my life.”

Now Ursula looked uncertain again and Stella felt cold inside.

She had intended to keep the woman calm, but it seemed as if remembering the violent scene that had played out, was tipping her all the way back into the maelstrom again.

“You don’t care either,” Ursula hissed.

She coiled herself like a cat, and Stella knew it was too late, that she was going to attack her again and this whole dreadful cycle would start up once more. This time, she didn’t know if she would have the strength to fight her off.

And then, footsteps pounded up to the front door.

Carrie Potts burst through the doorway, gun in hand, looking as determined and focused as Stella had ever seen her.

Without hesitation, she aimed her weapon at Ursula, even as the other woman was raising the knife again.

“Drop that now,” Carrie lashed out. “Put your hands up!”

Crying out in shock, Ursula let go of the knife and it clattered to the ground.

Stella felt dizzy with relief. Immediately, she staggered backward to grab her gun again as Ursula raised her arms.

After an almost fatal struggle, they had cut all the way down to the bare bones of the truth.

Finally, Patrick Coleridge’s killer could be arrested.

CHAPTER THIRTY ONE

A tap on the front door distracted Stella from her book.

Sitting up in her comfortable bed, she checked the time. It was eight-thirty on Monday morning. Wrapped in her dressing gown, she'd been reading, vaguely aware of the sounds of traffic outside as most people began their working week.

Roth had given Carrie and Stella two days off after they'd finally wrapped up the paperwork and the press conference on the Coleridge case, late on Sunday afternoon. It had been an exhausting weekend. Stella's emotions still felt frazzled. The graze on her neck was stinging and her hands and wrists were aching after the prolonged battle with Ursula.

Carrie had done the talking at the press conference, which suited Stella fine as by then, she'd completely lost her voice. Carrie's name would probably be mentioned first in the news stories, which Stella hadn't yet read, but she hoped that they would make Carrie's father proud.

She felt glad she didn't have to speak to anyone today. This was going to be her day for healing and relaxing. Tomorrow, she planned to treat herself to a manicure, to repair some of the rips and chips in her nails from the struggle with Ursula.

But now, someone was tapping on the door.

The case might be over, but she was not out of danger. Not by a long way. Stella felt nervous as she got out of bed, padding across the small bedroom and across the lounge to peer suspiciously through the peephole.

Outside, she saw a delivery man. He was holding a platter, wrapped in cellophane.

Curious, Stella opened the door.

"Morning, ma'am," the delivery man said. "Ms. Fall?"

"Yes. That's me," Stella said.

"Your delivery."

"Thank you."

Feeling totally confused, Stella took the package.

It was a platter of fruit and pastries. How weird was that? Someone had sent her a large plate piled high with fresh fruit, dried fruit, and delicious-looking croissants and Danishes.

She pushed the door closed with her foot and carried the plate back inside. There wasn't much food in the house. Her stomach was rumbling at the mouthwatering aroma of the pastries.

There was a card attached to the cellophane.

Stella put the platter down and removed the card. Turning it over, she read it.

"We didn't get much chance to eat in the past couple of days," the card read. "Here's something to catch up. Good working with you. C."

The card was from Carrie!

Stella felt overwhelmed with amazement. Carrie sure did things in style, and she had great taste in food. Unwrapping the packaging, she broke off a delicious, crisp corner of a croissant and munched on it hungrily.

She'd never thought that she and her ex-rival would ever be on a firmer footing. Of course, that did not mean everything would be sunshine from here. Stella was sure they'd have many clashes, and she knew that would mostly be a good thing. Differences of ideas and opinions could drive a case forward, as long as they were not destructive. But at least they now understood each other better.

Quickly, she went back to her bedroom and grabbed her phone.

"Thank you so much for the food! Very welcome! Enjoy your break," she keyed back.

Carrie was no longer her arch enemy. She'd had a choice, whether to try and destroy Stella or to work with her. She'd chosen to work with her and by doing that, she had moved away from the undeniably toxic influence of her father.

Stella respected her immensely for making that choice.

At that moment, she heard another knock on her front door. Rushing back, she checked the peephole again. To her shock, she found herself peering out at Maxwell.

Maxwell? What on earth was he doing here? Should she even open up to him?

Emotions clashed within her. For a moment, Stella considered the very appealing option of not opening the door, and just shouting at Maxwell to go away. But she was sure he wouldn't. He'd been messaging her nonstop for the past couple of days. She hadn't replied, so now here he was.

She guessed that at some stage they would have to talk things through, and that time was now. Even though it couldn't actually be a worse moment.

Stella looked down at her gown in dismay. She was literally straight out of bed. There wasn't time to change. She had croissant crumbs on her chin.

She felt at a disadvantage. If she was going to confront Maxwell, she wanted the armor of clothes and make-up. It was a small but meaningful layer of emotional defense.

Now she had no armor and no defense.

Oh, well, if Maxwell was going to pitch up at her front door unannounced, he'd just have to take her as he found her, Stella decided. After this case, she'd had enough of lies to last her a lifetime. He'd get the raw truth of her, and that was it.

Brushing the crumbs away, she opened the door and stared out at him.

It was actually more of a glare, as she wrapped her gown, and the remainder of her dignity, more tightly around her, aware of her bare feet and that she hadn't even brushed her hair yet.

"I'm sorry," Maxwell said, clearly noting her embarrassment. "I should have called first."

To her confusion, he was also carrying food. A large box of chocolates which he held out to her, looking hopeful.

"I should have called you yesterday. I know you were worried," Stella found herself saying, to her surprise. "It was rather busy, but I should have made the time."

"I heard you solved the case. Roth told me everything. I feel hugely impressed, because that was a minefield of an investigation. Also, I feel envious at the same time, because I wish I could have worked with you on it. I wanted to bring you something as an apology. I thought of flowers but then I thought you're more of a practical person. I thought you'd rather have a gift you could use." He glanced down at the chocolates, and then back up at her.

Stella pressed her lips together. While she appreciated the thought, neither flowers nor chocolates could make up for the fact he hadn't been honest with her.

"You need to know why I did what I did," he said.

"Why?" Stella challenged.

She felt a complex mix of emotions as she waited for him to speak. Mainly relief, that there was a reason, and she was going to hear it. But also nervousness, because she had to admit, her feelings for Maxwell hadn't gone away. She was way too emotionally invested in his answer, she realized.

"Brigitte is not okay. She's mentally unstable."

Of all the things she'd expected Maxwell might say, that was not one of them. Stella stared at him, feeling utterly floored.

She hadn't looked unstable, she thought, suspicion darkening her mood again.

Hastily, Maxwell continued.

"She's had psychological issues for most of her life. I knew her back from our school days. She came from a very unhappy home and there were things that happened in her childhood that damaged her terribly. I always looked after her in school. Then we moved apart, we went our separate ways, and I met up with her after university. She was so different. She'd really blossomed, and I saw for the first time what an amazing person she was. So we dated, and we married just a few months later, which was a big, big mistake."

"Why was that?" Stella asked.

"She hadn't overcome her problems. They'd gotten worse. She's extremely jealous. Destructively so. She threatened my previous girlfriend when she found out who she was. She caused trouble for me at work. Tried to interfere with my relationship with my brother and sister. Accused them of trying to take me away from her."

"I wish I'd known this," Stella said.

Maxwell looked deeply unhappy as he nodded. Finally, the harsh truth of his dysfunctional marriage was being told, and Stella believed him. He was no longer hiding anything from her, but this was difficult for him to talk about. She could see the stress in his face. Hear it in his voice.

"I didn't know how to tell you. Didn't know where I should start. When our problems worsened, I knew I couldn't carry on as I was, so I decided I was going to follow my calling, join the FBI, and use it as an excuse for a clean break. We eventually agreed that we would separate for a year, and after that, we would divorce. But of course, it didn't work out like that. Just a few months later she began calling, messaging. Saying she was sorry, and she'd sorted herself out, gone onto medication, that she was a different person now. And that she wanted to try again."

"Did you believe her?" Stella asked.

Maxwell shook his head. "Of course not. I didn't believe a word she said. I knew it wasn't true and that it wouldn't happen. But the problem is her vindictiveness. Her ability to destroy. She's so scarred, so damaged. Now I'm in a career where I can't risk any interference. And I've met you. So I was literally paralyzed, not knowing what the best decision would be. I think I came up with a plan to let her down gently, but I saw straight away that wouldn't work."

"Is there anything that will work?" Stella asked, feeling intrigued, and much more sympathetic to his plight than she'd ever believed she could be.

Maxwell shook his head.

"I have to be honest with her. I have to move on. I want a divorce. But I want you to know, in case there are consequences. For me, for her – even for you. I don't want that to happen, and I'll do anything to stop it, I'll try my utmost to manage this whole disaster, but I think you need to know – she can be vindictive."

"Okay. Thanks for telling me this."

Finally, Stella understood why he'd done what he did. It was a complicated situation and there hadn't been an easy choice. She felt relieved that there had been complex reasons for him doing what he did. He'd been caught in a difficult predicament.

He stared back at her and in his dark gaze, she saw only truth and integrity.

"Thanks for hearing me out." Finally, a ghost of a smile hovered around Maxwell's face. "This hasn't been easy. But it feels easier knowing I've got this off my chest and that I'm not holding anything back from you. And I won't, Fall, no matter what happens. No matter what the future brings. I've learned my lesson."

Now, to her astonishment, Stella found herself smiling, too.

He was calling her by her last name. That was good. She needed the distance and respected that he was giving it to her by using it.

"I appreciate that, Maxwell."

"I know that it's too soon to think about us. But would you agree to be partnered with me again at work? If I request it?"

Stella thought about that.

Her case with Carrie had allowed her to grow and learn. She'd been able to mend and heal a relationship that could have been destructive to both of them.

But she had to admit, she'd missed working with Maxwell. She'd missed the synergy that they had, the camaraderie they had shared.

Now that things were resolved between them, it made sense to try again.

"I'd like that," she said, and his face lit up.

"I'll also request it," she continued. "I think Roth saw that Carrie and I have sorted out our issues, so it will make sense for us two to partner together again."

"I look forward to it." He glanced down at the box of chocolates, realizing he was still holding it. Stella hadn't yet taken it.

Again, Maxwell held the box out to her. This time, Stella accepted it.

"I'd better get to work," he said.

"See you on Wednesday. And thanks," Stella said.

Maxwell turned and hurried away, and Stella closed her apartment door. She walked back to the lounge table and put the chocolates down.

Partnering with Maxwell again. Her spirits lifted at the thought. Feeling a deep sense of relief, she replayed the conversation in her mind, assessing what he'd said, taking in the complexity of his predicament.

It wasn't easy, but at least she now knew. It was always better to know.

At that moment, her phone pinged. She picked it up and saw that she had an incoming email.

"Well, this is good timing," Stella said, as she saw the email was from Detective Harding, in the Leavenworth precinct. There were a few large attachments and she felt excited to see them. They would be the list of old cases her father had been working on.

Finally, she'd be able to read the crimes that George Fall had been busy with at the time of his disappearance and see if there were any that could have triggered the catastrophe that had redefined her life.

CHAPTER THIRTY TWO

Opening her laptop, Stella sat at the dining room table, focusing all her attention onto her father's past.

She clicked on the first document and read through. As she did so, she felt surprisingly emotional. She imagined her father working on the file. That was his actual handwriting in the scanned document. Stella recognized the neat, forward-slanted lettering.

The first case was a smash-and-grab crime. A lady's purse had been stolen while she walked in the street. Reading anxiously through, Stella thought this looked like a straightforward case. She couldn't see anything that might have been problematic here. A suspect had been arrested but had later been released due to insufficient evidence.

Feeling impatient, she moved onto the murders. There had been three murders active at the time of his disappearance, with a handful of other minor crimes. The murders were clearly where she needed to focus.

The first had been a shooting. Domestic violence. A husband had arrived home late and drunk, and a fight had ensued. He'd pulled his gun and shot his wife twice. One of the bullets had hit an artery. She'd bled out before the paramedics had arrived. A tragic death. The husband had been found guilty and sentenced to twenty years. A later note in the case file, added in a different hand, had updated that he'd been paroled after six years. But that was far down the line.

Too far to be relevant to her father's situation, unless an angry relative had threatened him?

Stella cupped her face in her hands. There were so many possibilities. But she didn't see how an angry relative would have complicated things to that extent. Not when the husband had been to blame all along. Nothing her father could have done would have changed things.

What was the second one?

She opened the document and read the account of a bar fight. A man had been stabbed with a broken bottle. The perpetrator had fled and turned himself in the next day. He'd spent five years in prison. So again, not him, and if he'd turned himself in, then nobody could have had an interest in covering for him.

So it had to be the third case then, Stella thought.

Expectantly she opened the file. And frowned, confused.

This was not a case that would arouse suspicion. An employee who'd been fired had confronted his boss. Things had gotten violent. They'd fought. The boss had slipped, and the employee had kicked him in the head before fleeing. The injury had been fatal. Three days later, the employee had been tracked down and arrested in Missouri. He'd committed another two robberies by then. He'd since been paroled, had reoffended, and was currently serving his second sentence.

Stella read and reread the file. This seriously did not make sense at all. None of the three murders were ringing alarm bells in the way she'd hoped. She had no idea how to go forward from here. What should she do?

Her father couldn't have abandoned his family for another reason. Surely, he could not?

What could she do?

Surprising herself, Stella picked up the phone. Never in a million years had she thought she would end up doing this. She keyed in her mother's number. Hesitating only a moment, she dialed.

As she heard the phone start to ring, Stella immediately she wished she hadn't done this. It was stupid and reckless, and she should have known better. She was not going to get any information, and the question itself might destroy the tenuous understanding she seemed to have recently achieved with her mother.

But at the same time, she had no other recourse. Her mother was the only person who might possibly know more. Her finger hovered over the disconnect button, but she didn't press it.

Instead, she listened to the call ring and ring, feeling a growing sense of doom. Rhonda Fall wasn't going to pick up. She wasn't going to get the answers she needed. Not now, not ever.

And then, to her relief, her mother took the call.

"Stella," she said briefly.

"Mom."

Stella took a moment to gather her thoughts. She'd done this far too impulsively. She wished she'd taken the time to prepare, and to plan a few moves ahead.

"I got the money wire. It was very generous of you. Thank you," Rhonda said.

“I’ll send the same amount each month,” Stella promised.

“I’m using some of it to buy the medication my new psychiatrist recommended. I must say I feel more balanced on it. Calmer.”

Stella hesitated. This was a completely unexpected development. Was her mother trying to fix the issues that had plagued her for so long? What would this mean? Would those terrible rages and mood swings lessen, or even disappear?

This possibility felt like a bright ray of light shining through a doorway she’d never thought could be unlocked, never mind actually opened.

This brought even more conflict into the decision. Rhonda needed to rebuild now. She didn’t need the trauma of questions.

But there was no other way to find out.

As Stella agonized over what to do, her mother shocked her again.

“I know you’ve been asking about George’s old cases,” she said conversationally.

That silenced Stella completely. Her mouth opened, but nothing came out. How, how had her mother found this out?

As she did a good impression of a fish out of water, her mother continued.

“I have a friend in the police precinct. She’s been there a while. She told me you’d gotten in touch.”

Stella felt shivers prickle down her back. Rhonda’s tone was loaded with meaning.

“I want answers,” Stella finally managed to say, surprised by how resolute she sounded.

Rhonda was silent for a moment.

Stella had expected that her mother’s reply would bring the screaming, the diatribes, the volleys of insults and abuse. She mentally prepared herself for it, trying to strengthen herself for the tirade to come.

But when she spoke, Rhonda’s voice was gentle.

“If you interfere, it’s going to mean danger. Danger for you. Danger for me.”

“I won’t interfere. I just want to know,” Stella whispered.

“Danger for George. I don’t know if he’s dead yet.”

“What?” Stella’s eyes flew wide. Her father, dead?

“It wasn’t a murder. I’m sure that’s where you’re looking. You won’t find answers there. It was a runaway.”

"*What?*" Stella spoke the word in a different, more intense tone. Her mother knew about this? She'd known all along?

"Please, now you know, leave it alone. If you value all our lives."

Her mother disconnected, leaving Stella in mid-gasp.

A runaway?

Turning back to her screen, she checked out the case document headings.

Here it was.

Feeling now terrified, she stared at the description.

A runaway – well, that was how the police department had described it – had been found, hitch-hiking on a rural road outside Leavenworth. She'd been discovered late at night, a week before her father had disappeared. The person who stopped to pick her up had called the police immediately.

That was the start of the case. Did she dare to open it to read more?

Her mother's warning burned in her mind. She'd never sounded more serious. Stella had the feeling Rhonda had not been exaggerating. She might learn more, but what if her actions unleashed a Pandora's box of consequences, with catastrophic results?

Stella shook her head. She had to know more. She had to! Only then could she work out what, if anything, she could do.

With a trembling hand, she clicked to open the full document.

Reading anxiously through the case file, Stella learned that the young woman had been seriously off-kilter mentally. She'd been incoherent, unable to speak. She'd been wearing old, dirty clothes. A long, jagged wound down her side had recently been stitched. The female police officer who had examined her had noted that the stitches looked rough. She'd had two fingers and a big toe missing.

They had taken her into police custody and had phoned around to hospitals and institutions in the wider area. She'd had no ID on her and had been unable to answer any questions. Only two wide-eyed photos in the case file confirmed her identity.

Stella stared at them. She saw terror in those eyes.

Based on her condition, the police had made their initial calls to psychiatric hospitals and mental institutions in the wider area, but none had reported a missing inmate. They been planning to investigate further but, in the morning, the woman had disappeared.

Somehow, someone had managed to get in through the back door of the police department, go down to the holding cells, and either find the key or pick the lock.

Nobody had seen a thing. They'd searched for her and notified the surrounding precincts, but it was as if she'd vanished into thin air.

Stella felt ice prickle down her spine.

What had happened? Had this really been an escaped mental patient?

Or had she fled from someone who had been keeping her? Who'd subjected her to such torture that it had destroyed her mind? Someone so intelligent and cunning that he'd been able to recapture her swiftly and without a trace?

Stella felt sick with fear as she thought about that possibility. Her father would have determinedly tried to find such a man. Without a doubt he would have wanted to trace that traumatized runaway and help her. She guessed he would have started out by looking at every single missing person report in the state, and then in the neighboring states, to see if any matched up.

So, what had happened when he began his work?

Suddenly, a memory flashed back into Stella's consciousness. It was an innocuous scene that had escaped her mind completely, but now she remembered it had been a couple of days before her father's disappearance.

He'd walked in, late in the evening, and even as a ten-year-old, Stella had picked up on the stress that emanated from him. She'd seldom seen her father look scared, but at that moment, fear had filled his eyes.

"Let me see your bag, Stella-bella?" he'd said, using the nickname he sometimes gave her.

"My bag?" she'd asked, puzzled.

"Your school bag, hon."

"Sure." Confused, Stella had handed over the worn backpack that she used for school. She'd wondered why her father had asked. She'd thought he needed to borrow a pen or pencil – or that, perhaps, he was going to hide a surprise in there for her to find, as he occasionally had done in the past.

He opened the bag and looked through, removing her books one by one. He had an expression in his eyes she'd never seen before.

As he worked his way through the bag, something fell out and fluttered down to the floor. Stella remembered feeling mildly curious – the folded page was bright white and didn't look familiar to her – but by then she'd turned back to her dinner and wasn't paying him too much attention.

She saw her father pick up that paper and open it, and for a moment he lowered his head into his hand.

Stella had wanted to ask him about that piece of paper, but he'd turned and walked swiftly out of the room.

"Carry on with your meal!" The whiplash of her mother's voice had distracted her. Thinking back, Stella realized that she, too, had sounded more fearful than normal.

Nothing more was said about it. Her mother went through to the kitchen, where pots and plates banged as she dished up a bowl of stew for her father. Having finished her meal, Stella asked to be excused. She took her bag and went to her room, wondering briefly if she might find a surprise hidden away.

Now, with a cold feeling, she realized how close and how real the threat had been. Undoubtedly, that paper had been a message that her father had been told about.

"Leave it and walk away or your daughter will be next. And if you think I can't get to her – I already have."

That was all she could theorize, given the sparse information she had so far. There might be more to it. Stella was certain that a dire threat had been made and that, for her father, walking away and disappearing had been the only option, or perhaps this action had been demanded. At any rate, it had been the only way he could ensure the safety of his family.

She'd been thinking at first that this was the work of one evil psychopath. Now another, even more chilling idea occurred to her. What if this person had been part of a hidden, powerful network?

She shook her head, feeling overwhelmed by the possibilities. She knew she had to speak to her father. She was FBI now. Even if it was a network, she had far more resources at her disposal to help crush it. Surely, she could act, somehow? And now that she knew more, she had a way she could contact him. She could send a letter to the PO box in Ouray, Colorado. She knew the box number. She could write him a note and mail it, the old-fashioned way. And then, when he cleared his box, even if it was months later, he would hopefully get in touch.

Stella decided to keep it simple.

With shaking hands, she penned the short message, hoping this might be the first step toward seeing her father again.

"Dad, I know the situation. I want to help. Please call me." Below that, she wrote her number, and signed it, "*Stella.*"

Before she could change her mind, Stella pulled on a pair of jeans and a jacket and ran downstairs. She headed into the Staples across the road and bought a book of stamps. Quickly, she attached a stamp, and walked further down the road to the mailbox.

Holding her breath, she dropped it into the slot and turned away, visualizing its journey and praying that some unknown time later, her father would read it and call her.

It was only as she walked back up the stairs again that the recklessness of what she had done hit her like a rush of ice down her spine.

She had no way of knowing who was clearing that box. Someone else could have obtained the key and be looking out for just this kind of note.

When her mother had said, "I don't know if he's dead yet," Stella had assumed she'd been talking about her father. But now, replaying the words in her mind, she understood that Rhonda Fall had in fact been referring to somebody else.

Too late, Stella realized who it must be.

EPILOGUE

On this wintry, drizzly night, the winding roadway leading down to this section of the beach was all but deserted. Even so, Gordon Marshall looked around him carefully before parking at the point where the blacktop ran out and was replaced by a short dirt track.

He opened the door, glancing at Cecilia's sister Kathy in the passenger seat before they both climbed out. The track led down to a small, wooden hut, long overdue for refurbishment, but providing some shelter against the blowing wind and the crashing waves.

The biting sea breeze chilled him, even though he was wearing a thick, woolen coat. Kathy wrapped her black fur jacket more tightly around her as she followed him.

Carefully, Gordon used his flashlight to navigate the way. It was completely dark out here. Only a faraway twinkle of light shone from the luxury homes at the edge of the park. The route was familiar to him, but in the dark, his heavy, leather shoes slipped and slid over the wooden boards of the walkway.

"Where is he?" Gordon asked.

"He said he would park elsewhere, so that he wasn't noticed."

Kathy's light, clear voice was tinged with acid. Her features were sharp and determined-looking. Gordon held out his arm, giving her a hand across the slippery boards, but Kathy refused it with a disdainful shake of her head.

Gordon put the flashlight on the ground in the hut and placed his briefcase nearby. Their shadows looked harsh in the light's low beam. They waited in the ramshackle shelter, staring into the darkness.

"Here he is," Kathy sounded relieved.

As if from nowhere, the dark-haired man materialized, walking swiftly toward them, brushing rain back from his hooded face.

He stood under the shelter. Flexed his hands, which were protected by soft, dark gloves. He stared at the Marshalls, looking from one of them to the other.

Gordon Marshall let him stew for a while before speaking.

“That didn’t go as planned,” he said heavily. “You told me you had a track record of total success with your kills. We hired you for two kills. You have completed zero.”

The man shifted his feet uneasily.

“I’ve never had to take down an FBI agent before. And it was very short notice. Usually, I have more time. The circumstances were not ideal. There will be a better time soon.”

“What about the other target? The second woman we asked you to get rid of?” Kathy pressured the man.

“She wasn’t at the charity event yesterday. You told me she’d be there and that would be the place to get it done. I overheard someone saying she’d had to cancel at the last minute due to illness, but she wasn’t at her home when I went there. I need time to track her. I think she might have been warned and gone into hiding.” He sounded frustrated.

“You didn’t get us the results we needed,” Gordon chastised him harshly, feeling the hatred and resentment swell inside him again. Damn Stella Fall. She’d been trouble from the moment he’d seen her. How could one insignificant little nobody have caused such destruction to him and his family?

He craved revenge. He needed results, and fast. Failure was not acceptable.

The man pressed his lips together angrily.

“Doing this correctly takes weeks. Not days. If you’d given me weeks, this could have been done.”

“So you’re saying you want more time?” Gordon asked.

He nodded. “Two more weeks, and I promise you, I’ll have done both jobs. But you owe me money.”

There was a shocked silence in the hut, broken only by the thundering of waves.

“Money? Money for what?” Gordon asked him angrily.

“You’ve paid me half the fee for one target. Then, suddenly, you told me there’s another target. My terms are fifty percent upfront. Fifty percent on completion. So, give me the other prepayment. Now.”

The threat in his words was audible as he stared them down.

“Okay,” Gordon said. “I’ll give you the money.”

He walked over to the briefcase that he’d left leaning against the hut’s opposite wall.

He bent down, rummaged inside.

When he turned around, the light gleamed faintly on the silver pistol he held.

"What the hell? Hey! Wait!" the other man cried. He spun around, clearly intending to make a run for it, but he was too slow.

Gordon gritted his teeth. Aimed carefully. With a whiplash crack, he fired three times, holding his nerve, telling himself that at such a close range, he couldn't miss.

He didn't. The running man stumbled, and then collapsed.

Gordon Marshall put the gun away. He was filled with a cold resolve. His hand was trembling, and his heart was pounding hard, but he was pleased by how calmly he had handled the situation.

"There's no way of tracing him back to us?" Kathy asked anxiously, as they hurried back up the wooden boards.

"No way," Gordon reassured her. "We used a burner phone, and we'll get rid of the gun. Put it in a black bag and throw it into a dumpster. It's trash collection day tomorrow."

"How are we going to find someone else to do this?" Kathy asked, sounding at once annoyed and scared by the prospect.

Gordon shook his head.

If there was one thing he'd learned in the past weeks, it was that you couldn't trust other people. Not even his wife. At a critical time, when she should have kept her mouth shut and let the lawyers do their job, she'd caved and weakened and spilled out a whole lot of stuff that had incriminated her, influenced the jury, and worse, smeared the family's name.

On the night she had died, Cecilia Marshall had been raving, crying, saying that she regretted what she'd done and that she wished she could start afresh. That she was going to serve her jail time willingly, because she deserved it. She had mistreated the staff. She had trafficked them.

She'd been as drunk as he'd ever seen her. The plan had come to him in a flash. Desperate times, Gordon thought. She hadn't been sleeping well for months, and he knew where she kept the tablets.

He'd commiserated with his wife. Told her that he agreed with what she'd decided, and that he'd be there for her.

Then he'd made Cecilia a mug of thick, sweet hot chocolate, laced with brandy and rich with sugar and cream, containing all twenty-five of the remaining tablets. He'd hoped to hell it would be enough, along with all the alcohol she'd had. He'd sat with her as she drank it.

By the morning, she'd been dead. Public sympathy had swung in his direction immediately, thanks to the tragic suicide of his wife. Suddenly, the pressure had been off, and Gordon had felt as if there was a way forward.

Now, he saw again what he needed to do.

"We're not going to hire anyone else," he said to Kathy. "This time, we handle it ourselves."

NOW AVAILABLE!

HIS OTHER TRUTH
(A Stella Fall Psychological Suspense Thriller—Book 6)

A couple is found murdered in a suburban neighborhood, and all clues lead to dead ends. When Stella investigates, the neighborhood and its inhabitants seem peaceful, charming, and perfect—too perfect. Could darkness be lurking behind these manicured lawns?

HIS OTHER TRUTH is book #6 in a new psychological suspense series by debut author Ava Strong, which begins with HIS OTHER WIFE (Book #1).

As FBI Special Agent Stella Fall tries to enter the dark canals of the killer's mind, she realizes that this case may just have a link to something that happened in the past—the far past. Or with another life on the line, is that just another dead end?

With few leads and a ticking clock, Stella must put her brilliant mind to test to solve this seemingly impenetrable case.

Can she find the killer in the nick of time?

A fast-paced psychological suspense thriller with unforgettable characters and heart-pounding suspense, HIS OTHER TRUTH is book #6 in a riveting new series that will leave you turning pages late into the night.

Future books in the series will be available soon.

Ava Strong

Debut author Ava Strong is author of the REMI LAURENT mystery series, comprising six books (and counting); of the ILSE BECK mystery series, comprising seven books (and counting); of the STELLA FALL psychological suspense thriller series, comprising six books (and counting); and of the DAKOTA STEELE FBI Suspense thriller series, comprising three books (and counting).

An avid reader and lifelong fan of the mystery and thriller genres, Ava loves to hear from you, so please feel free to visit www.avastrongauthor.com to learn more and stay in touch.

BOOKS BY AVA STRONG

REMI LAURENT FBI SUSPENSE THRILLER
THE DEATH CODE (Book #1)
THE MURDER CODE (Book #2)
THE MALICE CODE (Book #3)
THE VENGEANCE CODE (Book #4)
THE DECEPTION CODE (Book #5)
THE SEDUCTION CODE (Book #6)

ILSE BECK FBI SUSPENSE THRILLER
NOT LIKE US (Book #1)
NOT LIKE HE SEEMED (Book #2)
NOT LIKE YESTERDAY (Book #3)
NOT LIKE THIS (Book #4)
NOT LIKE SHE THOUGHT (Book #5)
NOT LIKE BEFORE (Book #6)
NOT LIKE NORMAL (Book #7)

STELLA FALL PSYCHOLOGICAL SUSPENSE THRILLER
HIS OTHER WIFE (Book #1)
HIS OTHER LIE (Book #2)
HIS OTHER SECRET (Book #3)
HIS OTHER MISTRESS (Book #4)
HIS OTHER LIFE (Book #5)
HIS OTHER TRUTH (Book #6)

DAKOTA STEELE FBI SUSPENSE THRILLER
WITHOUT MERCY (Book #1)
WITHOUT REMORSE (Book #2)
WITHOUT A PAST (Book #3)

www.ingramcontent.com/pod-product-compliance
Lightning Source LLC
Chambersburg PA
CBHW030617310726
48979CB00003B/753